SEE
ROCK CITY

ALSO BY DONALD DAVIS

Story Collections

Listening for the Crack of Dawn:
A Master Storyteller Recalls the Appalachia of His Youth

Barking at a Fox-Fur Coat: Family Stories and Tall Tales

Jack Always Seeks His Fortune:
Authentic Appalachian Jack Tales

Novel

Thirteen Miles from Suncrest

Instructional

Telling Your Own Stories:
For Family and Classroom Storytelling,
Public Speaking, and Personal Journaling

Children's Picture Book

Jack and the Animals (Illustrated by Kitty Harvill)

Audiotapes

Christmas at Grandma's

Jack's First Job

Listening for the Crack of Dawn

Miss Daisy

Party People

Rainy Weather

The Southern Bells

Uncle Frank Invents the Electron Microphone

SEE ROCK CITY

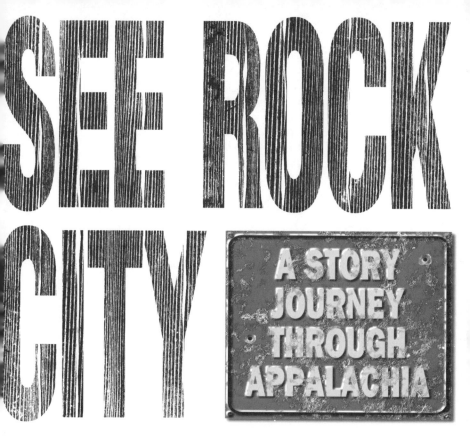

CITY

A STORY
JOURNEY
THROUGH
APPALACHIA

By the Author of *Listening for the Crack of Dawn*

Donald Davis

AUGUST HOUSE PUBLISHERS, INC.
LITTLE ROCK

Published 1996 by August House, Inc.,
P.O. Box 3223, Little Rock, Arkansas, 72203,
501-372-5450.

Printed in the United States of America

10 9 8 7 6 5 4 3 2 1 HC
10 9 8 7 6 5 4 3 2 1 PB

Library of Congress Cataloging-in-Publication Data
Davis, Donald D., 1944–
See Rock City : a story journey through Appalachia / Donald Davis.
p.   cm.
ISBN 0-87483-448-1 (hc : alk. paper).
ISBN 0-87483-456-2 (pb : alk. paper)
1. Appalachian Region, Southern—Social life and customs—Fiction.
2. North Carolina—Social life and customs—Fiction. I. Title.
PS3554.A93347S44   1996
813'.54—dc20   96-4609

"See Rock City" is a trademark of See Rock City, Inc.
and is used by permission.

President and publisher: Ted Parkhurst
Executive editor: Liz Parkhurst
Assistant editor: Karen Martin
Cover design: Byron Taylor

The paper used in this publication meets the minimum requirements
of the American National Standards for Information Sciences—
permanence of Paper for Printed Library Materials, ANSI.48-1984

AUGUST HOUSE, INC.   PUBLISHERS   LITTLE ROCK

To Miss Merle, Miss Linda, and Mrs. Davis,
and all the children
who passed through their classrooms.

OH, I SAVED THE ONE FOR ANOTHER DAY,
YET KNOWING HOW WAY LEADS ON TO WAY,
I DOUBTED THAT I SHOULD EVER COME BACK...

Robert Frost, "The Road Not Taken"

TAKE THEREFORE NO THOUGHT FOR THE MORROW:
FOR THE MORROW SHALL TAKE THOUGHT FOR THE
THINGS OF ITSELF. SUFFICIENT UNTO THE DAY IS
THE EVIL THEREOF.

Matthew 6:34

Contents

The Place

SULPHER SPRINGS, NORTH CAROLINA—1948

When I was still too young to go to school, Thursday was my favorite day of the week. From the time of my earliest memory, Thursday was always the day we went to town.

Daddy would get up early to milk, feed the chickens, and touch up the garden. He left home by seven-thirty, driving our nine-year-old '39 Plymouth to work. He was the cashier—whatever that meant—at the First National Bank of Sulpher Springs, North Carolina, and he always got to work at least an hour before the bank opened at nine.

It never occurred to the rest of us that we could ride to town with him as he drove our one and only car to work. No, going to town was too important to get there that fast. We *walked* to town.

The walk was so much a family ritual that we would have walked even if there had been a second car and even if Mama had been able to drive that non-existent second Plymouth.

In fact, we started getting ready for the walk even before Daddy left for work. Mama saw that Joe-brother and I ate breakfast, bathed, and dressed while she, who had slept with pink plastic and aluminum porcupine curlers in her hair all night, brushed her hair so many times that all of the slept-in curl was brushed back out.

Finally, about an hour after Daddy had left, we closed the kitchen door behind us—the key long ago lost and forgotten—rounded the back of the house, and trailed, three in a row, up the driveway and toward the road.

We lived on Plott Creek, two miles from town, on a dirt road. Mama insisted that it was not dirt but rather "a gravel road," just as she and some of the neighbors tried to rename Plott Creek "Fairview Road."

Daddy found the "Fairview Road" business quite amusing. "It's always been Plott Creek and it'll always be Plott Creek," he answered her suggestion. "It even *smells* like Plott Creek. Call it whatever you like … but some things never change!"

Through the thin soles of what Mama called our "barefoot sandals" we could feel the hard and irregular gravel as we walked, following her instructions, "on the left-hand side facing traffic," though there really wasn't any traffic. If a car did come, it would be, according to Mama, "one of those crazy, wild Plott boys running wide open in one of those flat-head Fords," and we would have to be ready to jump the ditch and land in the Queen Anne's lace.

When on those rare occasions the dust of the "gravel road" got stirred up, it really did smell like Plott Creek. Joe-brother and I loved the smell of the dust. Even if we encountered no Fords, I knew exactly how to walk, hiding behind Mama so that she wouldn't catch and scold me, dragging the edges of my sandals in the gravel so that I could stir up my own private cloud of that good-smelling dust.

In about a half mile we came to the end of the gravel and met the summer-hot smell of road tar as we left the Plott Creek road and followed the now-paved county road on to Sulpher Springs. Just as we turned right and onto the pavement, we were flooded by a new smell, for there beside the road was McCaul's Slaughterhouse.

I could never understand how cows, whose bodies and breath smelled so sweet to me one at a time on the farm at home, could smell so differently all penned up at the slaughterhouse. Perhaps some sense of their impending fate produced a different odor after all.

Daddy called McCaul's Slaughterhouse "the abattoir." Then it was Mama's turn to be amused. "It's always been a slaught rhouse," she would smile, "and it's always going to be a slaughterhouse. It even *smells* like a slaughterhouse. Call it whatever you want to call it ... but some things never change!"

Around the next curve in the road the smell changed for the better as we approached Mrs. Roper's house. Mrs. Roper was an old lady, a "widow lady," Mama called her. She lived in a fresh, white house that Mama called a cottage. Beside Mrs. Roper's cottage there was a huge garden plot that was fresh-plowed every spring of the year and then planted—not with vegetables, but from end to end with rows and rows of annual flowers. The yard was promiscuous with zinnias and huge yellow marigolds, strawflowers and asters and gigantic dinner-plate-sized dahlias.

There was no floral shop in Sulpher Springs, but people could come to Mrs. Roper's house, pay a dollar, and cut all of the flowers they could carry home in their own two hands.

Around the cottage were roses, and in the springtime, tons of daffodils.

I loved to drag back as we passed Mrs. Roper's and take in the sweetly aging smells of the changing summer season. I would beg Mama, "Could we please save a dollar and take home a handful of flowers?"

"Not today," she would answer. "We don't have an extra dollar, and if we did, the flowers would all be dead by the time we got home with them."

The W.G. Allen Leather Company sat across Plott Creek, on the west side, and the prevailing wind from the west carried the awful rotting odor of tanning hides and chemicals straight across the road we always walked down. As soon as Joe-brother and I got our first whiff of tannery smell, we would turn back toward Mrs. Roper's house and take the biggest, deepest breath of flower smell that our lungs could hold, then *run* through the tannery smell, trying to make it past that awful odor in one breath. We never made it. No matter how fast we ran, we would run out of air and have to breathe "tannery breath" for at least twenty steps until we reached the cut-lumber yard at the furniture plant, where the acid-smelling oak finally covered the tannery scent.

The walk past the furniture plant took us all the way to the railroad tracks, which meant we were almost in town. Just before the tracks we came to the sign that proclaimed SULPHER SPRINGS, CITY LIMITS. I did not know until I was in the fourth grade that the name of our town was spelled wrong! Then we learned that an unknown traveler had been the first to label the spring of sulphur water—for which our town was later named—with a sign that read: SULPHER SPRINGS — DRINK AT YOUR OWN RISK! Even the misspelling had stuck.

Joe-brother and I loved the railroad tracks. The wonderful puffing steam engines were so strong and magical to watch. The trains were wonderfully frightening when they roared by, shaking the air and the ground. Even when they idled beside the station they huffed and sighed and seemed to breathe like they were alive. The passenger trains and most of the freight trains were pulled by single steam engines, but occasionally we would see a double-header engine pulling a long freight train. Most of these engines were black Baldwin locomotives.

Whenever we encountered a passenger train there at the tracks, I would tug at Mama's hand and beg, "Couldn't we please ride the train?"

"Just where is it that you want to go on the train?" she would always ask.

"*Anywhere!*" was the only answer I knew.

"Maybe someday," she would answer. "We just don't have time to do that today."

The trains were not the only thing Joe-brother and I liked about the railroad tracks. We also loved it because the train station was there, and the train station had a bathroom. Almost always that was a regular stop on our trip.

The train station was a long, white building with a platform that ran alongside where the trains stopped. The ticket office was in the middle section of the building, and there was a waiting room on either end. I knew all of the people in both waiting rooms, but I never knew how important the difference between the two was until one day when we stopped to use the bathroom and the door of the bathroom I always used in the big waiting room was latched by someone else inside. Joe-brother was dancing around and about to wet his pants.

"I know what," I offered. "We can go and use the one in that other waiting room!"

"Oh, no, boys!" Mama lowered her voice as she took our hands, "That's the colored side." Then I noticed the difference: white people sitting, black people standing, apart.

One of the black men was a man I knew well. It was Mr. Arthur Washington. He was old, but still Daddy hired him to come and work at our house from time to time. Mr. Arthur Washington knew how to do a lot of things that Daddy didn't know how to do. He knew how to climb high ladders and paint the gable ends of our house while Daddy stood on the ground and painted the lower parts. This old, black man could tear English sparrow nests out of the porch eaves. He could burn the bagworms out of our apple trees with flaming, rolled-up newspapers. He could even find where the septic tank line was stopped up with willow roots, dig it up, and put in a whole new section. I thought he was the smartest man in the world. He knew how to do everything!

The next time Mr. Arthur came to work at our house, I told him what had happened that day at the train station. He held my little, weak white hands and showed me his big, strong black hands, explaining to me all about the differences between people, differences I had never heard of. He showed me his hands and made me look at my little, pale hands. Then he said that the world was changing and that things wouldn't always be the same.

"Some day," Mr. Arthur looked far away as he talked, "some day we will all sit together … but when that time comes, I probably won't be around to see it."

When all the bathroom business was taken care of and we finally crossed the railroad tracks, we were all the way in town.

Main Street in Sulpher Springs started at the railroad depot and ran no more than a quarter mile before it bumped against the courthouse at its far end and gave up trying to be a street at all. As we started our walk down the left side of the street, our first stop was almost always the post office.

Mama had seven sisters, all of whom had married Yankees and gone north to seek their fortunes. Every week at least one of them needed something that you couldn't get up north, so we usually had a package to send. We could mail letters in our mailbox at home, but packages required a visit to the post office.

The post office was a big red brick building with a double flight of marble steps leading up to the heavy front doors. It never occurred to anyone that a physically handicapped person might want to mail something back in those days.

A set of big brass block letters lined across the brick high up on the front declared: UNITED STATES POST OFFICE, SUL- PHER SPRINGS, N.C. Underneath this declaration was a second statement, mostly a list of weather conditions, promising: *Neither snow, nor rain, nor heat, nor gloom of night stays these couriers from the swift completion of their appointed rounds.*

Inside there were six service windows. Five of them were always closed. We would get in the one open line and wait our turn.

Finally Mama would step up and hand the package to Mr. Lonnie Walker, the postmaster. While he weighed Mama's package, Joe-brother and I stood on our tiptoes and pulled ourselves across the counter. If we stretched as far as we could, we could see a big .45 pistol in a holster that was fastened to the wood under the counter.

"Nobody ever robs the post office," Daddy always said. "If somebody should try, why, Mr. Lonnie would just pull that pistol and blow them away!"

Wow-eee! I thought. *Now that's the way the world ought to work!*

After leaving the post office, we resumed our journey down the left side of the street. All of the business buildings in town were two stories high. Except for Belk's Department Store, however, which did have an upstairs, none of the other businesses I had ever been in occupied anything more than the downstairs. Over and over again I wondered what was in the second stories of all those buildings.

Then one day it all came clear. As we walked down the sidewalk, we passed a set of stairs I had never noticed before. The stairs led to the conjoined second floors of all the buildings on that side of the block. Beside the stairs was a sign that read: RADIO WHSP: 5000 WATTS OF DAYTIME BROADCAST POWER. When I saw that sign next to those stairs, I knew! Upstairs in all of those buildings lived all of the different people we listened to on the radio!

Up there somewhere lived Bobby Benson, who would come on the radio at four o'clock every afternoon to tell Joe-brother and me about his adventures on the B-Bar-B Ranch. Surely Oxydol's Own Ma Perkins lived on that second floor, eavesdropping on neighbors and gathering gossip for Mama to listen to while she fixed our supper each weekday afternoon. Our Gal Sunday probably lived behind the windows with the flower boxes; and somewhere, way in the back, Gabriel Heatter was typing out The News. Why, the Shadow could even be living up there in a closet!

Some years later my theory about all the radio people was confirmed. One Thursday, as we walked down below those half-opened second-story windows, I heard Hank Williams practicing! He was up in his room working over a song we had all heard him sing so many times on the radio that Daddy now sang it to Mama. "Hey, good looking,/what you got cooking?/How's about cooking/about cooking/about cooking/about cooking/about cooking"—until finally he got unstuck and finished the verse—"something up with me?"

I felt very smart. Very few people in town knew the secret of how the radio worked. As we walked on, Hank Williams was still practicing the part about the hot-rod Ford and the two-dollar bill, and his voice gradually faded behind us. Sure enough, that very night after supper, he sang that same song on the radio and he got it right all the way through!

My favorite store, the one I could spend a lot of time in, was the dime store. WOOLWORTH'S 5-10-25¢ STORE, the sign over the front door said.

The dime store had its own smell, with wooden floors and wooden display tables that ran from the sewing notions just inside the front door clear back to the goldfish department near the back wall.

I loved the entire store, even the sewing notions. One of the sewing supply tables had an angled display case that held slanting stacks of thread in at least two dozen different colors. Most of the case was glass-fronted, but you could choose your color and pull the spool out from the bottom of the case. If Mama was looking at something else and if Joe-brother and I were fast, we could pull several spools of thread out at the bottom and watch all of the others drop—*clunk, clunk, clunk, clunk, clunk*—then slip the loose ones back in at the top before she turned around and caught us.

I watched with envy as customers would choose a goldfish from the big bubbling fish tanks in the back of the store.

Their chosen fish would be captured in a net wielded by Miss Victoria Francis, the store manager, who balanced precariously on the top of a three-step ladder and wobbled around with a little green net, lunging all over the fish tank until she finally trapped the poor fish. Then she would drop it into its own water in a folded cardboard carton just like those I saw in later life in Chinese takeout restaurants.

Joe-brother and I would beg for a fish, but Mama would only say, "If you get one, it'll be dead by the time we get home with it." And when we finally badgered her into letting us get one ... it was!

We always ate lunch at Conard's Drugstore. Dr. Conard ran the place. He filled the prescriptions in the pharmacy in the back of the store, made the grilled-cheese sandwiches at the lunch counter, and sold shampoo in the cosmetics corner. The drugstore was a one-person operation.

Mama, Joe-brother, and I always got the same thing at the drugstore, lunch after lunch. We each ordered "a grilled cheese sandwich and a small Co-cola, please!" I would beg for ice cream, but Mama always said, "We just don't have enough money for ice cream, boys."

But one day, the day when we bought new shoes, there was suddenly enough money left over for ice cream. That day we went to the Belk's shoe department at the back of the second floor. Mr. Kirkpatrick, the skinny, black-suited shoe man, patiently led us through trying on what seemed like a hundred pairs of black and white Buster Brown saddle oxfords until we each finally found the pair that was, in Mama's judgment, "just the right number of sizes too big ... so they can grow into them."

Mama and Mr. Kirkpatrick looked in the top eyepieces of the fluoroscope, a gigantic box-like contraption that x-rayed our feet in our new shoes. We stuck the toes of our feet in the openings at the bottom and, at his instructions, wiggled our toes.

Later, while Mama was paying for the new shoes, Joe-brother and I skipped back to the fluoroscope. We took turns—one of us sticking his hand into the port at the bottom of the big active x-ray cabinet, the other peering into one of the metal eyepieces on the top to watch the bones wiggle.

After Mama paid for the new shoes, she took us in tow and announced, "That was a bargain. All of those Buster Browns were on sale. We have enough money left over today so that when we get our lunch at the drugstore, both of you can have ice cream!"

Neither Joe-brother nor I had either one wanted the new shoes to begin with, and we wondered why we couldn't have just kept wearing our old shoes and then had enough money to get ice cream every week.

On this proud day I looked up at Dr. Conard and boldly placed my order. "One grilled cheese sandwich, one small Co-Cola, *and* a cone of ice cream, please!"

There were two flavors: brown and white. Being a farm boy, I just didn't trust brown. Joe-brother and I walked out of the drugstore carrying our first ice cream cones. I gave mine a big lick and the round ball of white ice cream rolled off the cone and landed smack on the toe of the Buster Brown shoe that I didn't want to begin with.

Dr. Conard saw it all. He came running with a handful of paper napkins, picked up the ice cream, wiped off the new shoe, and fixed me a new cone before Mama even had time to fuss about it.

No matter what we did or where we went on those wonderful Thursdays in town, we were always headed toward the same final goal. Every week, at precisely four o'clock in the afternoon, we would stop whatever we were doing and leave wherever we happened to be as we followed Mama's quickening step toward the door of the Ladye Faire Beauty Parlour for her every-Thursday four o'clock hair-transformation appointment.

Joe-brother and I loved the Ladye Faire. The old beauty parlor smelled like someone had taken Mrs. Roper's flower garden and the tannery chemicals and stirred them all up together in one big pot. It was a place of magic.

The Ladye Faire was a very proper establishment. Women were not transformed right out in the open where anyone looking in from the sidewalk could see them. No, there was a row of little private booths all across the back of the shop, booths of plywood painted the color of a flamingo. A woman would disappear into one of those booths as one person, then emerge an hour or two later completely trans-formed into someone else. No one knew the mysteries or the secrets of what went on inside those booths—no one, that is, except little boys who could get down on the floor and look up under the swinging doors and spy on the entire operation.

While Mama was being transformed by Mrs. Bryson, Joe-brother and I were told to wait out in the front part of the shop. At home we had *Life* magazine and some very old copies of *National Geographic* that had come to us from relatives who actually subscribed. But here at the Ladye Faire we could look at *Modern Romance!* While Mama was safely out of sight in the transformation chamber, we looked at pictures of people who were almost kissing and at advertise-ments for what the magazine called "support garments."

The seats in the waiting room all had arms that looked like chrome pipes and were covered with brown plastic upholstery. Each chair had a high back and a huge hair-dryer unit that tilted back when not in use, or forward for baking the heads of transformed women.

If no one else was in this waiting area, Joe-brother and I would get up on our knees in the seats, tilt the dryers into the "down" position, turn them on, and stick our heads up inside. Then we would *hmmmmm*, up and down the scale until we found just the right note that would make the whole building vibrate. Soon, from back in the booth, Mama would call out to us, "Boys?"—just that one word—"Boys?" That was all it took to put our behavior back in order.

We always hoped that Mama would be the last customer to be finished on those days at the Ladye Faire. If all of the other customers and beauticians were gone, we got a special treat. On those days, Mrs. Bryson would bring out a big horseshoe magnet with a string tied to the middle. Joe-brother and I got to take turns dragging the magnet through the hair clippings on the floor to pick up all of the bobby pins that had been dropped throughout the day.

I loved to start the magnet sweeping back and forth across the floor in an arc, gradually letting the string out more and more, trolling for bobby pins. The hair would fly and bobby pins would jump through the air until the whole magnet was gradually transformed into a giant hairy porcupine.

Once we finished, Mrs. Bryson would take the magnet covered with bobby pins and blow the hair off. Then she would drop the pins in a jar labeled *Sanitary*, and they were ready for the next day.

Now that Mama was finished (and beautifully frothed and curled) we would walk down to the bank and meet Daddy at the end of his work day. Then we would all ride home together.

Even though Daddy always liked to say, "Some things never change," in the nourishing and eroding flow of time, some things did change.

The year I started the first grade, the diesel engines came. They were beautiful, the big, green Southern Railway diesels with their loud, double horns … the first time you saw them. After that, though, they were not nearly as interesting as the huffing and puffing steam engines we had always loved to watch.

When the green diesels came, the passenger trains stopped running. "Too many people have cars now," Daddy said as Joe-brother and I complained that we had waited too long and now our family never would get to take a trip on the train anywhere.

With no passenger trains, we couldn't stop at the depot to use the bathroom anymore. Both sides of the waiting room were locked shut, and the spaces where white people once sat and black people once stood were now overflow storage space. The Railway Express agent could now deliver packages more slowly than when he had nowhere to store them for a few days.

About the time that I was in the second grade and Joe-brother started the first, they built a new post office. By now I could read, and I noticed that the newspaper called the new post office building "modern."

The new post office was built of cement blocks, not of brick. And it didn't have all those weather conditions listed up there either, all that stuff about "Neither snow, nor rain, nor heat, nor gloom of night …" In the new post office, our daddy said, they didn't much care whether they ever delivered the mail or not!

By the time I was in the third grade Mama learned to drive. Now on Thursdays we *drove* to town, moving so quickly that all of the smells ran together and you couldn't see or feel anything. Nothing was ever, ever the same after that.

In the fifth grade, 1954, we got a television. By now we had several new neighbors, one with a television set. The Mocks, who had bought the lower corner of our cow pasture and built a brick house there, even invited us over on Saturday nights to watch Red Foley from Renfro Valley and sometimes even George Jessel or their favorite, Lawrence Welk.

Mama and Daddy said that they didn't ever want one of those television things, until, on the day before New Year of 1955, Daddy read in the newspaper about all those football games that were going to be shown, *free*, on television. By that very afternoon we had a black, metal-cabinet RCA with a twenty-one-inch screen and two antennae mounted on the chimney of the house. The next day we watched the games and tried to figure out why all that snow we saw on the television set never did cover up the ground.

In the sixth grade we moved. Daddy sold the pasture off as two building lots and the garden as a third. With what came in from that and the sale of our house itself, we were able to move to a new, treeless neighborhood they called a "subdivision." It was all the way on the other side of town, with paved streets and cement sidewalks that nobody ever walked on because every single family in that subdivision had two cars to begin with. The move meant that Joe-brother and I changed schools and a new life began.

Now, forty years later, Mama still lives in that house, the "new" house, now with big trees in the yard, the house where Daddy lived out all the remaining years of his life. The trees grew as he aged, and I remember so well how he sat under them more and more as their shade spread and softened the earlier harshness of the new yard. Sometimes change isn't all bad.

I remember so very well the day when I stopped by for a visit in the last year of his life. Both Daddy and Mama were sitting out under those trees when I drove up in the driveway.

Without even getting out of the car, I rolled the window down and spoke. "Hello! I need to run up to the post office and mail some things before I come in. Anybody want to go along for a ride?" Daddy loved to ride and he was up and out of his chair and heading for the car before he ever even answered out loud.

Mama didn't move. She just laughed and warned us both: "You come right back. *Both of you!* I know how you are!"

We laughed, and I backed the car out of the driveway.

Daddy looked all around as we drove silently up to the "new" cement-block post office. We drove into the lot and he showed me how you didn't even have to go inside to drop mail anymore. We just drove up close to a blue, drive-by mailbox, and I handed him the letters I had brought. He rolled down the car window and dropped them in. Then he said, "Maybe somebody in there will come out here and get those letters one of these days."

I pulled the car up to the exit from the post office driveway and started to turn right, toward home, when Daddy poked a stiff finger in the opposite direction and said, "Go that way!" For the rest of the afternoon I took every turn that he told me to take.

We rode back out to Plott Creek and passed the little house where we had lived in those long-ago years when we used to walk to town. The house was still there, amid a whole neighborhood of red brick neighbors. There was not a cow pasture within miles.

It looked, though, like someone had scooted the little house much closer to the road. My childhood memory of a big front yard was suddenly spoiled by seeing that the real yard was small enough to cross in a half-dozen adult steps.

We drove down Plott Creek Road, all paved now, with two yellow stripes down the middle because there is a lot of traffic now. Some things do change!

McCaul's Slaughterhouse was gone. Oh, the building was still there, but now it is some kind of fabric outlet store.

Mrs. Roper's house was gone, and so was the flower garden. Daddy had apparently not been out this way in a long time, and he commented on this change. "Well, look at Evelyn Roper's old place. Why, they've pushed it down and parked four trailer houses in there. I reckon her children must not've cared anything about their home place."

Suddenly I noticed. There was no tannery smell! As I looked across through the trees toward the old, brick tannery plant, I could see that the space around the buildings was all grown up and had been for some time.

"What happened to the tannery?" I asked Daddy.

"Oh, you know how it goes," he went on. "Back when you were little, the men who worked at the tannery got paid less than anybody else in Nantahala County. But they did have jobs. And a lot of farmers made side money hauling tan bark.

"But on after the war," he seemed to be thinking mostly to himself now, "we heard that there were people in other countries who would work for even less than that. The leather company just closed down, son."

On into town we rode. Since the train no longer ran at all, the tracks had been taken up, and there were not even any bumps in the road any more to remind us of where the big engines once puffed and steamed.

But the old depot building was still there! Now it was called The Station, and I could see that it was dressed up into a very fancy restaurant. A paved parking lot was surrounded by expensive landscaping, and some of the old wooden windows even had stained-glass panels. Through those windows I could see that there were cloth-and-candlestick covered tables in *both* of the old waiting rooms, and I knew that people of any color could now sit to eat in either waiting room ... but only if they had enough money to pay the bill. (There was a vestige of prejudice, however, in that the smaller waiting room was now the smoking section.)

We rode on through town, past the new FM radio tower with a little brick studio at the bottom which was not big enough to hold an androgynous rock star, let alone giants of radio days like Ma Perkins and Hank Williams. We even rode up to the Oak Hill Cemetery so that Daddy could show me the plot he and Mama had picked out as their final resting place. "Don't you think we'll like it up here?" I had no idea what I was supposed to say about that.

Then, finally, with nowhere else left to go, we went on back home.

Mama was out in the yard waiting for us. She looked fit to be tied, almost jumping up and down.

"*Where* have you been?" she started. "I thought you were just going to the post office."

I heard Daddy start to answer, then his voice seemed to stumble and catch in his throat. As I turned to look at him, his eyes brimmed with tears. Finally, he answered. "That's where we went ... *but it took fifty years for us to get back home!*"

Mother calmed a bit, then went on. "I thought you'd *never* get home. Why, you almost made me late for my appointment at the Ladye Faire!"

Daddy laughed out loud, and when I looked at him next, all the tears were gone. He punched me on the shoulder and almost danced a little jig as he said: "I always told you, son … *some things never change!"*

Daddy is gone now, and Mama is older. As it turned out, he was wrong to the very end. Things *do* change because the people who hold the world in their memories finally die, and those who come after them don't remember the stories it takes to shape their new world in that same old way.

As the place changes, the people and happenings which that space contained gradually slip from their container inside our memory, until finally, there are no more memories there.

And so, while that changing place still holds a few of its old stories, perhaps it is time to pull them out and tell them, so that, even if the place is finally lost, if the stories do not die with it, perhaps you will know those people who walked through Sulpher Springs, and the happenings with which they filled their most ordinary precious days.

Mrs. Rosemary

1948–49

*T*here was no public-school kindergarten program in North Carolina in the 1940s, but when I was five years old, instead of just staying at home, I attended Mrs. Rosemary's kindergarten.

Mrs. Rosemary's kindergarten was in the basement of the old Methodist Church in Sulpher Springs. Every day, on his way to work at the bank, Daddy took me there for my first experience of "school."

The church basement was actually half below and half above the ground, like so many church basements of the day. Daddy would take me to the top step, and then on my own I would descend the six cement steps that took me into the wonderful new world created and shaped by Mrs. Rosemary.

The windows in the kindergarten room were high up on the basement walls, which were the first rough and randomly trowel-textured plaster walls I had ever seen, much less touched. I loved those walls. I could look at them and day-dream just like watching the clouds in the springtime. I could see and feel the shapes of lions and birds and sailing ships. Why, I could stare at those walls and easily keep myself awake during nap time.

It was never very hot in the basement room. In the winter when it was really cold, our heat came from a gas heater that stood out from the wall on the side of the room away from the windows. The gas heater was covered by a cage made of chicken wire fastened to a metal framework for support.

When it got too cold, a condition determined by Mrs. Rosemary's count of how many of us were shaking at the same time, we would all assemble in front of the heater, get down on our knees on the floor, and watch her light the gas. We had no television in those days and we would watch anything. Mrs. Rosemary would remove the protective screen, strike a big wooden match, and turn the gas handle. The hot blue flame would leap with a tramping sound from one end of the heater to the other. The whole class would applaud her success! Then she would carefully replace the protective cage, and we would huddle until we all warmed up.

Mrs. Rosemary was a strong, short little woman of inde-terminate if mature vintage who was absolutely the same size all the way up and down from top to bottom. She could have worn her clothes front to back or front to front; clothing without sleeves she could have worn sideways … it would have been just the same.

Her glasses had gold earpieces that seemed to brad through the outer top corners of their frameless lenses, lenses that were slightly rounded on top but had three distinct sides on the bottom halves.

Mrs. Rosemary's hair looked like an old-fashioned bathing cap with flat, brown curls glued all over it. It looked for all the world like she could take it off, hang it on a big bedpost at night, and iron it all flat again before returning to school the next morning.

There were fifteen of us in the kindergarten class, and we *loved* Mrs. Rosemary.

Mrs. Rosemary could have taught television's Mr. Rogers. Mrs. Rosemary knew that the only way to stay even with a five-year-old is not by speeding up, but by slowing down. No matter what we started, there was never any time limit about when it had to be finished. "Why not?" she said. "It's kindergarten."

Almost every day we had rhythm band. Once rhythm band started, we could keep right on marching and making music just as long as we wanted to! When time for rhythm band was announced each day, I always tried to raise my hand just as fast as I could so that I wouldn't get stuck with the wood blocks. All the slow kids got stuck with the wood blocks, those flat blocks of wood covered with sandpaper that were supposed to make a musical sound when you rubbed them together. I thought that maybe I could never get mine to work because the sandpaper was worn out, but when I finally got a set with new sandpaper, they didn't work either.

If you were lucky (and quick), you might get to play the one triangle, the one tambourine, or the one set of cymbals made from flattened aluminum pot lids. But best of all was "the whip." The whip consisted of two thin, flat boards about two feet long. They were hinged together at the bottom and had handles like drawer pulls on the outside. If you opened them wide by the handles and then smacked them together as hard as you could, they made a crack you could hear for half a mile.

One specially selected person got to lead the rhythm band each day. There was a baton made from a fat dowel stick with glitter glued all over it and a rubber ball stuck on its bottom end. The leader marched in front while the rest of us followed, outdoors, all around the block where the church was. Around and around we marched, without limit, until we had had enough.

There was one bad boy in Mrs. Rosemary's class: Bobby Jensen. Bobby Jensen was so bad that he would spend an hour working his way around the room until he got in exactly the right place where he could see a girl's underwear! One day Bobby Jensen came to school and told us that his mother had read in the newspaper that a lion had escaped from the zoo in Atlanta and it was still on the loose. When we asked, "How far is Atlanta?" Bobby Jensen sneered, "Not very far!" He would have cheated at rhythm band if that were possible.

It was Bobby Jensen who first inspired me to worry about untimely death. I knew that things finally died when they got real old, but I had not ever noticed that sometimes life ends prematurely until Bobby Jensen came along.

The realization came one day when we were having free play time outdoors. Davey Martin, Billy Stockwell and I were in the sandbox, but Bobby Jensen was, as usual, playing alone. He was sitting on the sidewalk and had his sandal off his foot. He held it in his hand. A column of red ants was crossing the sidewalk single file. Just as my playmates and I, curious, walked close enough to notice the ants, Bobby Jensen came down on them with the sandal—*smack!*—and about six of them completely disappeared!

That night as I was trying to go to sleep I kept seeing that scene and thinking. What if somebody came along with a bigger sandal, then a *bigger* sandal, and then a BIGGER sandal? Finally somebody could come along with a sandal so big that they could go *smack* right on me and I would just disappear! It was a terrible thought.

After a few weeks of kindergarten, Mrs. Rosemary announced that the coming Friday would be Pet Day and that we could all bring our pets to school for the day. This was the same week that the North Carolina State Fair was taking place in Raleigh, and Pet Day was to be our version of the state fair livestock show. I was not very happy about this whole idea because the only pet I had was the dead goldfish from the dime store and it was buried in the flower bed where the nasturtiums grew. I probably wouldn't even be able to find it. When I told Mama she said, "Mrs. Welch has some kittens ... why don't we just get you one?" That very afternoon we visited the Welches' house and I came home with a yellow-black-white kitten whom I named Judy.

Judy went to school on Friday. Everyone loved her softness, and she even won the prize for Youngest Pet. She was so good that I thought she might have won the ribbon for Quietest Pet also, but that one went to a big earthworm that Billy Stockwell brought. Pet Day turned out to be a great day after all.

On that Sunday afternoon we got in the car to go to Grandmother's house. As Daddy started to back the car out of the driveway, we all heard a ker-thunk noise under the car. He stopped quickly. We got out in time to see Judy run out from under the car.

She went about ten yards before she fell over onto her side. We watched while her legs kept going in a running motion, then stopped. When I got to her, blood was coming out of her mouth. Instead of a trip to Grandmother's house, we had a Sunday afternoon cat funeral.

I tried to talk to Mama and Daddy about what had happened, but they didn't much listen and said silly things like, "Oh, it was just a cat," and "You can get another one." The next day I had to go to kindergarten and tell Mrs. Rosemary that my kitten had died—*"for no reason!"* I wailed.

Mrs. Rosemary listened carefully, then she gathered us all into a circle on the floor.

"Boys and girls," she began, "you have all heard about what happened to Hawk's kitten, Judy. He has told us that he believes that Judy died for no reason.

"Now, boys and girls, sometimes things do die. But nothing ever dies for no reason. If something dies, it is either because it got too hurt to get well, or too sick to get well, or, if you are really lucky, just plain too old to get well. That kitten just got too hurt to get well."

In my five-year-old mind that took care of everything. Mrs. Rosemary had listened, and she had given me a reason. My kitten had just been too hurt to get well. Now life made sense again after all.

Mrs. Rosemary's assistant at kindergarten was Mr. Rosemary.

Mr. Rosemary was tall and bald and definitely old. We were all afraid of him. He came to school at some time or another nearly every day, often quietly taking pictures with a little black box camera that he squinted down into the top of. Mrs. Rosemary told us that Mr. Rosemary had been gassed in the war and that he only had one lung.

Mr. Rosemary had a hole at the base of his throat that he breathed through. He wore a little bib over the hole, but when he bent down we could see it, and we couldn't escape the sound of his rattling breath. He talked with a little white plastic speaking tube, which he held with one end in his mouth and the other end against his throat. When he talked, he sounded like a creature from another planet.

One day Mr. Rosemary was at school, talking robot-talk with Mrs. Rosemary. All of us were huddled on the other side of the room, watching and listening. When he left, Mrs. Rosemary came over to us.

"Are you afraid of Mr. Rosemary, boys and girls?"

We all nodded in solemn unison. Davey Martin actually said, "Yes!" out loud.

She looked at us and thought for a moment. "Then just wait until tomorrow!" She smiled as she made the promise.

I could hardly sleep that night for fear of the unknown activity planned for the next day.

Mr. Rosemary was already at school when we got there the next morning. As soon as all fifteen of us had arrived, he got down on the floor with us and taught us how to mix up a recipe for finger paint. Then, to try out the paint, each one of us got to take a turn at finger-painting his bald head! While some of us were painting, the rest of us got to try out the little speaking tube to see if we could indeed sound like space creatures. We were never afraid of Mr. Rosemary again.

Mr. Rosemary made all of our toys. In the back of their house he had a little shop, where he had made all of the rhythm band instruments. He had also made our Maypole. The Maypole was mounted on a heavy base that looked to me a lot like a giant's Christmas tree holder. It had a wheel mounted on the top, to which were tied sixteen ribbons: one for each child and an extra one for Mrs. Rosemary. We could all go in one direction and the wheel would turn freely with us. We could face partners and "dip and dive" in opposite directions and the blue and yellow ribbons braided themselves right down the pole, encasing it on the way.

The Maypole was such a great thing that Mrs. Rosemary introduced it to us in September, and after that we had May Day on the first day of each month. "Why waste a good Maypole?" Mrs. Rosemary said.

In fact, holidays in general were so important to Mrs. Rosemary that every Monday was a holiday. Before September was over we had already had Labor Day, Columbus Day, Halloween, and Thanksgiving. In October it was Christmas, New Year's, Valentine's Day, and St. Patrick's Day. When we passed the Fourth of July, it wasn't even December yet, so we just started all over again. We had every holiday at least three times and some of them four. Why not? It was kindergarten and we would never again get to have a full-scale holiday every week in all our lives.

Fridays were birthdays—over and over again. When the list ran out, we just started over. By the time the year was over, with only fifteen kids in the class, all of us had had three birthdays each. Why not?

Before his retirement, Mr. Rosemary had been an ice cream maker at the Fresh Meadow Dairy Company. When he retired he bought an old cream-colored Chevrolet Fresh Meadow Dairy panel truck, or maybe he just got to keep it. It had one small seat in the front just for the driver and was all empty with no seats in the back. Though faded, you could still see the green and black *Fresh Meadow* insignia on the side of the truck. The panel truck was our kindergarten field trip school bus.

Normally kindergarten got out at noon, but on Thursdays we were with the Rosemarys all day. Thursday was field trip day, and on many Thursdays we weren't delivered to our homes until dark.

We weren't very conscious of child safety back in those pre-seat-belt days. Mr. Rosemary simply opened the back door of the panel truck and he and Mrs. Rosemary tossed all fifteen of us inside. We were so tightly packed in that there wasn't actually enough room for us to bounce around. Once we were loaded, Mrs. Rosemary would climb onto an up-turned milk carton next to the front seat, and off we would go to explore the town and the countryside and to learn about the whole world around where we lived.

We took the same trips over and over again. We would go to the fire station, see all of the fire trucks, climb on the one old one we were allowed to touch, and beg to slide down the brass fireman's pole that came through the ceiling from the sleeping room above. We never got to do that.

We would go to the armory. The Sulpher Springs National Guard was a tank company, and they would let us climb all over the tanks. "A five-year-old can't hurt a tank," Sergeant Griswold at the armory told Mrs. Rosemary, "but they might get dirty!"

"They're already dirty!" she said, and let us climb all we wanted to.

We would sometimes go to the bank where Daddy worked and get to look at the big bags of money in the vault. He would even close us up in the vault and turn out the light so we could see how really dark it was in there when the big door was locked up.

We especially loved our field trips to the Fresh Meadow Dairy Company where Mr. Rosemary had once made ice cream. We would look through a glass window and watch the fast-moving and endless row of full milk bottles as they went under a machine that plugged and capped them so fast that we couldn't even see it happen. (Mr. Rosemary had told us that they moved at the rate of 120 a minute.) We loved to go back into the big, walk-in ice cream storage freezer and see how long we could stay there until we got so cold we had to run back outside, secretly hoping that Bobby Jensen got locked in. Before leaving the Fresh Meadow Dairy Company, we always got free Dixie Cups of ice cream and flat wooden spoons to eat it with.

Our favorite field trips, though, were those Thursdays when we got to go to the Rosemarys' house. It was a little rock house—our mama called it a "stone cottage." The roof shingles wrapped around the edges of its rounded eaves, giving the roof a thick, almost thatched look. In the back was the little workshop where Mr. Rosemary had made our toys and the rhythm band instruments.

The best thing of all about the Rosemarys' house, though, was that it had a rock and cement goldfish pond right in the front yard. I thought that the Rosemarys had to be very wealthy because I couldn't imagine how much that wonderful goldfish pond must have cost. It must have been so expensive that the Rosemarys couldn't afford to build a very big house with the money that was left over.

The goldfish pond was in the shade of some old oak trees. It was dark and shady and the goldfish in it were very large. Mrs. Rosemary told us that they were tough. She said that when it got so cold in the wintertime that the goldfish pond froze, the goldfish would just sit right there and take it. (Later on I wondered, *What else could they have done?*) "Then," she went on, "when the ice thaws out, they just swim on away!"

Sometimes when we went to the Rosemarys' house their one daughter, Ernestine, was there. She was maybe old enough to be in high school, and we liked her very much.

On one of those field trips to the Rosemarys' house we got a special treat. We got to change the water in the goldfish pond. Ernestine was our "special helper." She helped us dip the water out of the cement pond one bucketful at a time until it got so shallow that the big goldfish were flopping around. Then she waded into the low water with a bucket and caught each one of the fish in it.

After that we finished dipping out all of the water that we could. Then we formed a bucket line from a pump on the top of the Rosemarys' well and passed buckets of well water down the line until it was fresh and full again. It took all of the kindergarten day, but it seemed very important, and we were never bored for a single moment. We had, after all, had the very lives of those fish in our own hands.

There was only one thing about Mrs. Rosemary's class that I didn't like. I did not at all like the way she handled trouble. At home, when I had trouble with Joe-brother, all I had to do was to tell Mama on him and that took care of things. The only problem with that plan was that if he had trouble with me, all *he* had to do was to tell Mama on me, and that also took care of that!

Mrs. Rosemary had a different plan. One day Bobby Jensen made me so mad in the sandbox that I just wanted to kill him. He had been picking and pushing all day. By the time he deliberately squashed a whole row of frog houses Billy Stockwell and I had worked hard to make in the damp sand and then said, "It was an *accident*," I had just about had it. I went to Mrs. Rosemary and tried my best to tell on Bobby Jensen.

Mrs. Rosemary stopped me and wouldn't even let me finish telling. She said, "If you need to say something to Bobby, then *you* will have to tell him. I will sit with both of you and just listen if it will help." Then she made me talk to that "bad boy."

After that Mrs. Rosemary had one of her little talks with all of us. We sat in a circle on the floor and she said, "Boys and girls, any time you have something important to tell someone, you never send a messenger. You must always tell them yourself. I do that with you, and all of you must do that with one another." I listened, but I still didn't much like it.

One day not long after that Mrs. Rosemary had another woman with her when we all arrived at school in the morning.

"Boys and girls," she began, once we had all arrived, "let's come into our talking circle." The strange woman joined us on the floor. "Boys and girls," Mrs. Rosemary went on, "this is Mrs. Halley. She is going to be your teacher for the next four days. I know that you will take care of her and teach her how everything works in our class.

"I am going to have to be away from school for the next four days because, boys and girls, last night Mr. Rosemary died."

She could have sent someone else to tell us this, or just have had Mrs. Halley show up without any warning, but that would have broken her own rule about "important messages."

Before we even had a chance to feel sad or be upset, Mrs. Rosemary was talking again. "Now remember, boys and girls, what I told you. Nothing ever dies for no reason. If something dies it is either because it got too hurt to get well, or too sick to get well, or, if very lucky, just plain too old to get well. Do you remember what I told you about Mr. Rosemary's one lung? Well, boys and girls, he finally just got too sick to get well."

We all felt much better after that.

Mrs. Rosemary kissed each of us, and then she was gone for four days, just like she had told us. During one of those days we heard something going on upstairs above the kindergarten room in what all the grown-ups called "the big church." We could always tell when something was going on up there because the electric bellows that pumped air up to the organ was in a closet off our kindergarten room and we could hear it every time it came on.

When we heard the sound of the organ pumping, Mrs. Halley told us that Mr. Rosemary's funeral was going on upstairs in the church while we were having kindergarten underneath in the basement. I thought later on that maybe it would have been a nice thing if the rhythm band had marched up there and played for the funeral, especially since Mr. Rosemary had invented so many of the instruments, but I didn't think of it in time. I guess that Mrs. Rosemary hadn't thought of it either or surely she would have suggested the same thing.

The day after the funeral, Mrs. Rosemary was back.

We missed Mr. Rosemary. After he died, the field trips were not quite the same. Ernestine was old enough to drive the panel truck, but Mrs. Rosemary would not let her drive us on our field trips. Instead it took two and sometimes three parents' cars to haul the fifteen of us around.

Finally the year ended, and after the summer I started to "real school." Things were different in real school. There was no rhythm band. Everything we did had to be finished "on time." And we only got to celebrate holidays that the school board decided had really happened. Worst of all, we each got only one birthday, and, since mine came in the summertime, I didn't even get that.

As the years passed and I got older and bigger, I began to forget about all of those things we had done in kindergarten. Once in a while, even after I had gone away to college and was just home visiting, Mama would turn to me and say: "Remember Mrs. Rosemary, your old kindergarten teacher? You know, I saw her in the grocery store this week … and she asked about you."

I thought, *So what? Is that all?* It never occurred to my adolescent self that Mrs. Rosemary might have had more than one class of kindergartners to ask about.

No matter where I went or what I did—college, graduate school, first job—each time I ventured back home, the story was always the same. A visit home could never be successfully completed unless some time or another Mama paused to say to me, "Oh, I almost forgot … I saw Mrs. Rosemary not long ago, and she asked about you!"

On one particular trip home—it must have been a dozen years after college—I realized that there had been no mention of Mrs. Rosemary. However, just about the time I realized that, Mother brought her up again. "Remember Mrs. Rosemary, your old kindergarten teacher? Well, she died about a week ago. Ernestine still lives over there at their little house. I saw Ernestine in the grocery store this week, and, she asked about you."

I started thinking about my year with Mrs. Rosemary, and before the afternoon was over, I found myself in the car going over to see if I could find Ernestine at home.

There was the little house. Small and stone, it *was* a cottage, with the thick, rounded eaves just as I remembered them. As I turned into the driveway I could see Mr. Rosemary's old workshop there at the end of the driveway.

As I got out of the car I was drawn not to the front door but straight into the oak shade of the front yard. There it was!

The goldfish pond. There were the giant multi-colored gold-fish lazing about in the shade. I stood there and visited the great-great-great-grandchildren of those old goldfish we had changed the water for all those years ago.

It was beside the fish pond that Ernestine found me. She had heard the car enter the driveway and had come out on the porch to see who was there. She knew me on the spot, and even after all those years I knew her too. Ernestine was the very image of Mrs. Rosemary, same size up and down from top to bottom, same flat-brown curls clinging close to her head.

We looked at the fish and visited by the fish pond. After a few minutes, Ernestine said, "Come inside, I was just going through some things you might want to see."

Inside, in the living room, Ernestine showed me a long bookshelf which was filled from end to end with what looked to me like notebook binders. She fingered the binders and counted them off, moving about two-thirds of the way down the shelf. Then she pulled one out. I realized then that this was a whole long shelf of photograph albums.

I followed Ernestine to the kitchen table with the one she had pulled out. As she placed it on the table I saw the cover. Hand-lettered, it read, *Hopes and Dreams—1949.* Looking back at the long shelf I realized that there had to be at least forty volumes of *Hopes and Dreams.* I also realized, with some embarrassment, that when my mama had through the years reported that "Mrs. Rosemary asked about you," that she had been keeping up with at least forty groups of little hopers and dreamers.

Ernestine placed the album on the kitchen table. As she opened it, we began to look at it together.

There were black and white photographs on the left-hand side of each page. (Now I remembered how Mr. Rosemary had always been taking pictures with that little black box camera, but I had never seen any of these photographs before now.)

There we were, the class of the 1948-49 year, pictured page after page. There were three whole pages of the rhythm band marching all around the church, all around the block. There we were, all clustered around the back of the Fresh Meadow panel truck. There we were, again, posing on the fire truck, dancing around the Maypole ... the pages and the photographs went on and on.

On the right-hand side of each page we saw, not more photographs, but newspaper clippings where Mrs. Rosemary had followed the lives of each of her students as far as the newspaper had kept up with them. Right there in Mrs. Rosemary's *Hopes and Dreams* book I read about the time I made all A's in the third grade. I read about my rock collection, which won the sixth grade science fair. I read about being in the high school band and about speaking at the Latin banquet in the twelfth grade. I read about my own high school and college graduations. The album was filled with newspaper clippings that my own mother hadn't even kept.

Ernestine and I looked, a page at a time, remembering pictured events and reading the newspaper clippings, all the way through the whole book. Then we were at the end.

There on the last page was Bobby Jensen. On a yellowed newspaper page was a picture of Bobby Jensen *wearing a Marine uniform!* The article told all about his joining the Marine Corps.

I pointed to the picture and then said to Ernestine, "I'm not surprised he ended up in the Marines. That Bobby Jensen, he was a *bad* boy!"

"Oh," she answered very politely, "Mother was always so proud of that picture. You see, she always said that when she first got Bobby Jensen he was the only real crybaby she ever had."

We looked back and forth through the photographs once again before I felt that it was time for me to go. It seemed to me that, sitting there with Ernestine, I was really getting to know her mother for the first time.

"I must go," I finally told her. "Thank you for this wonderful afternoon. You've helped me see a lot that I was too little to see way back then. I think that maybe I really met Mrs. Rosemary for the first time only today. I am really sorry that she is gone. Now that I know her ... now I miss her! I'll bet that you miss her too."

"I do, of course," Ernestine answered, "but it's OK. You see, she probably never told all of you this because you were too little back then, but Mother always told me that nobody ever dies for no reason.

"'If somebody dies,' she always said, 'it's because they were either too hurt to get well, or too sick to get well, or, if they were very careful and *very* lucky, just plain too old to get well.'

"I think that all of us who knew her were very, very lucky, because she got to be with us until she was just plain too old to get well."

Taking Care of the Bank

1948–52

*T*he same year I was in Mrs. Rosemary's kindergarten class, I discovered the wonderful world of First National Bank, where Daddy went to work each day. Mama had not yet learned to drive, and that transportation dilemma introduced me to the world of adult business.

Except for the Thursday field trips, Mrs. Rosemary's kindergarten ended at noon each day. Since Mama could not drive she could not pick me up the way other mothers did, and we had no close kindergarten neighbors with whom I could ride home. But in those days, the banks closed at one o'clock in the afternoon, and the bank where Daddy worked was just one block from the church-basement kindergarten.

Each day, as soon as kindergarten got out, I proudly walked down to the bank. I had free run of the place until it closed at one p.m. While the accounting and balancing process was put into motion behind locked doors, Daddy could leave his bookkeeping long enough to take me home during his lunch time.

The bank didn't use armored car service in those days. They simply sent currency and coins by the United States Mail. Once in a while, in order to keep the cash inventory at some sort of proper balance, Daddy would get a call from Mr. Lonnie Walker, the postmaster, saying that a big load of money had come from the Federal Reserve Bank in Atlanta and was waiting to be picked up at the post office.

Since that money had to be at the bank early in the morning, I got to help Daddy make the big pickup and transfer before being delivered to kindergarten. Since the post office wasn't open to the public that early in the morning, we drove the Plymouth around the building and up to the back door. Daddy pulled up to the platform where the mail trucks loaded, parked the car, and left the back door of the car open. Then together we would make a dozen trips back and forth carrying cloth bags of coins and canvas containers of paper money.

Daddy would always let me try to lift one of the cloth bags of quarters, but I couldn't even budge them from the floor. When I asked him how much they weighed, he told me, "About sixty pounds, I guess."

I was amazed. I barely weighed forty! My job was to carry the canvas containers of currency; paper money wasn't heavy like the coins were. The flat, square containers had heavy metal zippers with locks at the end of them. I never realized at all that in my weakness I was carrying much more money than was contained in the heavy sacks of quarters.

We never locked the car or even closed the back door between the trips. Theft was a remote possibility. We knew everybody we ever saw anywhere in town.

Once the Plymouth was loaded, it was time for the big transfer. Daddy would drive the few blocks down Main Street from the post office to the bank. The bank building sat on the main corner of one of the two red lights in town, and a No Parking zone occupied a space from that corner all the way to the front of the bank building. Daddy would not only park in the No Parking area, he would actually pull two wheels of the Plymouth right up on the sidewalk so the car would be closer to the front door of the building.

He would unlock the brass-plated front door of the bank, prop both it and the glass set of inner doors open, and open the door of the parked Plymouth. The process was simply the reverse of what we had just done at the post office. Back and forth a dozen times we carried the money. Though the car was always out of our sight between trips, we never felt any risk.

The main vault at the bank was marvelous to behold. It had a wonderfully massive silvery door, highly polished in swirly patterns. Huge shiny steel bars ran across the front of the door; moved by a wheel about the right size to steer a steamboat, the bars dropped and then tightened into slots on the sides and sealed the vault door shut.

Even if you knew the combination, the vault could not be opened until eight o'clock in the morning because inside the back of the door were three time clocks; the dial could not be turned, even if you knew the combination, until they went off. (Besides that, Daddy often showed me what he called a "tear gas bomb" that was built right into the vault door just behind the combination dial. He said if anybody tried to drill a hole in the lock or burn it out with a blowtorch, the tear gas would go off. He said they would cry their way all the way out the door!)

At eight o'clock, Daddy would spin the combination dial. Opening that vault was *art* when you watched him do it. He was so fast and smooth that it was like watching someone playing a musical instrument. It was *spin* to the right, *spin* to the left, *spin* to the right, *spin* to the left, and then *click*, it was open.

He would then let me turn the big ship wheel, and the huge door would magically unseal and swing open. A hinged floor plate swung into place over the tapered fittings at the bottom of the door, creating a smooth little bridge to walk and roll money carts over. Now we completed our mission by carrying the bags of money a third time, from the floor of the lobby where we had left them all the way to the very back of that big vault.

No matter how much I loved Mrs. Rosemary's kindergarten, I was never really unhappy when the day was over, for then it was time to go to the bank. In the afternoon, the bank was a different place. The privacy I enjoyed with Daddy on those early morning trips was now replaced by the business and bustle of a world filled with people of all sorts, shapes, and sizes.

Between the outer doors, which pushed in straight off Main Street, and the second set of glass inner doors, which pushed into the lobby, there was a little alcove. On the left-hand side, marble stairs ran to floors above and below. The right-hand side was the domain of Mr. Roy Batchelor the Blind Man, who sold newspapers and magazines, cigars and cigarettes, candy of every kind, soft drinks and chewing gum.

The Blind Man's shop was my first favorite hangout at the bank. Mr. Roy Batchelor was the only blind person in town, as far as I knew. I thought that his name was funny because I knew he was married. I also thought it strange to be married to somebody you had never seen—and even stranger for a woman to be married to someone who had never seen her!

Mr. Roy Batchelor had a little dog named Blackie, whom he called "my eyes." (I always wondered how he knew what color Blackie was.) Once, when I asked him how he got to work each day, he told me, "Blackie knows the way," but later on I heard him counting his steps out loud to himself as he came down the sidewalk with Blackie. "One-forty-nine, one-fifty, one-fifty-one ..." On that count he turned left and pushed open the entrance to the bank without even feeling for the door.

Mr. Roy Batchelor the Blind Man could recognize anyone who came into the bank by the sound of their footsteps. Every time I went to hang out with him, as soon as my footsteps on the marble floor got close enough he would say, "Hello, Little Hawk." He could call everyone in town by name as they came into the bank. If someone with an unfamiliar step came in, he would call out, "Hello, stranger! Welcome to town," leaving everyone, especially the stranger, totally amazed.

It was so curious to me how someone who could not see could manage the world. I watched everything he did. Mr. Batchelor could easily tell coins apart by touch. I even suspected he could feel the difference between denominations of paper money, and I would close my eyes to see if I could feel any difference between a five-dollar bill and a one. He also had an amazing wristwatch with a hinged crystal that he could open to feel the hands and the numbers on the face.

The Blind Man's best customer was Mr. Angus McCrae, the mayor of Sulpher Springs and one of the vice-presidents of the bank. (All of the men who worked at the bank were the vice-president of *something,* and all of the women who worked there were called "tellers.") Mr. McCrae was a heavy man, a fancy dresser who sat at a big desk right out in the lobby. He didn't seem to really do any work but just sat there to greet people and answer questions about who they needed to see for the help they needed.

Every time I saw Mr. McCrae he was holding an un-lighted cigar in his mouth. He neither smoked it nor chewed it. He just held it there in one side of his mouth while he talked out of the other side. He bought Muriel cigars and Juicy Fruit gum from the Blind Man's shop and, even though it was not ten steps from his desk to the shop, he would often call me over and send me to buy the chewing gum and cigars for him. He always tipped me with a stick of gum.

I hated the taste of Juicy Fruit gum. Spearmint was my favorite flavor. I tried every way I could think of to get Mr. Batchelor to send Mr. McCrae the wrong flavor of gum, but the Blind Man knew so precisely where every single item in the shop was—and could hear so instantly if I tried to move things around—that we were stuck with the Juicy Fruit.

The whole inside of the bank seemed to be made of marble and brass. The floors were marble, the countertops and tellers' windows were marble, the walls were marble halfway up. Brass railings ran along the tops of the tellers' cages and all the way around the counters. I was both fasci-nated and revolted by the giant brass spittoons. There was a well-used spittoon in every corner, with a speckling of splashed near-misses decorating the surrounding floor and walls. All of the men who worked at the bank either chewed tobacco or smoked, some both, and most of the male custom-ers did as well. It was a world of tobacco: chewed, dipped, smoked.

I knew everyone who worked at the bank, and, with a few well-understood rules, I was free to play anywhere I wanted to. One of the rules at the bank was that nobody—not just me, *nobody*—was ever allowed to go into a teller's cage unless that teller invited you in there. The tellers' cages had little doors on the back of them with locks on the doors. I knew how to open those locks. You just felt along the bottom of the lock and pushed up on an invisible button your finger would find there even if you couldn't see it. But I was never, never allowed to do that unless one of the tellers invited me in, usually to send me on an errand or sometimes to give me a piece of chewing gum or candy.

The rule about the tellers' cages helped me figure out which of the men was the president of the bank. In kindergarten we had learned that the president of anything was always the person who was in charge, and besides that, Daddy had said that the president of the bank was his boss. Armed with that information, I figured out that Mr. Ardis Carpenter was the president of the bank. I knew that he was the boss and that he was the one in charge because in spite of the rule about the tellers' cages, Mr. Carpenter could go in and out of all of them without ever asking anybody and he could do this anytime he wanted to. Mr. Carpenter, who was black, emptied the trash cans and cleaned the brass spittoons, and I knew he was the president because not only could he go anywhere in the bank he wanted without even asking, he was the only man who worked there who didn't have to wear a necktie to work.

The bank was filled with toys. There were the big National Cash Register adding machines. You could punch in a whole row of numbers, and when you hit the ADD button, metal bars with numbers on them jumped up out of the top and—*chunk*—printed the numbers on the paper tape as it came out around the roller. I would add the numbers in the telephone book, most of which were just three digits, and try to create a paper tape—pluses in black, minuses in red—that would reach all the way to the floor before my play time ran out.

Sometimes I got to play with the coin-rolling machine, but only with pennies. This wonderful machine had a flat wheel where you dumped the pennies. Off of the edge of the wheel was a tube that held an empty paper coin roller. It was like magic. You turned a crank and pennies flew off the wheel until exactly fifty of them filled the tube. Somehow the machine knew when it had thrown fifty, and the handle would lock until you took that roll out and put an empty one in to start again.

My favorite business machine, however, was the check perforator. This was before the days of modern self-inking rubber stamp pads; instead, checks were processed through the perforating machine. (Some of the tellers called it the "check canceler," but Daddy insisted that it be properly called the "check perforator.") It had a slot to slide the check into and a side-mounted handle. When the handle was pulled, the machine punched a pattern of tiny holes (perforations) in the check to spell out the name of the bank, the transit number, and the date of the transaction (which was changed each day with dials on the front of the machine).

Of course, the great wonder of this machine was that the many-colored remnants from all those tiny holes fell into a tray in the bottom. They made a wondrous and beautiful miniature confetti.

The check perforator was located in the basement of the bank, just underneath the Blind Man's shop. I thought this was so that the confetti didn't get spread all over the bank, but it was probably because there were big storage closets downstairs for outdated checks and other documents. One of my favorite pastimes was to slip downstairs and run blank sheets of paper through the perforator. I could create a whole drawer full of confetti, whose fine texture felt so good to your fingers that it was simply impossible not to handle it.

The game I played with the confetti and the way I disposed of the evidence were one and the same. There was a bathroom there in the basement. I would take the full drawer of confetti into the bathroom, flush the toilet, and, as the toilet-ocean swirled below, play Second World War Bombs over the Pacific. I would sprinkle the confetti into the swirling water of the toilet and watch it all go down the drain as the big white commode went *ggguuuggghhh!* in cooperation.

The older I got, the more fun it was to hang out with Daddy, Mayor McCrae, the tellers, President Carpenter, Mr. Roy Batchelor the Blind Man, and all the others who populated the bank. Whenever there was a chance, whenever Mama needed to do a few things in town, I would now volunteer, "Oh, you go on … I'll just stay with Daddy at the bank!"

By the time I got to be seven years old, Daddy gave me a special job—taking care of the Board Room. The Board Room was upstairs, above one side of the entrance alcove where the Blind Man's shop was located. Opposite the Board Room was a small office that the bank rented to Dr. Baker, an older, round, bald, pink man, whom I often saw come in the front door and go up the stairs to his office. Dr. Baker didn't seem to have many patients. Maybe he was so old himself that they had all died on him.

The Board Room had portraits all around the walls that Daddy called The Dead Bankers' Gallery. There was a long mahogany table surrounded by a dozen big chairs, all upholstered in old, soft, cracked, dark-red leather. They were the first leather chairs I had ever smelled. To me the smell of the leather was expensive and almost delicious.

About the time I was assigned to maintain the Board Room, it got what I heard the tellers call "a good sprucing up." This meant that the portraits were all taken down and cleaned while the walls were repainted a monkey-vomit green and the floor was carpeted with the most beautiful dark red carpet anyone had ever seen. The carpet was so thick that it felt like walking on a cloud, and it showed every step you took on it!

Daddy described my duties to me. I was to carefully dust the big mahogany table and the wooden parts of the chairs with a rag soaked in red Old English Scratch Remover, then I was to carefully vacuum the rug with a torpedo-shaped Electrolux vacuum cleaner. When I did my very best job, the room ended up smelling strongly of scratch remover and looking for all the world like no one had ever been in there.

The hardest part of the whole job was being sure that all of the carpet nap was pushed in one direction so that the finished and un-walked-on carpet looked like a lawn of freshly mown dark-red grass. It took a long time to get the carpet groomed to perfection. On my first few tries Daddy kept coming up to the Board Room to see what was taking so long. Finally he realized that this job just took a long time, and he left me alone. Once I was completely satisfied with my work, I would go and tell Daddy and he would come to inspect.

After the work was checked and approved, it was time for me to get paid. My regular pay for taking care of the Board Room was fifty cents, always paid as two quarters. I usually spent part of one of the quarters at Mr. Roy Batchelor's shop. It was possible to get a Baby Ruth or a Peanut Plank for a nickel and an Orange Crush in a wide-mouth brown bottle for a dime. Mr. Batchelor would ring up the two items as separate sales in order to save me a penny. There was a one-cent tax on sales of fifteen cents, but below that it didn't have to be paid.

Out of the rest of the fifty cents I took a dime to church and saved a quarter. My goal was to start a savings account and it took five dollars to do that. At twenty-five cents a job, it would take twenty times of cleaning the Board Room to get enough. Since the cleaning jobs averaged less than one per week, it took a full year of saving before that much money accumulated.

I was probably in the third grade by the time I had all of the five dollars in hand. Finally the great day came. With five dollars in quarters in my two front pants pockets, I was almost afraid the weight of all that money would pull my pants down. I wanted to do this all on my own, so I walked up to Mr. Angus McCrae's big desk (just the way I had seen other people do) and announced, "I would like to open a savings account, please!"

Mr. McCrae helped me himself. He took some papers out of his big desk drawer and had me tell him our post office box and telephone number. He put down my full name and birthday and had me sign my name twice: at the bottom of the papers and also on a little blue card, which he stuck in a box.

Now it was time to get down to business. "What will your initial deposit be?" Mr. McCrae asked.

I proudly answered, "Five dollars, *in quarters!* I have them all right here." I started pulling quarters out of both pockets and piling them up on the glass top of his wooden desk. Mr. McCrae stacked the quarters in piles of four. When he had five piles, he counted them off out loud, "One, two, three, four, five. Five dollars!" Then he swept them off of the desk and into the open end of a brown envelope and carried it up to Mrs. Millie Crawford at the first teller's window.

When he came back to me he had in his hand the most beautiful little red book I had ever seen. It measured about two inches by four inches and it looked just like it was made out of pebbly red leather. "Here you go," he said, and he handed it to me.

There, typed sideways inside the front cover, was my name. And written on the top line of the first page was:

OPENING BALANCE: $5.00 ... Mar. 9, '52

I looked at Mr. McCrae and said, "Thank you ... but how much do I have to pay for this little book? I didn't bring enough money for this."

He laughed out loud and said, "You don't have to pay for it. It's yours. It's called a passbook. Every time you put some money in your savings account, we'll write it right down there in that passbook. Then at the end of the year, we'll put in your interest." During all of this time I didn't notice that Daddy was watching me from over at his work place in the loan department.

I held that little red passbook in my hands all the way home and could hardly wait to get in the door so I could show it to Joe-brother and Mama.

"It is a very important thing," Daddy began to tell them, "to have a savings account. It means that Little Hawk is now a part-owner of the bank. That's the way it works ... everybody who has money in the bank actually owns a little bit of the whole operation."

After hearing how important I was, I could hardly get to sleep that night. I could not believe what a wondrous day this had been. I had not only reached my goal, I was now an investor in the bank!

The next time I went to the bank, I took my red passbook with me. Whenever I cleaned the Board Room and got paid, I wanted to be ready to put another quarter in my savings account, right on the spot.

It was a Thursday afternoon after school. Instead of going with Mama to her appointment at the Ladye Faire, I asked to stay with Daddy at the bank, knowing it was time for another cleaning job. Sure enough, I had hardly gotten my first piece of Juicy Fruit from Mr. McCrae when Daddy said, "The Board Room could use some cleaning. Are you up to it?"

"Sure I am," I replied. I headed up the stairs across from the Blind Man's shop, pulled the Electrolux out of the closet, soaked the rag with Old English, and started to work. I did the best job I had ever done. Dr. Baker not only watched me work, he actually said, "Now, that's what I call clean!" As pink and clean as he looked to me, and being a doctor to boot, I knew he was an expert on what it meant to be clean, so his remark made me especially proud of my work.

On this day I even cleaned the windows. I had noticed that Mr. Roy Batchelor the Blind Man had a bottle of blue Windex that he used to clean the glass-topped candy counter in his shop. I couldn't begin to figure out how he managed to tell when the glass needed cleaning. Once, when he cleaned the glass while I was hanging out there, he told me his secret. "I clean this glass after I hear five people put their hands on it! That's what I do!" He not only sprayed the Windex on the glass but also on the wood and even on the cash register keys. After that he wiped everything off with the same blue towel.

I went down the steps to see if I could borrow Mr. Batchelor's Windex. "I heard you turn the vacuum cleaner off, Little Hawk," he told me. "I didn't think you had finished that fast. Most of the time it takes you about an hour to get done." (I never knew it had taken me that long, nor that his sharp listening reached all the way upstairs.) He lent me both the Windex and the blue towel, and I made those windows shine. I figured that might be worth at least an extra dime.

Finally, when the carpet was well curried, I reported to Daddy for inspection. The late afternoon sun was slanting through the Board Room windows as he stood at the open door and surveyed my work. He saw that I had polished those windows before I even had time to tell him. He admired them especially and pronounced my work to be an "A-plus job."

Then, without paying me, Daddy went back downstairs and started closing things up for the day. I thought he had liked the windows so much that he had just forgotten about the two quarters, so I reminded him.

"You forgot to pay me!" I said. "You always give me two quarters—" though I secretly believed that this time I would get more.

"Oh, I didn't forget, son," he began. "It's just that now things have changed."

"What do you mean?" I asked. "What's changed?"

"Remember … the savings account? Now that you're a part-owner of the bank you don't get paid anymore. When you own something, it's your responsibility to help take care of it! No pay for taking care of what you own."

I couldn't believe it. What was the point of having an old savings account if you couldn't earn any money to put in it? I wished that I had never heard about savings accounts, but had just kept my money in a jar under the bed and forgotten about the stupid three percent interest. I was about as mad as I could be.

For a while after that, I didn't want to go to the bank or hear anything about what was happening there. I didn't volunteer to hang out there with Daddy, I never mentioned my savings account and I surely didn't suggest going up there to clean the Board Room.

In fact, I almost stopped even thinking about the bank until one day Daddy told us about the funniest thing I had ever heard in my life.

There was a man named Roddy Fancher who worked at the bank. I knew him very well and liked him because he joked with me a lot. I had heard Daddy and Mama talk about Roddy Fancher having a "drinking problem" and a "hollow leg," but I didn't know what any of that meant.

The previous day, it had been Roddy Fancher's turn to close up and lock the big vault at the end of the day. Everybody else had already gone home when Roddy went to lock up. He had turned off all the lights and then set the time clocks inside the vault door to keep it locked until eight o'clock the next morning. Since he was the last one to leave—and, Daddy said, probably in a hurry to get to the beer joint—he was in a big rush. He swung the big door of the vault shut, spun the wheel to tighten the door, and clicked the lock handle. When he started to step back, he couldn't. Then he discovered that he had locked his necktie in the tightly sealed door of the vault.

"Yep," Daddy said, "he had wound both ends of that silk necktie right down into the slot the bars go into. He couldn't get either end loose, and he couldn't get enough slack to loosen the tie and slip it over his head. And, you know, those silk ties are so strong you could hang a bull with one of them."

So, Roddy Fancher had just stood there, with neither a pocketknife nor a pair of scissors in reach, and hollered for help, with nobody anywhere near to help him. His wife, at home, thought he had stopped off at some beer joint and maybe even a card game with some of his drinking buddies. She didn't start to worry until about eleven o'clock, when he still hadn't come home.

I had been asleep the night before and didn't know that Daddy had gone back out in the car in the middle of the night. Mrs. Fancher called Daddy to tell him that Roddy hadn't come home. Daddy told her he would go and look for him. Of course, Daddy figured that Roddy was out drinking beer and so he had first looked at the pool hall and in all the beer joints. Finally, as he drove through town, Daddy had seen Roddy's car still at the bank, so he had stopped and was real surprised to find that the front door was still unlocked.

As soon as he pushed the door open, Daddy heard Roddy holler. "Oh Lord, please get me loose. Oh Lord, get me out of this mess and I won't ever drink another drop!" Daddy told us he was tempted to hide right there in Roy Batchelor's shop and listen in for the rest of Roddy's Prayer Meeting before going in to the rescue. But he didn't. He went on in and turned on the lights. There was Roddy, still tied into the door of the vault by his necktie. Daddy took some scissors and got him loose. When he opened the vault door this morning, he told us, he kept the two tail ends of the silk tie as a souvenir!

After I heard this story I started thinking about all the old fun at the bank. I missed Mr. Roy Batchelor the Blind Man. I missed all of the tellers and President Carpenter. I especially missed playing with all of the business machines. I wanted to go back up there again.

Not even a week passed before the opportunity came. Mama was going to a church women's meeting. When Daddy came home for lunch, Mama asked, "Can Little Hawk go back to the bank with you? I really ought to go to this women's meeting. It's church, you know." And of course, Daddy agreed.

It turned out to be a great day to go back to the bank. It was the time of year for the 4-H Fat Calf Show, and the bank always bought the winner in order to support the projects of the 4-H clubs. Each year the winning fat calf, now a yearling weighing a half-ton, was displayed in the bank lobby after the show, awaiting its demise as a gift to the kitchen of the local Baptist orphanage.

Just as I was about to speak to Mr. Roy Batchelor the Blind Man, I heard the sound: *"Mmmooo-OOO-uuunnn!"* There, right inside the inner door of the bank lobby, was a little wooden pen about eight feet square, and inside that pen was the winning fat calf. The floor inside the pen was covered with straw and there it stood, right inside the civilized bank! Its name, Red Boy, was displayed on a sign declaring that Tommy Kirkpatrick of the Old Smoky 4-H Club was the winner, and its blue ribbon was also displayed on the side of the pen.

It was all that Mr. Ardis Carpenter could do to keep that calf under management. He just seemed to stay right there by the pen all of the time. Mr. Carpenter was either feeding or watering or cleaning up a mess or just making sure that none of the customers got too close to that fat calf. As soon as I saw this, I knew right off that the Board Room would need cleaning, because there was nothing in the bank that had been cleaned by Mr. Carpenter at all since he had begun baby-sitting the calf show winner.

Pretty soon Daddy brought up the subject. "Don't you want to clean the Board Room? You used to be good at it, you know. We haven't had much cleaning of any kind done around here since Red Boy moved in with us."

"Well…" I thought about it. It didn't seem to me like I had much of a choice. "I guess I could do that." It had been so long since I'd been there that I was hoping he'd forgotten about the no-pay rule.

But the last thing he said as I went toward the steps to the second floor was, "Remember, it's your responsibility now … you're a part owner and you have to help all of us take care of this place."

That was just too much. I was sure that he had forgotten and that he would be so glad to have me do some cleaning now that Mr. Carpenter was occupied that I would end up getting paid. No such luck. I was into work and out of pay all at the same time.

I decided that I just wasn't going to do it. Up the stairs I went, all the way up to the Board Room, trying to come up with some kind of creative plan.

The door to Dr. Baker's office was closed. So much the better. He was preoccupied with one of his rare patients. That meant he couldn't watch me, whatever I did. While I pouted and slowly began dusting the furniture I could hear Mr. Roy Batchelor below, talking with a customer. Then I remembered that when I had the vacuum cleaner running, Mr. Batchelor knew that I was working.

All of a sudden an idea came. *If I leave that vacuum cleaner running,* I thought, *I could be doing* anything, *and anybody who has any sense of hearing at all will just think that I am vacuuming for a long time.* Besides, Red Boy would make enough extra noise to cover up whatever I did. Mr. Batchelor had told me that it usually took about an hour for me to get finished, so I knew I had plenty of time to devise and execute a plan.

I thought about what to do instead of cleaning. If I went back downstairs to the bank, Daddy would see me. That was no good. Then I remembered the check-perforating machine. It was in the basement, not on the main floor. If I could sneak past Mr. Batchelor and down to the basement, then I could play Bombs Over the Pacific while I just let this old room clean itself for a while.

I took my shoes off so I could sneak down the marble stairs in my sock feet. I put the vacuum cleaner in the middle of the room and turned it on. Then, leaving my shoes up there, I slipped out of the Board Room and silently crept all the way down to the basement. I held the air in my lungs so that Mr. Roy Batchelor wouldn't even hear me breathe as I passed through.

Oh, did I have fun! Since I hadn't been there in so long, plenty of scrap paper had accumulated in the room where the perforator was located. I ran sheets and sheets of paper through the machine and made a big drawer full of confetti. I flushed the commode and sprinkled thousands of "bombs" into the swirling Pacific Ocean. I did it over and over again.

I realized that my play time was limited. I could hear the vacuum cleaner running all the way up on the second floor, and I had to admit that it didn't sound like someone vacuuming for a long time, it just sounded like a vacuum cleaner running while it was doing nothing. *One more time,* I thought, *and I better get on back up there.*

Quickly I ran paper through the machine and made one last drawer full of confetti. Quickly I went to the commode, which had not yet finished refilling from the last flushing. Quickly I flushed it again, and quickly I *dumped*, not sprinkled, the entire drawer of confetti in the slowly swirling water.

The partly filled commode reservoir did not send down enough water for a good clean flush, and I watched as the big wad of paper confetti started to disappear, then stuck in a glob, and the rest of the water began to back up instead of going on down. My panic only lasted a moment. *Oh well, one more flush ought to do it!* I reasoned.

I waited for the reservoir to slowly refill, not knowing that all the while the water-soaked paper glob was swelling up in the crook of the porcelain drain just out of sight down the bottom of the commode. The second flush was a disaster. The water that was already in the commode never moved, and the new water simply backed up and up and up until, as I held my breath in horrible disbelief, it stopped, absolutely level with the top rim of the big white commode.

I am caught! was my only thought. It was like a bomb ticking away as I listened to the suspicious sounding vacuum cleaner, running on its own upstairs. I knew that I had to get the commode unstopped. Everyone in the bank would surely know that nobody else would possibly have stopped it up with check perforations but me.

Once, when our commode at home had stopped up with too much toilet paper, Daddy had gone to the back porch and returned with what he called a "plumber's friend." I had watched as he pumped the plunger up and down in the stopped-up commode and dislodged not only the toilet paper but other things that I would just as soon not have seen. *That's what I need,* I thought. *There's got to be a plumber's friend around here somewhere.* But there wasn't. I looked everywhere, and there was no plunger.

I began to try to figure out whether there was anyone at all in the bank that I could get help from. *Mr. Roy Batchelor,* I thought. *He can help me.*

"My daddy wants to know if you have a plumber's friend," I said when I got to his stand. "Somebody stopped up the commode downstairs."

"Little Hawk," Mr. Roy laughed, "your daddy knows I don't have any plumber's friend. I don't even have a bathroom. I use the same bathroom you just stopped up!"

How did he know?

"You go up there and tell Dr. Baker what the trouble is and he can help you take care of it. And put your shoes back on. It's silly to have to listen to somebody run up and down these stairs in his sock feet all day long."

I had a sudden sinking feeling that I was not going to get away with anything. But I headed up the stairs, following Mr. Batchelor's orders, to find Dr. Baker and get help.

The door of his office was standing open now and I could see the retired doctor sitting at his desk reading a magazine. His feet were propped on the trash can, which he had turned upside-down to serve as a footstool. He was dressed in a gray striped double-breasted suit and had on a hand-tied bow tie. He looked as pink and clean and shiny as could be and was reading through his little gold-rimmed glasses.

I was scared to approach him, but I knew that Mr. Roy Batchelor was listening to my every breath. I was more scared not to carry out the Blind Man's orders.

"Dr. Baker," I stood in the open door of the office. "Mr. Batchelor sent me to get help from you."

He raised his head and looked, then took off the glasses, and looked again. He sat up in his chair.

"What can I do for you? You're not sick, are you? How come you left that vacuum cleaner running over there in the Board Boom? I thought you were supposed to be cleaning. I did wonder what you were running up and down the stairs for, though."

"Well, I stopped to take a break ... and I got the commode stopped up down in the basement. Mr. Batchelor said that you might have a plumber's friend that I could use."

"I don't have a plumber's friend. Roy knows that. But he sent you to the right place. Take me down there and show me what you've done. Don't you want to turn that vacuum cleaner off before we go?"

I knew that if we turned off the vacuum cleaner Daddy would come up to inspect the cleaning job for sure and then everybody in the world would know what I had done.

"I think I'll just leave it running. I think it takes the dust out of the air."

Dr. Baker let out a snorting laugh, and we started down the stairs. As we passed the Blind Man's shop Mr. Batchelor said, "Good luck, boys. I hope it all works out."

The water in the stopped-up commode had not gone down a single bit when we got there. It sat there, level with the top of the ceramic bowl, still hiding the sins of my confetti flushing adventures. "This is it," I pointed out to Dr. Baker. "I don't know what got it plugged up. How are you going to help me get it fixed?"

Dr. Baker took one look, then he pulled off the coat of his gray double-breasted suit and hung it carefully on the door knob. Next, he took the gold links out of his shirt cuffs and rolled up his sleeves.

What came next was hard to believe. I watched as Dr. Baker got down on his knees and plunged one hand down into the water of the commode. He reached as far as he could up out of sight in the curve of the drain, then, to my chagrin, pulled out a big handful of soaked and water-swollen confetti. As he pulled it out, the commode seemed to flush on its own and the rest of the water went swirling down with a loud sucking noise.

The way in which this pink and shining-clean doctor had unstopped the commode so amazed me that for a moment I totally forgot about how I had stopped it up to begin with. I must have been staring at him, mouth open, because he started answering questions I hadn't even figured out how to ask.

As he washed his hands, dried them, and put himself back into full dress, Dr. Baker turned to me and said, "Oh, son, that wasn't so bad. Why, if you ever become a doctor, you'll put your hands in stuff that's a lot nastier than that almost every day!" I was so taken aback that I didn't even remember to thank him.

As soon as Dr. Baker was gone, I wiped up the water that had splashed on the floor with a wad of toilet paper (which I threw in the trash can, not in the commode), ran back up the stairs, slipped my shoes back on, and started vacuuming furiously. I had not vacuumed five minutes until Daddy did indeed come up to the Board Room to check on my progress.

"You sure are taking a long time up here today. You must be doing a real good job!"

"Well," I said, hoping that the tremble in my voice did not betray me, "you know how it is. When you know that something belongs to you, you just feel like taking care of it. Since I'm a part owner, I'd be willing to clean up this whole bank if you needed me to."

"Oh, that's not necessary. This one room will do. Things will get back into shape downstairs when that calf goes on to the orphanage.

"I'm almost ready to go home," he said. "Come on down to the basement with me while I run a few checks through the perforator. I've already shut the big vault. As soon as we cancel those checks we can go on home from there."

We returned to the scene of the crime, and I waited, silent and still, while he punched all of the checks. While he was filing them away he said to me, "Son, how about emptying the drawer in that check machine, will you? It's about full."

I took the drawer out like I had never done it before and carried it over to the wire-sided trash can.

Then Daddy said, "Wait ... don't dump them in there. If you dump them in there, they run out the sides to start with and then Ardis spills them all over the floor when he's emptying the trash. I usually just flush them down the commode, it's neater that way. But don't dump them all in at once. One time I did that and it stopped the thing up so bad that I had to go all the way home and get the plumber's friend to get it running again."

"Oh," I said. "I'm glad you told me. I never would have thought of something like that." And with that, I dropped Bombs over the Pacific one last time.

As it turned out, Daddy did decide to pay me again for cleaning the Board Room. I tried later to give one of the quarters to Dr. Baker, but he said he didn't take a consultation fee on anybody's first visit.

Instead of laying any aside for the church or my savings account, I spent the entire fifty cents at the Blind Man's shop. Call it a bribe? Mr. Roy Batchelor didn't call it a bribe, he just thanked me for always supporting his business.

Party People

1951

*T*here were no neighbors' houses close enough that we could see them from our house at Plott Creek, so early on there was no one for me to play with except little Joe-brother. My well-thought-out opinion was that a little brother was worse than nothing at all.

I never met any human children who were interesting enough to play with until that year when I started to school in Mrs. Rosemary's kindergarten. In kindergarten I learned not only those lessons taught by Mrs. Rosemary but also the secrets of home life that slipped from the lips of those new playmates.

The first time Mama asked, "Well, what did you learn at school today?" I was proud to reply, "Donnie Duckett's daddy's been drunk for four days!"

When she gasped and tried to recover by asking, "No, I mean about letters and numbers," I looked dumb and replied, "I don't think Mrs. Rosemary teaches about letters and numbers."

The next day, when she asked the same question, I was glad to report, "When Charlotte Greene's mama gets real mad, she slams the door and sleeps on the davenport in the living room."

After that, Mama never asked about my school days again.

It wasn't long, though, before I had to fill her in on something I had learned at school whether she asked for it or not. On one of those first Friday afternoons of the kindergarten year I came home and asked, "Mama, did you ever hear of something called a *birthday?* Mrs. Rosemary says you're supposed to have at least one a year!"

My family had held out on me for five years about this. Much later, I realized that this omission was because my daddy had come from a family with thirteen children and Mama herself had ten brothers and sisters in all. Before Joe-brother and I were born most of our aunts and uncles were already married and had even *more* children. Our nearby extended family was so large that they had apparently figured that we just couldn't afford to take a day or two out of each week for somebody's birthday.

I did not give up. Every Friday afternoon from then on, after we had celebrated someone's birthday at Mrs. Rosemary's weekly observation, I would make a report on it. The reports—which Mama had the nerve to call "pitching fits"—went on through the first grade, whenever anyone in my class of fifteen had a birthday party. I was getting desperate, and the whining reports of my kindergarten year had now improved to include floor-wallowing and sometimes even outright kicking in the air. *"Somebody else had a party, and I never have had one!"*

The real injustice was that with a June birthday, I didn't even get a school party, much less a real one at home.

Our mama was a tough woman. She held out on the birthday business until about the middle of the second grade. Finally, though, she either saw the light or just got tired of all the whining.

"All right," she said one day, after one of my birthday party fits. "I've heard enough! You know you just haven't been old enough until now"—whatever that meant—"but now you're almost old enough. This year, when you're eight years old, we will have a full-scale birthday party."

I couldn't believe it. This was going to be great!

My birthday comes on the first day of June, which that year was to be on a Monday. The last day of school would be on the Friday before that. Mother told me the plan. On the last day of school I would take birthday invitations to my fourteen classmates. The party would be held at our house on Monday.

We got down to that last Thursday before school was out. Our family ate supper, cleared off the table, and washed the dishes. Once everything was done, Mama sat down at the kitchen table and began writing out the fourteen birthday invitations. She was mostly finished when Daddy came into the kitchen and walked over to the table to watch what she was doing.

Mama immediately stopped writing. She looked up at Daddy and with hard eyes said, "Just what am I supposed to do about that Barbara Blackwelder?"

"Don't worry about it," Daddy answered her. "Those Blackwelders don't have a car. Send her one of those invitations anyway. She won't come—no way to get here. Besides," he added, "they are really not party people!" That seemed to be the end of it.

Not quite eight years old, I didn't understand all of that. So when Mama was putting me to bed that night, I questioned her. "Mama, what's wrong with Barbara Blackwelder?"

She seemed to be looking off into space as if trying to think of an answer. "Well," she finally said, "she just doesn't *smell* right."

So? I thought to myself. *So what?*

Actually, when I really thought about it, it seemed to me that Barbara Blackwelder smelled *great*. She smelled to me just like she got to *live* on a camping trip. Wood smoke ... food that had been left over for several days ... that's what she smelled like. And a little bit like the woods and the earth itself. It was a pleasant smell. But Mama was also right: it was different. I went to sleep on that answer and didn't think any more about it.

The next morning I got up, took the fourteen birthday invitations, and headed out for that last day of school. As soon as I got there I gave one to every kid in the room.

Our second-grade teacher was old Miss Ethel Swinburne. All year long we had to listen to older kids who had been in her room in past years tell us how unlucky we were. "She's been teaching second grade for seventy-five years!" they said. Miss Swinburne was a teacher who could stop an eighteen-wheel Mack truck simply by speaking to it.

Still, she was a schoolteacher. And, like all schoolteachers, she had that basic belief that she could make up for a whole year of meanness, all on the last day. Miss Swinburne came to school that day with a big box of chocolate candy, certain that she could destroy our bad memories of her with caffeine and sugar.

She passed out candy and we ate it. We messed around all morning long. After lunch, Miss Swinburne said to us,

"Now, boys and girls, you have been *sooo* good, *aaall* year"—
it was the first time any of us had ever heard that!—"that we
just don't need to learn anything else between now and the
time that school's out."

Huh! I thought. *Big deal. Two hours!*

Miss Swinburne went on, "We will all just spend the
afternoon doing folded-paper cutting."

Now all of us knew about folded-paper cutting. It was a
trick that Miss Swinburne pulled on us every time she
wanted her room cleaned up. She would give each one of us
one piece of construction paper to fold and cut any way we
wanted to, and a little pair of blunt-nosed loose-jointed scissors that you couldn't cut anything with. Then, just about the
time we got started, she would call out, "Time's up! Time's
up, boys and girls. It's time for us to clean up this big old
mess that we have made." Somehow, the "big old mess" now
included the entire room, and through the trick of folded-paper cutting, Miss Swinburne got her entire room cleaned up.

On the last day of school, Miss Swinburne pulled a
version of this old trick designed to get her entire room
cleaned out for the summer. She brought paper out from
everywhere. She gave us paper in colors and sizes and shapes
that we had never seen before. Paper came out of closets and
boxes and drawers.

We folded and cut, folded and cut. She gave us glue and
we glued. She gave us tape and we taped. She gave us the
stapler and we stapled. Why, we even got to use the big
scissors with points on the ends! And on this day only, Miss
Swinburne herself folded and cut paper right with us.

She showed us how to make something I had never seen
before. She showed us how you could take a long strip of
paper and fold it just right, back and forth, back and forth,
zigzag, zigzag, zigzag. Then she mashed it together tightly

and cut out what looked like half a woman with her dress tail sticking off the edge. When she unfolded the paper there was a whole string of women with their dress tails connected, right there across the top of the table!

"Do it again!" we said, and she did. This time she cut out half a man with his arm stuck out, and, when she unfolded this cutting, there was a whole string of little men shaking hands right there on the tabletop.

Before Miss Swinburne was finished, she had shown us how to cut out whole rows of pine trees with their limbs touching at the tips, strips of stars, strings of snowflakes ... they were all beautiful!

By now we had made such a huge mess that, by the time we cleaned it all up, Miss Swinburne did in fact have the entire room emptied for the summer.

We all went home. I was glad that school was out for the year. But I was especially glad because I knew that if I could just manage to stay alive for three more days, I would have a birthday party.

On Saturday morning I got up, ate breakfast, went in the living room, and sat down. Mama came in and said, "What *are* you doing?"

"I'm waiting," I answered.

"What are you waiting for?"

"For my birthday party," I said proudly.

"That's not until Monday!"

"I'll wait," I assured her.

Pretty soon Daddy came through the living room. "What are you doing, Hawk?" he said, and we went through the same talk I had just had with Mama.

Then he looked at me and said, "I'll *help* you wait! You know, I'm going to try to finish building that picket fence between the yard and the cow pasture today, and while I finish nailing up the last part, you can start painting on the first part."

I was so excited! All of my life I had wanted to paint stuff, but every time I almost got to do it, Mama would show up and ruin it. "Don't let him paint," she would always say. "He's not old enough ... he'll just make a great big old mess."

I thought to myself, *Now that I'm going to have a birthday, I must be old enough.* I could hardly wait to get started.

Daddy gave me a big bucket of white paint and a brush about three inches wide. (Joe-brother was definitely *not* old enough. He would just have to stand and watch.)

The fence was made of wooden pickets, little boards about two inches wide and cut to a point at the top. There was a space between every two boards as wide as the boards were. *This is going to be easy,* I thought. *This fence is half holes to begin with! Why, I can just stand back and count all of those holes finished and be half through before I even wet the paintbrush.*

It *was* easy. I *was* old enough. All I had to do was dip my brush in the paint and then paint, with the grain of the wood, up and down, up and down. I was moving along just fine until Daddy came back to inspect the progress.

"Aren't you going to paint the edges?" he asked. "You have to be sure to paint the edges."

I had noticed the edges of those little thin boards, there in the open spaces, but I didn't think that anyone else would possibly pay any attention to a little thing like that. Daddy took the brush and got a little paint on it. Then he went up and down one of those edges and it was painted just as easy as could be. But when he had me try to do the same thing, all I managed to do was to mess up all the bristles on the whole paintbrush and have paint running all the way down my arm to my elbow.

"Just keep practicing," he told me, "You'll get it."

Just keep practicing, my eye! I thought, but not out loud. *If I practice until I get these edges just right, then I'll be fifteen before I get to the other end of this fence and I'll miss the next eight birthdays in a row.*

As I looked at the picket fence, it occurred to me that if you had something flat that you could hold up against the back side of it, something that you could sort of paint *against*, you would be able to paint those edges without tearing the brush all up.

It had gotten pretty hot by now, and Joe-brother and I had taken our shirts off. I looked at him, six years old, and I knew exactly what to do.

"Joe," I said, "Go around there to the other side and put your back up against the fence." I watched while my little brother marched right around and backed up against the first part of the fence.

As little as he was, his naked back still covered three of those spaces at one time! The rest was easy. All you had to do was to take a great big heavy brush-load of paint and just slop it up and down through there. Not only did it cover two edges at once, he was all primed up to move on over to the next place at the same time. He could even get so low down to the ground that I could paint all the way to the bottom of the fence without getting too much paint down his britches. It was perfection.

We went down that fence in no time. I thought, *See ... I am old enough to paint. I can even solve problems on the way.*

Mama came out in the yard to see how we were doing. We were just about finished. She looked at the fence and thought it was great.

"How in the world did you boys manage to do this?" she asked.

Then Joe-brother turned around.

Our mama had very pale, blue eyes. But all of a sudden they started turning red right in the center. By the time they were red all over, they had jumped out at me about three inches.

Then she looked at me and said the craziest thing I had ever heard. "Don't you think"—her voice was trembling now—*"Don't you think* you're a little bit too *old* to pull a trick like this?"

I was too shocked to speak! *I don't get it!* I thought. *I got up this morning "not old enough," about two hours ago I got to be "old enough," and now I'm "too old"—just like that! I don't know if I want a birthday or not. I mean, your whole life could be over in a week if it starts moving this fast!*

But at least Saturday was just about over. That left only one more day to wait.

Sunday started out moving along pretty well, but it stalled down during church. It seemed like the service went on forever, and, I kept thinking, "We're going to be sitting right here on *Tuesday,* I just know we are."

I was trying to move things along as well as I could. I had the church "Order of Worship" bulletin and a pencil. Whenever we did something, I took the pencil and marked it off on the bulletin. I marked off hymns, I marked off prayers, I marked off the offering, very slowly I marked off the sermon. I marked them off really well. Each time I marked I thought, *At least they can't back up on me!*

Finally we got out of church and got to go on home. We had Sunday dinner, and then the afternoon began to roll along. Pretty soon I began to think, *I'm going to make it! I can almost see Monday coming. I* am *going to have a birthday.*

And then, at about five o'clock on Sunday afternoon— out of nowhere—I got sick. It was instant, food-losing, floor-running, knee-walking, commode-hugging sick. I was blowing out one full meal about every ten minutes.

Mama sat next to me on the floor in the bathroom. She was holding my head and wiping, flushing, wiping, over and over again. Daddy was standing way back, against the wall across the bedroom. Once in a while he would offer, "Can I do anything? Can I do anything?" But he never made a move toward the bathroom to go with any of his offers.

Finally Mama looked up long enough to say, "You can call the doctor! At least you can do that."

Daddy disappeared into the kitchen and when he came back we got his report. "Dr. York said that I was the sixth person to call since he got home from church. He says there's a virus going around."

I whined, "What's a virus?"

"Oh that," he said. "That's just something they tell you when they don't know what's wrong with you!"

Later I found out that wasn't true. A virus, I discovered from experience, is something that waits to get you the night before what you've been looking forward to for weeks.

That virus cleaned me out from one end to the other. Finally, when things all slowed down, Mama put me to bed and tucked the cover in all the way around. As she walked from the bedroom back into the kitchen, I heard her say to Daddy, "Well, we can't have the party. I'll have to call all of the mothers and tell them not to come."

I could actually see her there, through the open kitchen door, as she stood by the black telephone on the wall, with her list of fourteen mothers, calling each one to tell them that I was sick, that there wouldn't be a birthday party after all.

Actually, when she finally walked away from the telephone, she had only made thirteen phone calls. Because

Barbara Blackwelder—well, besides not having a car, her family didn't have a telephone, either.

"Don't worry about it," I heard Daddy tell her when she reported her dilemma. "Remember what I told you? They don't have a car, she's not coming ... no way to get here. And, I have already told you, *they are just not party people.*" And that was the end of that.

After a good night's sleep, I felt a whole lot better the next morning. I wasn't losing food anymore, though there wasn't any food left to lose! But I did have a real bad headache left over from that virus the night before. I didn't feel at all like getting out of bed, so I just stayed there.

Pretty soon Mama came into the bedroom to check on me. "Don't get up," she started. "Don't even try to get up. You just stay right there in the bed until you're all well." She straightened and restuffed the cover all the way around the bed.

Then she started talking again. "I'm going to the grocery store. Not for long, just for a few minutes. Joe's going to go with me. I know that I've never left you alone by yourself, but we'll be right back. We'll even bring you some juice to drink. Don't you try to get up. You just stay right there." The last thing she told me before she left was, "I don't want you up out of the bed fanning around. I want to find you right where you are now when we get back." Then she and Joe-brother were gone.

There I was, for the first time in my life, all alone by myself in the whole empty house. It was very quiet.

We had new curtains in the bedroom that Joe-brother and I shared. Mama called them "drapes." They were long and green and heavy, and they made it real dark in there. It was not so bad when it was nighttime and you actually wanted to sleep. But now, in the daytime, especially with no one else in the house, those closed curtains made the room feel just plain depressing.

I know what Mama said, I thought to myself, *but I have just got to get out of this bed and fan around just enough to open those curtains.* So I got out of bed, eased over to the side of the window, and pulled the cord that opened those curtains. Then I got back in the bed.

The way the bedroom pointed, the morning sun, just coming up, came shining straight in the window. Once I was back in the bed, it hit me straight in the eyes. With that headache from the night before, I just couldn't stand that.

So I got back up out of the bed, pulled on the cord, and closed the curtains. All of a sudden it was dark, scary, and depressing again.

I got back up and opened the curtains. Now there was nothing but sun, sun, sun! The next few minutes were awful. I just could not get those curtains right. I tried everything: half-open, half-closed, propped up with a chair, propped back with a yardstick. I even tried to move the bed. Nothing worked.

Finally, trying to come up with some kind of better plan, I opened those curtains just as wide as they would go and then just stood back to think about it.

All of a sudden I noticed that when you opened those curtains just as far as they would go, they folded themselves in little flat pleats that went *zigzag, zigzag, zigzag* right back against the walls. For some reason those curtains, just hanging there, reminded me of that folded-paper cutting we had done in Miss Ethel Swinburne's room on that last day of school.

I'll bet, I was thinking clearly now, *that if somebody could find Mama's good, sharp sewing scissors and could cut a little half-pine tree right up there ... I'll bet it would let in just the right amount of sunlight!*

This was not an original idea. When we had been picking out those new curtains about two weeks earlier at Belk's store, Mama had fallen in love with a beautiful pair of curtains that had pretty little cut-out patterns in them. But when she saw the price tag, she had said, "We can't afford these pretty curtains, they're too expensive. We'll just have to get plain ones."

Well, I thought now, *not for long!*

I knew exactly where Mama kept those scissors hidden. I had watched her put them in the bottom drawer of her dresser after she had taken them away from me for cutting paper with them.

In no time I had found the good, sharp scissors and had pulled a stepstool from the kitchen into the bedroom. I was ready to work. I squeezed those curtain pleats up tightly together and cut the nicest little pine tree you ever saw. It was just about a third of the way down from the top. The material in the curtains was so thick, that every pine tree that came out was just a little bit smaller than the one that came out in front of it.

When I closed the curtain, there was a beautiful little row of tapered pine trees that started out pretty big toward the center of the window and gradually got smaller, smaller, smaller, right on towards the edge. I looked at that curtain and thought, *Now, that is what you call art!*

Then I thought, *If I can just manage to make the other side match, Mama probably won't even notice it!* So I opened the drapes again, moved the little stool to the other side of the window, and cut a matching tree in the curtain on the other side.

This time, when the curtains were closed, there was a perfect little row of pine trees that started little on the left, grew gradually taller up toward the middle, jumped across to the other curtain, and tapered down, smaller and smaller, on down to the right side. It was perfect!

Now, I thought, as I admired the curtains, *nobody would want just one row of pine trees in their curtains.* So I opened the curtain back up and added a nice little row of women with their dress tails just touching. On the left-hand side I put in a nice row of those little men shaking hands. Then, while I was doing such a good job, I added stars all across the top.

All of a sudden I looked around the room and discovered a bonus. There were rows of little sunshine figures running all across the wall above the bed. I thought, "You could trace around those with crayons and have *wallpaper!*" This was getting better all the time. By now I had completely forgotten about the headache I had started the day with.

As I began to study the room, I realized that I could see every one of those shapes four times each: once right there in the curtains with the blue sky and the morning sun coming up in the background; secondly in those projected sun shapes on the wall (they were sliding down across the bed as the sun got higher and higher). I saw the shapes a third time where I had kept all of the cut-out pieces and arranged them in a pattern on the bedspread. It seemed to me that surely they ought to be sewn down to the bedspread so that the bedspread and the curtains would match. And, by now, I had "fanned around" and stirred up all of the dust in the room until I could see all of those shapes a fourth time, in suspended dust, hanging in the sunbeams from each of those holes in the curtains right down to where the sunbeams connected now with the floor.

Looking at the whole wonderful scene I thought, *Mama is just going to love this!* I could hardly wait for her to get home.

After looking around the room one more time, I got back into bed, stuffed the cover in around me very neatly, straightened out the pieces making a nice pattern on the bedspread, and waited for Mama and Joe-brother to come home.

Finally I heard the car come into the driveway. Listening carefully, I could hear them talking as they came into the kitchen. Mama was telling Joe-brother to keep real quiet because, she said, "As bad as Little Hawk was feeling when we left, he's probably fallen asleep by now." I was smiling all over!

Silently I thought, *Come on in here! You've got to see this!* I thought they would never come.

Now I could hear grocery bags rattling in the kitchen. I could hear Mama opening a can of frozen orange juice. I could hear her pouring it back and forth, back and forth, mixing it as it melted. Finally she poured a big glass of orange juice to bring to me and here she came!

When she saw the curtains, I realized it was a good thing that she hadn't brought the whole pitcher of orange juice. Because when she saw the curtains, she liked them so much that she couldn't hold on to the orange juice. All of a sudden she screamed and the orange juice went *up,* spreading out to cover most of the ceiling before it began to rain orange juice back down. By the time I glanced up at the juicy ceiling and quickly back down again, Mama was already circling the bed, planning her attack.

Much later, I found out that what she was actually doing was trying to slow herself down. She was so mad that she didn't want to waste it by killing me all at once and getting it over with. What she was trying to do was to start in at a real low level so that there would be plenty of room to escalate. As she kept circling, she started in: "You don't *deserve* a birthday ... You think you're eight years old? You're not even ready to be *five* years old ... Why ... Why ... Maybe you *deserve* to be sick!" My headache was back all over again.

All of a sudden there was a noise on the front porch. Then we heard somebody knock on the door.

Mama left me right there in the bed. She started across the floor, sticking to that orange juice every step of the way. I heard her squishing through the living room, all the way to the front door. It was a shotgun house, and I could see from my bed as she opened the door.

There on the front porch stood Barbara Blackwelder and her mother. Behind them, in the driveway, I could see a yellow taxi, waiting with its motor running.

Mama tried to talk, but she couldn't seem to get a whole sentence to come all the way out. "I'm sorry—he got sick— you don't have a telephone—I'm sorry."

I could see that Barbara's mother was a lot older than Mama was. She stood straight and tall, very quiet and calm. Finally Mrs. Blackwelder said, "It's all right. We already knew ... Miz Moore that lives down below us has a telephone and she comes up and tells us whatever we need to know. We already knew he was sick. We wouldn't have come if you were having the party. We never were much 'party people.' But, you see, when I heard what had happened, I just knew he wouldn't get anything for his birthday.

"We're not coming in ... we just asked Miz Moore to call a taxi for us. We just ran to town. Barbara just brought him a little something."

Barbara Blackwelder handed a little box through the door to Mama. It was a plastic model car that had cost thirty-nine cents. Barbara's mother told Mama that she hoped I felt better soon and then they started to leave. Just before they stepped off the porch, Barbara looked in the door, shaded her eyes, and squinted to get a better look. Then she smiled, and I heard her say, "Oooo, Mama, look! Ain't them purty curtains?" With that they were gone.

I spent the whole afternoon putting that little car together. It was a 1912 Stanley Steamer, and they had even brought me the glue to put it together with. That glue smelled so good, but when I told Mama about it, she said, "Now don't you start that too. Not after everything else that's happened today!"

By supper time that night, I was actually well enough to eat real food again, but not quite well enough to sit at the table with my mother. I thought, *I just won't eat tonight ... I can just do without.* But in a few minutes, Mama brought my supper right into the bedroom.

As she came into the room, carrying a tray of food, she was already talking. "Well, I tried to tell you about birthdays. Not a good idea in our family. It never has been. Well, I guess at least you learned something. I guess you don't want to try another birthday."

I looked up at the curtains. It was dark now, and the full moon was just coming up outside. The moon was making little moon men and moon women right up there on the ceiling above the windows. As the moon rose, they moved across the ceiling. I knew that those shapes would keep moving with the moon until they had traveled all the way across the ceiling, down the wall to the bed, and all the way back across the floor. I thought, *I can stay awake most of the night watching that!*

Then I looked at the little car I had spent all the afternoon putting together. It had been, in fact, my only birthday present.

I looked at the glue. There was enough glue left to glue all kinds of stuff together!

Then I closed my eyes, looked up inside my head, and I could see Barbara Blackwelder and her mother, standing out there in our driveway beside the yellow taxi, counting their money, and then sending the taxi on its way, because, after spending thirty-nine cents, they didn't have enough left to ride back home.

I opened my eyes and looked at Mama. Then I finally said, "You know, Mama, I'm pretty smart in school. But I think I'm kind of a slow learner about birthdays.

"I really think that it's going to take me *one more* birthday to get it right. But it won't be hard. You see, next year I only want to invite two people ... Barbara Blackwelder and her mother. You see, Mama, I think they're the only real party people we know."

Dr. Franklin

1949–53

W ell, son," Mama said, "now that you're in school, it's time you had a real store-bought haircut. On one of these Saturday mornings I'm going to send you with your daddy to the barber shop. I know that I've cut your hair all of your life, but now it's time for you to start looking like a 'young man.'"

At breakfast that very Saturday morning, Mama said to Daddy, "I want you to take our big school boy down to the barber shop so he can get a good, fresh haircut to start to school. He's getting too big for me to keep on trimming it like when he was a baby."

The last thing she said to Daddy was, "Whatever you do, don't let Jim Caldwell be the one to cut it!"

I already knew who Jim Caldwell was. He and his twin brother, Dr. Bob Caldwell, went to our church and sat about two rows behind where we always sat. They were two old bachelor brothers; Mr. Jim was the barber and Dr. Bob was the dentist. They lived together and looked just alike, with straight posture and shocks of stiff, white hair. They drove together to church on Sunday and to work during the week in an old faded blue DeSoto.

The barber shop and the dentist's office were located around the corner from one another. The bank was on the corner between them and so the back ends of both Dr. Bob's office and Mr. Jim's shop nearly met behind the bank building.

As we started out the door to go to the barber shop, Mama repeated the orders, "Get it cut short all over, and, *don't* let Jim Caldwell cut it!"

Since it was Saturday morning and lots of people from the county had come for their weekly trip to town, Main Street was filled with cars. Daddy went to his regular parking place, through the alley beside the barber shop and into the corner lot behind the bank. There was the blue DeSoto of the Caldwell brothers, pulled up behind the barber shop. Daddy drove into the space beside it in our Plymouth and then he took me not around to the front but right in the back door of the barber shop.

The Sulpher Springs Barber Shop was a big and busy place. There were six heavy barber chairs in front of mirrors that ran all the way down the wall on one side. A big, hanging pendulum clock ticked away beside the front door.

Since I had never been inside the barber shop before, I didn't know the world could smell so good! When I told Daddy this, he said it was the smell of witch hazel and bay rum.

There were signs all over the barber shop. Each barber's name was on the mirror behind his chair. There was a sign that announced prices in the thirty- to seventy-five-cent range, including a haircut, a shave, a massage, and something called a singe. You could even go in the back of the shop and take a bath for seventy-five cents.

There was a sign that said NO SPITTING, and a bigger one that warned NO PROFANITY.

I watched the whole scene with real fascination while Mr. Angus McCrae, the mayor of Sulpher Springs, got tilted back in a chair, smothered with a hot towel, and shaved with a freshly stropped straight razor. Daddy said that Mr. McCrae got shaved every day of the week. It cost thirty cents, but he bet there was a special price for getting shaved every day.

There, at the last chair in the back, was Mr. Jim Caldwell. When I watched him cut hair, I saw what Mama had been worried about. In those days we didn't know anything about diseases like Alzheimer's or Parkinson's, and we didn't have proper names for illnesses and conditions that would be identified later on. So Mr. Jim Caldwell had what I had heard old people back then simply call "the palsy." His hands seemed to shake uncontrollably, including the one that held the electric clippers he was trying to aim toward some strange man's already half-bald head.

Daddy punched me and said, "See that bald fellow in Jim Caldwell's chair? I saw him in town one day last week and, you know what, he had a full-grown head of hair!"

I was not surprised! Jim Caldwell could zoom in with those trembling clippers and hit your head three times between your ear and the top!

Pretty soon I figured out that people waited in turn for the next available barber. Since it was busy on Saturday morning, it was a pretty long wait. Once in a while somebody would give up their turn, saying, "Oh, you go ahead of me. I'm waiting for Mister So-and-so ... I'm one of his special customers."

I knew that when my turn came I would have to go with whoever called out "Next!" because I was not anybody's "special customer." I kept watching and wondering just which barber would be the one to give me my first haircut.

By now I was watching as Mr. Jim Caldwell lathered around the ears of his now-mostly-bald customer. I watched carefully as he, with trembling straight razor, shaved around those same naked ears, drawing only a little bit of blood in the process. I watched as he applied witch hazel and talcum powder and then unfastened the sheet and let his now-finished victim go free. I was still watching as he snapped the hair from the sheet, shouted "Next!" and in the same breath turned to Daddy and said, "I believe it's your boy!"

I froze, hoping that Daddy would tell him that I was *somebody's* special customer, but at the same time knowing that, after an initial moment of hesitation, there was no kind way in the world to do anything except climb right on up there and seem glad to have Mr. Jim Caldwell cutting my hair! I got up and started the death march toward the big chair. Mr. Jim Caldwell smiled so proudly that I could see gold fillings in some of his teeth.

As I approached the big chair, Mr. Jim reached under the shelf behind him and pulled out a worn-smooth board. He laid the board across the arms of the barber chair and instructed me to climb up and sit on it with my feet in the real seat of the chair. This plan was designed especially to show me that I was not truly big enough for a real haircut and at the same time get me high enough to give him a better chance of actually connecting the electric clippers to my head. He tied around my neck one end of the sheet he had just shaken his last customer's hair off of. Then he picked up the clippers and switched them on.

The haircut reminded me of a day I had spent a good bit of the afternoon watching a big blue jay dive-bomb our tomcat. The bird got about one good peck in at the cat each pass, and that is about as good as Mr. Jim did with my head. With the electric clippers buzzing instead of a blue jay screaming, I thought I was being buzz-bombed by a little miniature fighter plane.

The haircut would have looked quite horrible in the end except for one final saving grace. Just as Mr. Jim cranked up the clippers he had turned to Daddy and asked, "How do you want it cut?"

Daddy answered the question. "His mama said to be sure to cut it short all over." This instruction meant that the buzz-bombing went on for an eternity, until finally all of the separately gapped places simply ran together and it was "short all over," sure enough.

When we got home later, I smelled of bay rum, and had so little hair left that Mama couldn't possibly have guessed who might have cut it. From that day on, I was Mr. Jim Caldwell's "special customer." He always announced the fact when I got to the shop and would sometimes even quickly slip my haircut in before some adult customer who was actually ahead of me in line. This arrangement helped account for the reason I wore my hair "short all over" by my own choice for a good number of years after that.

Even though I was now a "special customer" of Mr. Jim, I had not ever had any personal contact with his brother, Dr. Bob, the dentist. After all, I had not yet started to lose my baby teeth, and Daddy said there was no reason to even meet a dentist until your permanent teeth started coming in.

It was nearly a full year of haircuts later before the dental business began. Near the end of the first grade, my first baby teeth began to come out, and as the "real teeth" started to slide into the open spaces, the word came from Mama.

"It's time to start going to the dentist," she announced. "You have to make those new teeth last for the rest of your life, so we want to take good care of them." It was time to meet Dr. Bob.

Unlike the six-barber choice available at the Sulpher Springs Barber Shop, there was only one dentist in town. I guessed that since everybody had more hair than teeth, it just sort of evened out that way. So my first dentist's appointment was made for the very next Monday afternoon with Mr. Jim Caldwell's dentist brother, Dr. Bob.

I was not scared at all as the time came for the first appointment. After all, the point of going to the dentist was to get to keep your teeth, not to pull them out. Going to the dentist seemed like a much safer prospect than dodging the clippers at the barber shop.

When Monday came, I didn't think much about it one way or the other when Mama met me at school and we walked the short distance, past the barber shop, around the corner of Daddy's bank, and into Dr. Bob's dental office.

The office had the most peculiar smell I had ever inhaled. There was a good strong hint of clove with a definite undercurrent of alcohol running over the top of it. It smelled kind of like somebody had been making fruit cake in the bathroom.

A mixture of sounds coming from the back of the office created a real air of mystery. Somebody was talking, and somebody else was trying to talk. Pretty soon I realized that it was Dr. Bob who was doing the talking. He would say "Open up a little more now," and then some woman would say, "Owwooowwoowwwoooie!" while she sounded like she was gagging at the same time.

You could hear water running and a continual kind of sucking sound. In the middle of all of this I could hear a kind of grinding sound like somebody running a wood rasp real fast back and forth over the edge of an apple box. Once in a while I thought I could smell somebody singeing the pin feathers off of a chicken.

All in all, I wasn't real sure that this was a place that a six-year-old was going to want to spend the afternoon.

Mama signed me in at the desk, and we waited.

Finally all of the running and sucking and grinding noises stopped and the mumbling woman got to where she could talk again. She came out, paid her bill, and left. I was called up, taken back in the room that the woman had come out of, put in a chair that looked to me like it was an extra from the barber shop, and had a paper towel tied around my neck like a bib.

From what I had learned about taking turns at the barber shop, I had guessed that I was due to be next. Not true. What I did not know was that there was another little room just like the one I was in, and in that other little room there had been waiting a man who had been put in there ahead of me just so he could get progressively scared in the very same way I now had my own private room to get scared in.

I didn't have to sit up on a board in this chair, but still I was high up enough to take in the whole room, and the things I was seeing, along with the sounds coming from the room next door, helped me come up with a lot I questions I was not sure that I wanted to know the answers to.

There was water running in a little white ceramic bowl beside me that looked something like a little commode but was, I decided, both too little and too high off the floor to actually be one. There was a little funny-looking crane of a thing that was hanging over my head with a lot of little strings running around mysterious pulley wheels.

I figured out that the big spotlight was designed to shine in your mouth but I really didn't know what all the funny-looking pliers lined up in a big glass cabinet could possibly be for. I hoped they were to keep all of the other stuff working right, but I was getting a sneaky feeling that the business end of some of those pliers might end up in somebody's mouth once in a while. There was also a big wooden mallet, from which I quickly averted my gaze.

After what seemed like several hours, Dr. Bob Caldwell finished in the other room and it was finally my turn. He came in the room where I was, said, "Hello, how are you?" and, without even waiting for me to answer, picked up a metal handle that had a little round mirror on the end of it.

When Dr. Bob picked up that little mirror, I realized that he had "the palsy" just like his brother in the barber shop did. As he came toward me with that mirror shaking in his hand, I knew that he was going to need a lot of plain good luck just to get that thing into my mouth to begin with.

As it turned out, I was so scared that I was shaking as hard as Dr. Bob's hand was, and once we got our shaking kind of synchronized, he was able to hit my moving mouth without any problem at all.

That mirror hit every one of my teeth two or three times on its way around my mouth and when he later told Mama, "I didn't see anything," I thought, "Of course you didn't … that mirror never slowed down enough to even catch a reflection, let alone enough for you to see it."

Back then we didn't have fluoride in our water or in the toothpaste either one and the advice was, "See your dentist four times a year." So, during the remainder of the year, I went through that very same process three more times. In all those times, Dr. Bob never did see anything.

About the end of the second grade, my luck changed. I had lost most of my baby teeth by now (I was certain that Dr. Bob had knocked some of them loose with that mirror even before they started wiggling on their own), and on the next visit to the dentist, the report changed.

"Well," Dr. Bob said to Mama, "he's got a cavity in that first bicuspid ... and ... it's got to be filled." With that, Mama went back to the waiting room, abandoning me to a new adventure with Dr. Bob.

He came over to the big chair, pumped it up a little higher, tilted it back, and spoke what sounded like some kind of Latin to me. "You take Novocaine?" he asked. I had no idea in this world what he could be talking about.

Dr. Bob took my silence for an affirmative answer, nodded his head more to himself than to me, and turned his back to spend a few minutes rattling around in a little tool chest over on a side table.

When he turned back around toward me, I saw, in his shaking hand, a long needle with a two-fingered pistol grip. That needle reached halfway to the ceiling and it was weaving all over the room as Dr. Bob came jousting toward me, obviously planning some kind of attempt to get that thing in my mouth.

All of a sudden I understood the Latin that Dr. Bob had been speaking to me earlier, and I shouted, *"I don't need that Novocaine ... I never did care about pain very much!"*

If I live to be one hundred years old, I will never forget the filling of that first cavity. Dr. Bob yanked my mouth open with a jack you could have used to change a tire with. Then he hung a vacuum cleaner hose over a little hook on my lip.

It alternated between sucking spit out of my mouth and trying to suck a hole in my lip itself.

Then he unhooked one end of that little crane with strings running around the pulleys. He snapped a big burr-headed drill bit into the end of it.

Dr. Bob leaned across me and put his elbow on my shoulder and his wrist on my jaw. I knew that this maneuver was designed to hold his arm and hand still from shaking so he could at least hit the right tooth with that drill. He kicked the start switch, and the drill came to life. Then he attacked!

The last thing I heard was a sound like a truck spinning in the snow, and then I felt the pain. I completely stopped breathing and then squeezed the arms on that chair until I had flattened the ends of them. When he finally finished drilling, it smelled like somebody was singeing the hair off a pig in there. It felt good when he squirted warm water on the tooth and said, "Spit," but when he blew air on it after that, I just knew that the top of my head had come off!

On that day and for the next six cavities, Dr. Bob filled my teeth, while I refused to have any pain deadener at all.

So this was the way life was going to be: scalped every other week by Jim Caldwell and drilled every three months by his brother, Dr. Bob. What was the point of even wanting to grow up into a world in which adults *chose* to do things like this?

In the third grade I was in Miss Betty Sims' room at school. Every year since the first grade we had had the same fifteen children in our class. In fact, most of those same fifteen had been together from the days of Mrs. Rosemary's kindergarten. This year was different. When we got to Miss Betty Sims' room, right there on the first day of school, there was a new girl none of us had ever seen before.

Her name was Donna Sue Franklin. Even from the start she fit right in, and before long it actually seemed like she had been there with us all the time.

Donna Sue Franklin was, even to a third-grade boy, a very pretty little girl. She had clear skin with a scattering of tiny freckles across her nose. Her eyes were dark gray, and her hair was curly and just as black as it could possibly be. I liked her from the first time I saw her.

Not long after school started, I was invited to Donna Sue's house to play on a Saturday. Of course, I was not the only one who was to be there: as a *boy* I wouldn't have gone to a girl's house to play if I were the only one going! No, it was to be a "play party," not a birthday or any other special occasion, just a party, for no reason at all. I had never heard of such a thing, but Mama said, "Some people just do things like that."

It was mid-September and still as warm as summertime, so the party was mostly in the back yard of the Franklins' house. The house itself was beautiful. It was not a new house—there were hardly any new houses in Sulpher Springs—but it had been all remodeled and painted, and all the furniture looked modern and brand-new. There was a brand-new 1953 black and white Oldsmobile 88 in the driveway. But the best was still yet to come.

In the back yard of the Franklins' house there was a swimming pool! It wasn't a swimming pool set down in the ground, it was an above-the-ground pool. Oval-shaped, the outside walls looked like a blue metal fence of connected square panels. You went up some wooden steps to a little wooden deck, and there was the water! It must have been ten or twelve feet across and at least three feet deep, and the inside surface was blue with a lot of colorful tropical fish painted on the sides. Now I knew why Mama had had me bring extra short pants (no one in Sulpher Springs had ever even heard of boys' swimming trunks). I could hardly wait to get into that water.

The party lasted most of the day, and throughout all that time Donna Sue's mama and daddy not only fixed food for us but actually played with us, even right in the water! Now, my father was nearly sixty and my mother in her forties. But the Franklins were very young. Donna Sue's father taught us how to play keepaway with a blown-up rubber ball in the swimming pool. I saw where Donna Sue got her black curly hair. Her father had the blackest and curliest hair I had ever seen.

Up in the afternoon, Mr. Franklin got dressed and then thanked us for coming to the party. He said, "I am glad all of you came ... you'll have to come back soon. I wish I could stay until the party's over, but I have to go down to the dentist's office."

I spoke up quickly, "Oh, you don't have to go there. The dentist's office isn't open on Saturday."

He laughed and his eyes sparkled. "Oh, I know that, but, you see, I'm the new dentist! We moved here so I could be partners with Dr. Bob Caldwell. I have to go down there and do a little work in the lab."

I couldn't believe it! So Mr. Franklin was actually *Dr.* Franklin, and he was a dentist. Wow! I couldn't decide whether that spoiled my opinion of him or whether I hoped that he could be the one to see me the next time I had to have my teeth checked.

The next Saturday we were all invited to the Franklins' house again. When my mama questioned the invitation on the telephone, Mrs. Franklin said, "We won't do this all the time, but while the weather's still warm the children should get to enjoy the pool. We'll have to drain it when cold weather gets here."

By the time of my next dental appointment, I knew Dr. Franklin quite well and really did hope that he would get to check me out. Once we got to the dental office, my hope came true! Old Dr. Caldwell was in the front part of the office when we got there, and right off he told Mama, "I've taken on a new partner."

"Oh, we already know Dr. Franklin," she assured him. "Don't we, Little Hawk? His daughter, Donna Sue, is in Hawk's room at school. Why he's even been over to play at their house, *more than once!*"

"Well," Dr. Caldwell went on, "then you've got a head start. I'm going to give your boys over to him if it's all right with you. He is awful good with the young ones. And besides, one of these days I may decide to retire."

"Oh, you'll never retire," Mama smiled. "You've got too much old Novocaine in your blood!" They both laughed and I tried to pretend that I understood that it was some kind of a joke.

And so it was done. There was a new dental chair in the room that was now Dr. Franklin's room. It looked like something out of Buck Rogers' spaceship instead of a leftover from the barber shop. In fact, all of the equipment in the room was very shiny and new. I was still curiously looking around when Dr. Franklin came in. He got the mirror into my mouth on the very first try, and he looked around all over my mouth without hitting a single tooth.

When Dr. Franklin finished checking me out, he turned to Mama and said, "I see one little pit that ought to be touched up." In a few minutes he came back over to the chair and said to me, "Just watch that light … right up there." He pointed to the chrome frame of the big light that was focused on my mouth.

I never even saw what he was doing. He eased up from below my field of vision while I was concentrating on the light. He did some poking around back in my jaw that I hardly felt at all, and, the next thing I knew, it seemed like my whole face was getting hot and numb.

After that, Dr. Franklin filled my tooth and I didn't feel a single thing. I thought, *This is a great man ... he can even take away pain.* Whatever he did to deaden the tooth, I never even knew when it happened.

I told him that I was really glad he was my new dentist, and as I climbed down from the big chair he replied, "I'm glad too! You can be one of my *special customers!*"

Thinking back now to that first trip to the barber shop I thought, *At last ... I am glad to be somebody's special customer! Even if I end up baldheaded, at least I will have my teeth!*

Very soon after that, I was told that Donna Sue's mother had volunteered to start a children's choir at church. I knew right then that I wanted to be in that children's choir. We practiced every Wednesday after school, and when choir practice was over at five o'clock each week, we walked over to the other side of Main Street to Conard's Drugstore where Dr. Franklin would meet us and buy every one of us hot chocolate.

In just a few weeks I began to realize that I was turning out to be the boy soprano star of the children's choir. There was no question at all about that in my own mind, and when Mrs. Franklin picked me to sing a special solo I was sure that she knew it too.

This was to be no ordinary solo. It was the Easter season and the song was "The Holy City." I was singing it, not with the rest of the children's choir, but with the entire adult choir. My part was to sing the solo verse, all by myself.

> *Last night as I lay sleeping, there came a dream so fair,*
> *I stood in old Jerusalem, beside the temple there,*
> *I heard the children singing, and ever as they sang,*
> *Methought the voice of angels, from heaven in answer*
> *rang ...*

At that point the entire adult choir picked up the angelic chorus:

> *Jerusalem, Jerusalem, lift up your hearts and sing,*
> *Hosanna, in the highest, hosanna to our King!*

I was to sing the solo part from the balcony in the back of the church; the big "Angel Choir" would reply from the choir loft under the organ down in the front.

I sang beautifully, but there was a problem: being separated so far from everybody else, I could never figure out exactly when I was supposed to come in for my part, especially on the second and third verses, which I had to crank back up for after the "big angels" sang the chorus.

It was Dr. Franklin who came to the rescue. He sang tenor in the adult choir, and during a break at choir practice he got me off to the side and we made a plan. I listened while he lined out his idea.

"I can see the music real well," he said, "from up where I am. This is what I think we should do. I'll watch real carefully, and when it is almost time for you to come in, I will hold up my finger. You be ready then. When it is exactly time for you to sing, I will drop that finger. You start singing when my finger drops and you will be right on time!"

The plan worked perfectly! When the great Sunday morning came I put on my cape-like children's choir robe and proudly climbed the steps to the balcony. As I sat, I kept thinking, *Are they ever in for a surprise,* as the regular balcony sitters filed up and into their regular places, staring at me as they settled into their seats.

I carefully checked off each item in the bulletin as we worked our way down the page from the Introit on to *Special Music: "The Holy City."*

It was time. Dr. Franklin gave me the planned finger signals, and I came in on all three verses perfectly!

It sure is great, I thought, *to be Dr. Franklin's special customer!* I had by now just about decided that I wanted to be a dentist when I grew up. My dentist was like no adult human I had ever met.

I began to look forward to my quarterly dental checkups. But on my next one, Mrs. Caudill, the receptionist, said to Mama, "We'll have to reschedule you for next week … Dr. Franklin's not here today."

"Not here?" Mama asked. "But we had an appointment."

"Well, he's not here," Mrs. Caudill answered flatly. "We can try again for the same time next week."

The next week Dr. Franklin seemed just like he always did, but he made no mention of the missed appointment the week before.

That fall when school started, we were in Miss Daisy Boring's room for the fourth grade. The same old gang was back, including Donna Sue, who was prettier than ever. I was sure that the Saturday parties would start again, but the first September Saturday came and went and no mention was made of the house with the swimming pool.

The next week Donna Sue was absent on Monday. I paid no real attention, because someone was absent in our class almost every day. She was also absent on Tuesday and Wednesday, and by then I decided she must be quite sick.

On Thursday Miss Daisy called us to order. "Boys and girls ... we have lost one of our students. Donna Sue Franklin. She and her mother have moved away." She didn't say anything at all about Dr. Franklin and, somehow, all of us knew that we were not being invited to ask.

When you are in the fourth grade, no one ever tells you anything directly. Most of what you learn comes from eavesdropping on grown-ups, which was exactly the way I began to put together the story of what had happened to Dr. Franklin.

Mama was sitting on our front porch visiting with Mrs. Mock, our neighbor. Whenever they visited I liked to ease around the side of the house and see what—or whom—I could listen to them talk about. It was always about somebody I knew, and it was always interesting.

Without even hearing the name mentioned, I knew that they were talking about the Franklins. It was all the descriptive details that established the context: "Dentists have access to things like that" ... "I heard that they just left that swimming pool" ... "He did have the nicest tenor voice" ... "and that little girl, she looked just like him ..."

Just as I got all settled behind the butterfly bush at the end of the porch, I heard Mrs. Mock say, "Would you have ever guessed that he was a dope fiend?"

In my head I was trying to remember where I had heard that strange term before. It had been on a Saturday, long before, when Mama had taken Joe-brother and me to a movie at the Suncrest Theatre. I had to go to the bathroom as we left the theater to go home. While in the bathroom, I spotted an empty paregoric bottle sitting on the window ledge. When I took it back out to show it to Mama, she looked disgusted, scrunched up her nose, and said, "Shew! Throw that thing away! Some old dope fiend left that in there."

This memory completely confused me. I couldn't get hold of what it all meant. Dope fiends sounded to me like people who belonged in back alleys in dirty cities, people who had no jobs, people who had never finished school. It just didn't sound like a word that went with people who had swimming pools or pretty little girls with curly hair, or who had been all the way through dental school, who sang in the church choir. What I had just overheard couldn't be true; there must be some kind of mistake. I tried to not think about it.

It was on the next trip to the dental office that I got to overhear the whole story. I was back to being Dr. Caldwell's patient again now, and he was talking with Mama while he rattled the mirror around in my mouth.

"Yes, it's all true," he began. "First he started missing work. His wife would call in and say that he wasn't feeling well. Then a little later I began to notice that something wasn't adding up quite right with the narcotics inventory.

"And then ... oh, I hate to remember that day ... then, it was a Saturday and I came by the office to finish working on a piece of bridgework for Mr. Grover. When I opened the back door I walked right in on him, standing there injecting himself with morphine.

"The state board's pulled his license. I don't know exactly what is going to be involved legally. Right now he's in the hospital in Asheville. I understand that Mrs. Franklin and the daughter have gone back to her parents' home in Galax."

That night I couldn't sleep. I just could not understand what I had heard. I kept thinking, *Why did he do that? How could he do that?* I had never in my life been angry at any adults except my parents. But now, suddenly, a great well of anger boiled over as I thought about Dr. Franklin, my hero, the man I had come to love.

How could he do this to me? Why, I was his special customer! He was magic. I was talking out loud in the dark now. *He could take away pain!*

I lay awake in the quiet dark. There were no angels singing the answer, like when we had sung "The Holy City"—no, but suddenly there was my daddy standing at the foot of the bed.

"I heard you talking," he said. "I know that you heard all about Dr. Franklin today. Let's talk." He sat on the side of the bed and, still in the dark, listened through the quietness to a disappointed child's questions.

Finally his thoughts began to come together. "Maybe," my daddy said, "maybe ... maybe Dr. Franklin wasn't anybody's special customer ... Maybe being able to take away pain in someone else still doesn't mean you can take away your own pain, wherever it comes from."

Three months later it was time to go back to the dentist's office. To my surprise, Dr. Franklin's name was still up on the sign, right under Dr. Caldwell's name. I thought it was just a mistake, that they had just forgotten or not gotten around to taking it down yet.

Before the next three months had passed, another new dentist had arrived, Dr. Carter, to be Dr. Caldwell's new partner. I had heard all about him when he came to town and now maybe I would get to meet him.

When we drove up to the dental office, I couldn't believe what I saw: Dr. Franklin's name was *still* there. They had added Dr. Carter's name to the bottom of the sign but had still not taken Dr. Franklin's name down.

I didn't dare say anything about it, but as soon as we were with Dr. Caldwell, Mama brought it up. "Why are you leaving that man's name up on your sign? Don't you think it's time we forgot about all that?"

Old Dr. Caldwell looked at Mama, and he almost stopped shaking as he gently explained himself, very calmly. "No, it's not time to forget … it won't ever be time." She had asked the question and so now she had to listen to the whole answer.

"I'm leaving that name up there from now on, ma'am, and there are three reasons for doing it: in the first place, that man was the best dentist I have ever known—he was good with the children, and that is the real test. I don't want to ever forget that.

"In the second place, if he ever gets straightened out and comes back here, I want him to know that I want him back before he even has to ask."

Mama was not frowning anymore, just listening. She seemed to be beginning to understand.

"But that's not all. You see, even if we never ever see or hear from him again, I'm leaving his name up there. That way, every time somebody sees that sign and says, 'Who was that?' one of us will get to tell this story. And, ma'am, it's not a story to forget … it's a story I want your boys to remember."

Tonsils

1954

*A*ll through the winter of the fourth grade, I was sick over and over again. It was earache and sore throat, sore throat and earache, the same thing again and again.

Dr. York, our family doctor, called it "tonsillitis," a word that was so incomprehensible to me that it struck fear in my very heart, especially since it was usually whispered as a question by Mama—"Tonsillitis again?"—followed by Dr. York's solemn nod like it was a condition much like internal leprosy.

By late in the winter a decision had been made. Dr. York was talking to Mama in his office, but I could easily hear every word from where Joe-brother and I sat in the waiting room. "Those tonsils have got to come out ... and the adenoids too!"

I heard a tremble in Mama's voice, and in that moment I knew that the adults had conspired to kill me so that they wouldn't be bothered by having to nurse a sick child any-more.

"While we're doing it," Dr. York continued, "we might as well do the younger one too and get it all over with."

So, I thought, *they are getting rid of both of us.* I knew that Joe-brother had not been sick at all during the winter. Un-aware that in the 1950s tonsils and adenoids were removed as routinely as extraneous wisdom teeth, I could find no other explanation that made sense to me.

That Mama said nothing about this on the way home, but made the kind of chattering small talk that she never engaged in normally—"Did you have a good day at school? What have some of your friends been up to lately?"—just served to prove to me that something was indeed up. After supper that night, when all the dishes were dried and put away, we were called back to the kitchen table to have ice cream for dessert—another thing we *never* did. Then the big talk started.

"Boys," she started, "you know how sick you've been this winter." This didn't make sense. Joe-brother hadn't been sick at all. She went on, "I know that you are tired of being sick, and Dr. York knows a way to keep you from ever being sick like that again."

Sure he does, I thought. *Dead people don't get sick at all!*

"Both of you are going to have a little operation … It's called 'taking your tonsils out,' and it won't hurt a bit. They put you to sleep before they do it!"

Joe-brother was already crying and blubbering in his ice cream as he remembered (just as I did) that our neighbors, the Mocks, had had their big black dog "put to sleep" just the week before Christmas.

"Put to sleep!" Joe-brother wailed.

I remembered Mr. Mock saying, "We had to have it done … he had just served his purpose!" *And now*, I thought, *so have we!* I didn't sleep for a week after that.

After a lot of crying, a lot of bewildered queries from Mama, then a lot of talks after we finally verbalized our fears, Joe-brother and I began to understand that we were not being deliberately murdered, but that it was, as Daddy told us in one of the talks, "for your own good." My little brother and I settled down to try to accept the inevitable.

Dr. York himself was not going to perform the operation. "I could handle the little one," he said to Mama, "but that big one—he's got the worst tonsils I've ever seen. I want you to take him to a specialist in Asheville." And so we went to Asheville where I got to meet Dr. Vines.

Dr. Vines was, I thought, appropriately named. His entire brick office building was covered with ivy. The ivy even hung down over the doorway as we went in.

It was a pleasant enough office. There was even a gigantic fish tank out in the waiting room, which Joe-brother and I enjoyed examining, though there seemed to be more seaweed than fish living in it. There was no hiding the fact, however, that this was a real doctor's office. The smell gave that away.

Finally we went in to meet Dr. Vines. He was a small, soft-spoken man who seemed quite old to me and wore very round spectacles, which were strung around his neck by a black cord. His age was comforting to me. "At least," I whispered to Joe-brother, "he's done this before!"

Dr. Vines told me that I had a prize-winning set of tonsils, but later I overheard him telling Mama that I had the worst-looking throat he had ever seen in his life. That was not very comforting. It seemed that Joe-brother's tonsils were close to normal, but they were going to take his out at the same time anyway.

"We can do the operation either at Mission or St. Joseph's," he told Mama. "I would rather take children at St. Joseph's, though, because the nuns take such good care of them."

Mama agreed to the whole plan. It was decided that the operation would be done on Good Friday, so we would have the next week of school vacation to recuperate, and she would have that week off from teaching to be with us.

That night after supper, the plan that I had already overheard from the waiting room was publicly announced at the supper table. "It's going to be on Good Friday. We'll check into the hospital the afternoon before for all the lab work. The doctor says we'll do it at St. Joseph's Hospital because the nuns are so good to the children."

It was Joe-brother who asked the question that I was ashamed to verbalize: "What in the world is a nun?"

His eagerness to ask the question had saved me the embarrassment of revealing my own anxious ignorance. I vaguely knew what nuns were, but since I was soon to be at their mercy, I wanted to hear more.

"Nuns are Catholics," Mama answered. "Don't you remember, Little Hawk, seeing those two who came to town last summer to run the Catholic Bible school?"

At least ninety-five percent of the residents of Nantahala County were of pure Scots-Irish heritage; most of them were blood-related. The accustomed religious fights were between Methodists, Baptists, and a scattering of Presbyterian cousins.

But times were changing. As the mountains of western North Carolina were being discovered, one of the things outsiders brought with them was religious diversity. Now there were Episcopalians, a few Lutherans, and six families of actual in-residence Catholics!

During the summer before, Joe-brother had not been with us when Mama and I had seen the nuns. We were going to Ammons' Grocery Store. Just as we got to the red light at the corner where the store was located, I spotted the two strangest creatures I had ever seen. They were dressed in black and white robes with long sleeves, even in the heat of summer. The robes reached down to the pavement. They wore black hoods, which had what looked to me like little white wings protruding out and up on the sides. When we got close enough to get a glimpse of their faces it was downright scary.

Their faces were old, wrinkled, and nearly as pasty white as the white parts of the robes. Both wore rimless, wire-topped glasses, and there was a starched white band of cloth running like an oval frame around each of their faces, which kept me from seeing their hair and at the same time looked like its real purpose was to keep them from opening their mouths too far.

The most interesting things to me by far, though, were the gold chains the nuns wore around their necks. Gold links, these beaded chains came down to their waists and terminated in gold crosses. The wearers seemed to never stop fingering these chains, like it was a nervous habit.

"Look, Mama!" I had shouted when I first saw them. "What are those things?"

Mama hushed me in the open-windowed car, told me that they were "just nuns," and that she had heard that they had come to town to hold Bible school for the tiny band of Catholic children now resident in Sulpher Springs. I just nodded my head, without taking my eyes off of the strange visitors. I had neither enough knowledge nor experience to enable me to ask more questions.

Later on I wondered whether the things called "nuns" were men or women. From what I had seen there was absolutely no way to tell. I supposed that it was possible they were neither.

As my mind drifted back to the present, I listened as Mama explained about St. Joseph's Hospital. "It's a Catholic hospital," she told us, "and most of the nurses are nuns. Those that Little Hawk and I saw last summer were teacher-nuns; at the hospital you will meet nurse-nuns. They will take care of you!"

This scared me all over again. I remembered that when Mr. Mock told us about putting the old dog to sleep, he had said, "We finally had to *take care* of old Blackie." In my mind I saw the ancient, close-mouthed, chain-fingering nuns from the summer before, and I knew for sure that I was going to die!

On Palm Sunday the horror of the coming trip to the hospital reached its high point. It was one of those Sundays when relatives get together to spend the afternoon eating. Joe-brother and I had a cousin, Teddy Hawkins, who was two years older than I was. He was really a brat, and I hated him doubly because we had to be related to him. He lived way out in the county on a farm above the Clyde Valley, and he was a name-caller.

"City slickers ... townie-boys ... bird-legs ..." Teddy Hawkins always had new derogatory names to call us, and he seemed so sure of himself he could convince you that whatever he called you must be true!

Just as Joe-brother and I were finally getting to go through the food line, Teddy Hawkins pushed his way in front of us and said, "You-all don't need to bother with eatin'.

I heard you were going to get sent to get your tonsils yanked out. A boy in my room died when they yanked his tonsils out in the doctor's office … I heard he choked to death on his own blood! And even if you live, you're going to miss the Easter Bunny!"

Joe-brother ran off crying for Mama. I felt rage as I trembled and heat rushed up through my face and on to the top of my head—and all Teddy Hawkins' big, fat aunt-of-a-mama did was make him do without a second dessert. All this was just not fair.

I worried all week, scared and mad at the same time. It was one school week during which I never heard a single word the teacher said and didn't learn one single thing.

On Monday I thought all day long about Teddy's saying *yanked out*, over and over again. Did he know something that I didn't know? How did they get your tonsils out, anyway? I had an image of a giant corkscrew hooked to some kind of machine like the one in Dr. Caldwell's dentist's office!

On Tuesday I thought about choking to death on your own blood. I could even taste the salt my mind had memorized the first time I had stuck a cut finger in my mouth.

On Wednesday I doodled the day away drawing what to anyone else would have looked like tall, thin, sheet-covered ghosts. I knew, however, that they were legions of nurse-nuns wearing masks so that I couldn't tell which one had done what.

Thursday was the day we were going to, as Mama said it, "check in" at the hospital. Even so, we had to go to school all that day to start with, and then on to the hospital in the afternoon. I spent all that day finally realizing that on Easter Sunday we were going to be in the hospital, where, like bad cousin Teddy Hawkins had said, the Easter Bunny would never find us—if we lived until Sunday!

Once home from school, Mama gave each of us a little cloth duffel bag to pack our things in. She counted out four sets of underwear, which told me we would either come home in four days or linger that long on the road to death. Joe-brother and I half-heartedly added comic books, a few toys, and one stuffed animal each.

It was a forty-five-minute drive from Sulpher Springs to Asheville, and by the time we found St. Joseph's Hospital, parked the car, and started inside, it was nearly six o'clock in the evening. When Mama asked and Daddy told her what time it was, Joe-brother cried, "I'll bet we've already missed our supper!" Then came the next low blow. Mama told us that we weren't allowed to have supper the night before the operation. I silently remarked to myself that even condemned criminals got to have a last meal.

I was completely unprepared for St. Joseph's Hospital. We entered the lobby and went to the desk to find out how to check in. There was a nurse-nun sitting there who looked just like the two I had seen the summer before except that this one's outfit was all white. The nurse-nun's face looked like a woman's face, but when Mama asked, "Where is the admissions office?" the voice sounded like a man's. I was sure by now that we were dealing with a third gender.

While this was going on I was staring at two big pictures hanging on the wall behind the information desk. At school we had two pictures about the same size hanging in the hall beside the principal's office. One school picture was of George Washington; the other was Franklin Roosevelt. Even though Eisenhower was now president, Mr. Underhill, the principal, wouldn't put a Republican's picture on the wall.

At St. Joseph's Hospital, the big pictures were not of our presidents. No, one of them was Jesus. (Even I recognized that!) In his picture Jesus was standing out on a pretty poor-looking hillside with a pretty poor-looking bunch of sheep all around him. In fact, Jesus was pretty poor-looking himself. All he was wearing was a faded old robe, some thin sandals, and a little sweatband thing to keep his hair in place.

The picture beside him was of an old man who looked as rich as Jesus looked poor. It may have even been that the way he was dressed was part of what made Jesus look as poor as he looked. The old guy was sitting on a throne to start with, wearing gorgeous robes and a little white cap with no bill. He had on one of the biggest ruby-looking rings I had ever seen. The caption under the picture read: POPE PIUS XII. There was no message or meaning for me in the two pictures. I just wondered when I saw them which one really was more important around this place.

We followed the first nurse-nun's directions and went down the hall to the admissions desk, only to be met by another nun who was the very spitting image of the first one.

"How'd that one get down here so fast?" Joe-brother asked.

Mama said, "Hush, son ... they all look alike!"

Joe-brother and I sat and watched while Mama filled out a lot of papers and signed us in. Once we were finished with that, I found out we really were in a crazy house. The admissions nun picked up a telephone and, almost instantly, two black men dressed all in white appeared with big old wooden wheelchairs and ordered Joe-brother and me to get in. We hesitated, thinking there must be some mistake, but they told us, no, we were supposed to be rolled to our rooms. Patients weren't allowed to just walk around alone in the hospital.

At first the wheelchair ride was fun. But the two drivers were so jerky and unpredictable that I soon almost got carsick, especially when mine twirled me around three hundred and sixty degrees and pulled me backwards into the elevator.

Once off the elevator, we were rolled down the third floor hall and to our room. It had two metal beds that were so high off the floor they were scary looking to begin with. The beds had cranks at the foot which I had no understanding of at all. I figured you must wind them up for some reason, but I couldn't figure out what they might do once they were wound up.

Once undressed and on the bed, there was so much sliding and crackling from the plastic mattress cover under the sheet that I knew I would never get any sleep.

Then I saw it. The final blow, the thing that showed me for sure that I was going to die. We had crosses at the Methodist church, but I had never in my life seen anything like the thing I was now staring at above my bed. It scared me to death. Right there on the wall, above the head of my hospital bed, was a wooden cross with poor dead Jesus hanging right on it! I knew I was in bad trouble now. This was the final sign, for sure.

True to Mama's word, we got no supper and nothing to drink but water and one little cup of orange juice (which I gulped down quickly, thinking it must surely be a mistake). In place of supper there was, however, another activity—a general bloodletting!

A short, round nurse-nun with a low, constant, rattling laugh came into the room carrying a tray. On the tray was a rubber strap, two gigantic needles, and a round rack that held what must have been two dozen test tubes. I closed my eyes, gritted my teeth, held my breath, and turned my head away even though my eyes were already shut, while the nun tied the rubber strap around my arm, ran the big needle into the inside of my elbow joint, then jerked the rubber strap loose and drained enough blood to fill half of the test tubes.

I could not figure out how she held my arm with one hand, worked the needle with the other, and still managed to jerk the rubber strap loose. Later on, though, Joe-brother, who ignorantly watched the whole thing, told me that the nun had the end of the rubber strap by the teeth and jerked it loose with a good head toss.

Once finished with me, the nurse-nun turned to Joe-brother's bed. I truly hated my brother in those moments, as he not only watched the nun stick the needle right in his arm but kept saying, "That doesn't hurt … that doesn't hurt …" all the way through the whole procedure.

Finally the nurse-nun was satisfied that our blood levels had been dropped enough and left us in peace.

As soon as this one was out of the door, though, another one came in with a second tray. It was going to be tag-team bloodletting, I was sure! But this one had no needles. Instead, on the tray were what looked like two squares of ink blotter and a little metal contraption I couldn't begin to identify.

It turned out to be an ear-piercing tool! Before I knew what was going on, the nurse-nun held the little machine against my ear, pulled the trigger, and—*snap!*—my ear was bleeding! The nun looked at a stopwatch, and every few seconds touched the blotter to my bleeding ear. I made red spots around three sides of the blotter square and was starting on the fourth before the spots got smaller and the bleeding stopped.

"This one's a real bleeder," the nurse-nun said to Mama. "We'll have to give him a shot of vitamin K so his blood will clot."

Mama looked down at me and said, "I told you you better eat your eggs! Now see what happens?"

When the ear-bleeding trick was worked on Joe-brother as he sat up in the other bed, his ear bled only two drops on the blotter, and so there was only one vitamin K shot given in our room that night.

Soon after that, a little skinny nurse-nun brought us two small pills to take with "just a swallow" of water, and, before I knew what was happening, I had slept all night and was waking up on Good Friday morning.

It was not quite fully light outside yet. Before I could wake all the way up, the same two white-dressed black men who had driven the wheelchairs the evening before came pushing a rolling bed into the room, and as they lifted me onto it and we started out the door, Mama said, "Look outside, boys ... it's just starting to snow." I turned my head and got a glimpse of the soft, white flakes falling in the early morning light as my rolling bed disappeared out the door and Mama wept out, "God bless you!"

The bed rollers left me parked in a freezing cold room while they went back with another rolling bed and returned with Joe-brother. Soon two nurse-nuns—these even had masks over their faces—rolled me into a room so full of big lights and machinery that I knew this was where the actual tonsil-yanking was to happen. It looked like a gigantic version of the dentist's office.

In came Dr. Vines. I could recognize his shortness and his gold glasses frames even though the rest of his face was also covered by a white mask. Things started happening so fast now that I couldn't begin to keep up with them, let alone make sense of anything.

Dr. Vines stood by while one of the nurse-nuns held up a rubber mask on the end of a hose. The doctor said, "Son, I want you to count from one to ten, please."

As I started counting the nurse-nun put the rubber mask over my face, and by the time I got to three, I was back in the hospital room waking up just as they were rolling Joe-brother back into the room too.

I had never felt worse in my life. My head felt like it was overstuffed with cotton that had been soaked in something that smelled like a rotten version of the same stuff that had put me to sleep to start with. I couldn't even begin to start listing all the places that hurt.

As the two black men lifted Joe-brother onto his bed, the very sight of his rolling over made me nauseated, and while he was supposed to be the one getting attention, I was throwing up. One of the biggest of the nurse-nuns came running with a little silver pan shaped like a half-moon and I filled it full of stuff that looked as black as the molten tar that I had watched the work crew patch the school roof with. Later Daddy told me it was my own blood that I was vomiting! After this I didn't mind vomiting because all I could think of was that if I vomited the blood, I couldn't choke to death on it the way my bad cousin Teddy had told me I would.

I had never imagined that a boy as small as I was could possibly feel this much misery. It didn't help when I realized that it was Good Friday afternoon and I had returned from the operating room about the same time that Jesus had died on that first Good Friday. Besides that, there was that crucifix hanging on the wall to remind me of all of this. I knew that I was reliving that awful day and that forever afterwards I would appreciate Easter much more, having truly experienced dying on Good Friday.

One of the worst things about the entire remainder of the day was that Joe-brother did not get sick one single time. He seemed like the tonsil-yanking was no more trouble or trauma for him than having a haircut. His wellness was disgusting.

It seemed like I vomited all of Friday night and never slept a wink. But finally by daylight on Saturday morning, it appeared that I actually might pull through and live. The nurse-nuns had been there in shifts, one bringing a new throw-up pan while another ran out to empty and clean the filled one. Now they told Mama that I was going to be just fine and that maybe I could have a soft-food breakfast.

At this particular time I didn't really feel like eating, but that was not to be my choice. "Soft food" was on the way. From the time I had first helped my daddy kill and clean chickens for Mama to cook, I had had an aversion to eggs, especially eggs that were not very fully cooked. When the soft-food breakfast arrived, it was centered around scrambled eggs that were so soft they were running all over the plate, around the watery grits that accompanied them. They smelled very sulfuric. One view and one whiff sent me into the black vomits again. The breakfast tray was soon taken away.

At this time in my life I knew absolutely nothing about dehydration, and so I did not realize that all of this vomiting was stripping my systems of all of their fluids. I was not in the least bit hungry but was beginning to have a thirst that reflected my worst imaginings of the desert. More than anything else in the world, I wanted a simple drink of water.

I appealed to Mama. "Could I please get a drink of water?" It seemed a simple request, but it turned out to be quite complicated.

"We'll have to ask the nurse to see if it's OK. You have some stitches in your throat, you know, and we want to be sure that we don't do anything to mess them up!"

Stitches in my throat? Stitches in my throat! I had never heard of or imagined this, and the very image brought the black vomits back once again.

By the time the nurse-nun was finished cleaning up this latest episode, Mama relayed my question to her. "Little Hawk wants a drink of water. Is it OK for him to have one?"

"I'm sure it is … but I can't just give him one until the doctor gets here and we ask him," the nurse-nun answered.

"When will he be here?" I asked, desperately.

"Well," the nurse-nun went on casually, as if I were not on the edge of death, "he's already made his morning rounds … and it is Saturday … he will probably drop back by sometime before the day is over."

I was simply dying. My throat was dry and in pain. I knew that even if I got the vomits again that nothing would come out because there was nothing at all left to come out. No wonder I had vomited black blood. Everything else down there was long gone. And now I was not even going to have my question about water answered for hours.

Suddenly I got an idea. Back at home I never had to ask for a drink of water. I took care of drinks of water on my own. In our bathroom at home there was a big sink with two faucets. All you had to do to get a drink was stand on your tiptoes and put your mouth under the "cold" faucet and turn on the water.

If I could just manage to get from my bed into the bathroom, then I would be able to get a good, long faucet drink and I would feel so much better! It was a plan.

The hospital room at the old St. Joseph's Hospital did not have its own private bathroom. Instead there was a bathroom on the hall for several rooms to share. I did not realize that in those days, if you were in the hospital you were supposed to be too sick to be able to go to the bathroom on your own.

Still, I knew where the bathroom was. Joe-brother and I had used it and even brushed our teeth there Thursday night before going to bed.

I innocently whimpered to Mama. "I think I need to go to the bathroom." I even started edging toward the side of the high bed.

"You better hold it until the nurse comes back. I don't know what the rules are about that, and around here I'm a little scared to do anything without asking."

So! I thought. *Mama is scared of the nurse-nuns, too!* Knowing very well that I had no real need to go to the bathroom, it was actually no trouble to "hold it" until one of the nuns returned.

In a few minutes one of the mysterious neuter figures came into the room. "Well?" Mama was looking at me. "Ask your question." She was not going to help me even one little bit.

"What question?" I asked stupidly.

"What you were just wanting to do before the nurse came in … you know!" Mama just looked at me.

Now the nurse-nun looked at me too. It was the heavy one with the little whitish moustache on the outer corners of its mouth. "What is it, honey? Do you need something?"

"Yes, I do!" I jumped in. "I really do need to get up and go to the bathroom."

"Well, son," the nurse-nun went on, "what do you need to do in there?"

"I need to go to the bathroom! That's what I said and what I need to do … *I need to go to the bathroom!*"

Without so much as answering my question, the nurse-nun disappeared. In less than a minute the same one came back in the door. In one hand was what looked like a milk bottle with a handle on it and in the other hand an oval shaped silver-looking pan. She brought both of these things to the bed. I could see Joe-brother watching like he was glad

I was going through this first and that by the time he needed the bathroom he would know exactly how to deal with it.

"Now," the nurse-nun said to me, "which one of these do you need?" Even if I had really had to go to the bathroom, there was no way that I could have unclothed myself in front of this nun, whatever its gender, not enough to use either of the appliances that had just been presented to me.

"I've changed my mind," I whimpered. "I mean ... I must have been wrong ... I don't really need to go after all ... That operation just has all of my feelings all mixed up ... Thank you for your trouble very much ... I'm sorry!" Mother was still just looking at me.

The nurse-nun turned to Mama and said, "Well, I didn't think he could possibly need to go after all that he's vomited and without anything to drink. I'm sure that by tonight Dr. Vines will let us start giving him whatever he feels like drinking."

The snow that had made its false start just as we were on the way to surgery the day before had begun to come on strong. It seemed a shame to feel so horrible as such a beautiful Easter weekend snowfall was building up at the same time outside. While I was doing all of this suffering, Joe-brother was propped up on his bed reading funny books and watching the snow fall. I knew that he had no feelings in this world if he could behave like this.

About five or six o'clock that afternoon Dr. Vines finally arrived. He and Daddy came into the room together. They had met on the elevator and were still talking about the snowfall as they entered the room. Dr. Vines had what looked like a glass quart jar in his hands. It had a funny glass cover and it was filled with something.

"Here they are, Little Hawk! The biggest mess of tonsils I've ever taken out in my life! I'm sending these things down to Chapel Hill where they can take a look at them at the medical school. You win the prize."

The jar held what looked horrible to me. It looked like big wads of bloody bread dough soaking in alcohol. If there had been anything else in my body I could have vomited, I would have done it on the spot. But after a few retches of dry-heave nothingness, I realized that at least the throwing up was over.

Dr. Vines put the jar on a table and came over to my bed. He pushed back his gold-framed glasses and looked down my throat, using a flat stick as a tongue depressor. If he needed those glasses, I wondered, what could he possibly see down my throat with them pushed back on his head? Maybe he hadn't used his glasses for the operation and took out more than my tonsils. Maybe there was a lot more than tonsils in that glass jar!

"I think you're going to live!" he said, then he looked at Joe-brother and gave him the same verdict.

"Well, now, could I at least get a drink of water?" I pleaded directly to the doctor, with Mama and Daddy looking on. I didn't care whether they approved or not, I had to have a drink!

"We'll do better than that! I'll send down for a treat for both of you! This is a little something I cooked up for my tonsil patients ... my own recipe!"

Pretty soon one of the black men came in with a tray. When I saw that the tray was not brought by the nurse-nuns I knew that what we were being sent must not be on their "approved" list. Dr. Vines's special invention turned out to be something like a snow cone in a glass. It had white sugar sprinkled all over the ball of crushed ice, and instead of syrup in the bottom, it had 7-Up. Nothing ever tasted better to me in all my life! This was a smart doctor to know that a good little sugar kick helped more to bring a kid back to life than anything else.

Once I was started on the sugar-7-Up-snow cone diet, the world got better and better. I began to feel wonderful. Now I read funny books and propped up in bed just as well as Joe-brother could. The last thing I did that night was look out the window and watch the beautiful snow falling through the streetlights below as we welcomed the eve of Easter morning.

I slept one of the finest night's sleep that I had ever had in my life. I was not going to die, I was not going to vomit blood anymore, and I had not died of childhood dehydration. The sleep was deep and drifting without being exhaustingly dream-filled.

Early the next morning I was awakened by the skinny nurse-nun coming in to take my temperature with a thermometer that tasted like alcohol. "Wake up," the nun squeaked. "The Easter Bunny's been here!"

Before I even opened my eyes I knew that it was true. As I moved in the bed to raise up, I could feel something on the foot of the bed and hear the crinkle of the cellophane the Easter Bunny always used to wrap Easter baskets. It was really true! There on the foot of my bed was the biggest Easter basket I had ever seen! It had a handle over the top, and through the yellow cellophane I could see pastel-colored sugar eggs, colored foil-wrapped chocolate eggs, and a big marshmallow and chocolate rabbit right in the middle. There were even some little marshmallow ducks covered with yellow sugar nesting in the shredded cellophane grass in the bottom of the basket.

On Joe-brother's bed was an identical basket, but covered in purple cellophane, which he was already opening and digging into. Mama and Daddy were already there, watching us and beaming.

"The Easter Bunny found us!" I almost cried.

"I knew that he would," Daddy said. "I saw his tracks in the snow outside as we came in this morning. Come over here to the window and see for yourself."

Joe-brother and I crept out of the tall beds and over to the window. Down in the snow beside the parking lot we could see the giant rabbit tracks. There was no question: there were the sets of tracks: two close together, then two wide apart, just like rabbits always made as they hopped with their front feet together and their back feet wide apart. The funny thing to me was that it looked like the Easter Bunny had been wearing shoes when he made the giant tracks. *Oh well*, I thought, *maybe the Easter Bunny does wear shoes. They probably don't let anyone barefooted into this hospital!*

What a wonderful and miraculous Easter day this was. I felt so alive now that when I turned back to get into the high bed and saw the crucifix again, I was surprised that Jesus was still hanging there. I just knew that he would be up and going by now. Then I remembered that in the real story, Jesus had been up earlier that day than I was, and even if the crucifix was still there, everything seemed all right.

This was to be our last day in the hospital. This afternoon Dr. Vines would come by and check us, and if everything was all right, we would go home in the afternoon and be in our own beds that evening. I would be away from the mysterious nuns forever and ever!

I had free rein now, on this last day, to be up and out of the bed and even go to the bathroom on my own. Just before lunchtime I was reading a funny book in the bed when Mama said, "Hawk, you better go into the bathroom and wash your hands before they bring your dinner. Joe just got back, now you go on!"

I was at a very interesting place in a Bugs Bunny funny book where Bugs was really getting at Elmer Fudd. I didn't really want to stop just then and do anything until I got to the end. Mama pushed at me again, and with the kind of disgust I could not have managed when I was going to die on the day before, I jumped out of bed and dashed out of the room and into the bathroom just off the hall.

I had moved too fast. All of the extra blood in my body must have been in my feet at the time and there was none available to come to my head. I just made it to the bathroom when the whole world went black and I passed out cold. In falling I either hit my head on something or just split it when it hit the hard ceramic tile floor, because I was bleeding when it was all over.

Then next thing I knew I was being picked up. Mama had me and was picking me up and carrying me back to the high bed in the room. I could smell the bath powder she always wore and I could feel the soft, familiar round and comforting shape of her body as she held me even before I opened by eyes.

When I did open my eyes, I almost fell out of her arms. Instead of being held by my mama, I was in the arms of the heavy nun. She was a woman! She wore the same powder my own mama wore, and even through the white robe, the rounded shape of her bosom left me with no more doubts about her gender. She held me carefully, like she could have been my mama, and I knew that, after all, the nuns, who daily remembered Good Friday by living in a world inhabited by crucifixes even on Easter Sunday, had, just as I had been promised in the very beginning, taken care of me.

See Rock City

1955

*A*t the end of the fifth grade we moved. Mama had always dreamed of living in town, and after scrimping and saving money for years, we finally bought a house way across town from the little house on Plott Creek and became town residents.

Our family had very little experience with things like moving, so the three-mile move took us two weekends and the afternoon of each weekday in between. On top of everything else, moving week turned out to be the last week of the school year. With Mama herself now teaching school, this was not good timing. She was trying to clean out her school room for the summer, complete all of her report cards, decide who had passed and who had failed and, at the same time, supervise a moving operation not one of us knew a thing in the world about.

Daddy borrowed a pickup truck from Roddy Fancher (the one who had locked his necktie in the vault door at the bank) for the move. He thought that two loads would do it. It never occurred to us that actually packing things up might be easier. Daddy said we would pack things up if we were moving farther, but for three miles we would just "haul it loose." It took all of the first Saturday to move the living room furniture, rugs, pictures, and the dining room table and chairs.

We used up a lot of time disconnecting and taking out our Siegler oil heater and loading it on the truck. When Mama said, "Why are we taking that? Our new house has a furnace," a lot more time was spent taking the oil heater back inside from the truck and hooking it up again so the people who bought the old house from us wouldn't know how foolish we had been.

Since we couldn't really work on Sunday we did nothing after that first day but look at the new house and think a lot about where everything else needed to go. (We did cheat and take a load of clothes in the car, but Mama was pretty sure that nobody saw us doing it.)

Every afternoon of the coming week it was the same thing: get home from school, load up a room of furniture, take it to the new house, unload and move it in, go for supper at the E&W Drive In (even Mama couldn't be expected to cook during trauma like this), and then sleep at the old house. By Tuesday Joe and I were sleeping on the floor because the beds were gone; by Wednesday Mama and Daddy were also sleeping on the floor. But for some reasoning I never did understand, we couldn't consider spending a night at the new house until we were totally and completely out of the old one.

On Saturday, when it was finally time to depart with our last load, Mama looked wistfully at the old house she had waited so long to leave and said, "We shouldn't be doing this."

"Why not?" all three of us chimed in question. "You are the one," Daddy added, "who wanted to move to town. We've waited ten years for this day."

Years later I came to realize that when you come from a long-dammed-up Scots-Irish gene pool it is an OK thing to wish for something, but it is *not* an OK thing to get it. Mama went on, "We're leaving our home! Nothing good is going to come of this. I just know it!"

On the Saturday after the move was completed we took off to make our regular visit to Grandmother's house. After all, with the big move, we had missed our weekend visits for two Saturdays in a row.

The road to Grandmother's was awful. The entire mountain where the family farm was located was made of huge granite rocks, and this included the road itself. Daddy knew where all of the bad rocks were, and we crept along, keeping the tires on the high spots. Still, the car always scraped bottom a few times on the mile-long washed-out farm road. This time the bottom took a lick harder than usual.

The car had no oil-pressure warning lights, and Daddy was talking all the way and not watching the gauges. The first warning of trouble came when the engine started knocking. By then it was too late. We had knocked a hole in the oil pan, and before the Plymouth could even be brought to a coasting stop the engine seized up and died.

So just one week after we moved into the new house we had saved for years to move into, Daddy had to take a nine-year-old Plymouth with a blown engine and try to trade it for a new car. Somehow a trade of some kind was made, but we were now doubly in debt as we became the proud but mostly unwilling owners of a two-tone green and white 1955 Plymouth Savoy sedan.

But the trouble was not over yet.

The new house had an electric stove. Until we moved in there, Mama had cooked on a wood-burning stove all of her life. The electric stove was a totally new and unique experience in every way. Mama loved it. Without either splitting wood or building a fire she could cause, create, and control heat at any time she chose. She absolutely fell in love with the new electric stove.

On the second Sunday that we lived in the new house we got up for a breakfast of pancakes and bacon. While we were eating breakfast, Mama announced her Sunday dinner plan: "We're going to have a hen for dinner!"

Daddy answered, "That will take all afternoon! It will be time for supper before it's finished."

"Oh, no," Mama smiled. "It will be almost ready when we get home from church. See, I'm going to put it on the top of the new electric stove in my big enamel pot all full of water and let it simmer while we're at church. It will be nice and tender when we get home, and I'll just pop it in the oven to brown and we'll be ready to eat. We already have plenty of leftover vegetables to go with it."

Mama started the hen with the stove turned to *High* to get it boiling. As we left for church, she came through the kitchen on the way to the car and turned the burner down to *Simmer*.

Daddy was always the last one out of the house. When he came through the kitchen about half a minute behind Mama, the just-turned-down chicken pot was still boiling. Thinking that she had forgotten to turn it down, he turned the switch again. Since the *Simmer* setting was next to the setting for *High,* the chicken was now left cooking under full General Electric power.

Being too considerate to point out Mama's forgetfulness, Daddy said nothing about what he had just done, and we drove off for Sunday school with plans to stay for church.

Sunday school started at nine forty-five, and we were always a little bit early for that. Church started at eleven and got out a few minutes after noon. Daddy loved to talk, and we were always among the last to leave. So when we finally did get back to the new house in the new car, the chicken had easily had a full three hours to cook at the maximum heat.

"I sure am hungry," Daddy said as he got out of the car.

"We'll be ready to eat in fifteen minutes," Mama promised.

We walked into the carport and opened the door to the kitchen. You could not see inside the house at all. There was a solid and unmoving wall of heavy greenish-gray smoke that just stood there, filling the entire house.

Mama started crying and wringing her hands. Daddy immediately reconstructed the whole chain of events and knew exactly what had happened and why, though it would take him a full twenty years to admit his role in turning the stove "down."

Joe and I started gagging like we were going to throw up in the carport. The smell was like singed hair but much more nauseating. Our gagging charade simply made both parents madder than ever at the whole world, and the family degenerated into a comedy of crying and blame placing as we all tried to open doors and windows and air the place out.

One of the first things we noticed was that the tiled kitchen floor felt greasy when we walked on it. The carpet in the living room felt greasy. The walls were greasy. So were the dishes and the curtains and the furniture. Everything in the entire house was covered with a thin coat of burned-smelling chicken grease. It penetrated the closets and the bottom layers of the cedar chests and dressers. How one hen could have rendered so much lard was amazing, and the efficiency with which the smoke had carried it into every possible nook and cranny was beyond belief. Mama thought that there was even grease behind the paint on the walls.

Before it was all over, the entire interior of the house would have to be scrubbed and repainted. All carpets, upholstery, and draperies would have to be cleaned. All clothing and linens had to be cleaned or washed, as did every single dish, glass, and piece of silverware in the entire house.

Daddy spent most of Sunday evening on the phone, and by early the next day the house was running over with scrubbers, painters, and carpet cleaners. That afternoon, Daddy came home from work and made an announcement.

"Well, folks, we're broke! We've bought a new house, we've bought a new car, and now we almost burned the house down and we're going to have to redo the whole thing. What else have we got to lose? We might as well take a vacation!"

Now I had heard the word *vacation*, but only because it was on our spelling bee list for the fourth grade in school. Vacations were even more wasteful and outlandish than birthdays. No one in our entire extended family history had ever been on a vacation.

We were all so taken by surprise that we couldn't even think of a question to ask, so it was Daddy who broke the silence. "Where in the world do you-all think that we ought to go?"

Out of nowhere, Joe replied: *"Florida!"* Where he had even heard that word, let alone how he knew what it meant, was beyond all of us. Mama and I sat dumbfounded while Daddy went on.

"Why not? OK, we'll go to Florida. Let's get packed up, and we'll leave first thing in the morning."

For many years I blamed my parents for this trip with the mistaken notion that adults always know what they are doing. When I later realized that I was wrong about this basic premise, I recanted my accusations. They simply didn't have enough experience to know any better: they just didn't know what they were doing. After supper we walked around the neighborhood to let people know we were going to be gone for "a whole week," as Daddy described it. Our new neighbors, the Coles, had actually been to Florida. While Mama talked with Mrs. Cole, getting advice about what to pack for the trip, Mr. Cole told the rest of us all of the places we ought to be sure to go.

"Go to Daytona Beach," he said. "That's the best place to go from here. But be sure to stop in St. Augustine. While you're in St. Augustine you ought to go to Ripley's Believe It or Not. Whatever you do, be sure to take these boys to Marineland. 'Course, there's things to see all the way down there. It'll take you a little more than a day just to get there."

At the same time, Mother was making her mental packing list from Mrs. Cole's advice. "The main thing I remember about Florida is how hot it is. Hot, hot, hot! That's what I'd call it. You won't need sweaters, and those boys won't need anything but short pants. Just take them some short pants and sandals and some little seersucker shirts, and they'll be fine. Just remember while you're packing, *hot, hot, hot,* and you'll be just fine." That was the sum total of Mrs. Cole's remembrance of their recent trip.

And so the next morning—a cool, early-summer mountain morning—we left the new house in the care of the smoke cleaners, and we headed south, six hundred miles to Daytona Beach.

Nineteen-fifty-five was the first year Plymouth had produced cars with V-8 engines, but our new Plymouth was a six-cylinder "custom" model. It was also straight drive. (Mama had insisted, "I had a hard enough time learning to drive *with* a clutch! I just could not go through having to learn to drive without one!")

The new car also had no radio ("Why do we need a radio in the car? We already have one radio at home!") and, of course, no air conditioning. The Plymouth had come with nice cloth-upholstered seats, but the day after we got it, Daddy had taken it to the upholstery shop to have the brand-new seats covered up with slick green-and-white woven plastic plaid seat covers—"so the new seats won't get messed up," he said. In the wintertime, we would later learn, you could slide across these seat covers and generate enough electricity to electrocute a small animal. In the summer, as we were now about to learn, they could inspire enough pure sweat to drown one!

We made it about twenty minutes before Joe cried out, "How much farther is it?"

Three times each in the first fifty miles, Joe and I had to go to the bathroom—never both at the same time. After the sixth stop Daddy came out from the service bay of an Esso station carrying something in his hand. It turned out to be a wide-mouthed quart canning jar. "We're not stopping again!" he proclaimed. "From now on both of you can use this and empty it out the back window."

We had been gone less than two hours when we approached South Carolina. Boredom and heat were rapidly defeating adventure and excitement. As we came down out of the mountains and into the flat country of South Carolina,

Joe and I had begun sweating in the back seat. With no air conditioning, the choice was between keeping all of the windows rolled down and having your breath sucked out or closing them with the risk of quick death in a rolling steaming sauna. We were broiling, ill-tempered, and bored.

The green plaid plastic seat covers had stripes running in both directions, up and down, back and forth. Mama picked a wide green stripe that came down the center of the seat back and across the bottom cushion. She pointed it out to Joe and me and strongly forbade either of us to cross the line to the other's side. During the next hour, we responded by alternately and illegally crossing the line, accusing one another of being the first one to have done it, and slapping back and forth.

"How much farther is it?" Joe moaned again, sweat dripping down his face.

"Are we almost there?" I echoed. "This is a hot place. Hot, hot, hot! It must be Florida!"

We were, in reality, just now flattening out in the upper stretches of South Carolina with a full day and a half left to drive. We had already exhausted ourselves playing Find the Alphabet on the Road Signs during the first hour. There was no creativity left in either Joe or me.

"Let's sing," Daddy suggested. So we sang: "Down By the Old Mill Stream" … "When the Saints Go Marching In" … "Let Me Call you Sweetheart" … "Found a Peanut, Found a Peanut" … "Ninety-nine Bottles of Beer on the Wall" (much to Mama's objections). We sang every song we knew.

Daddy tickled us and entertained us by changing the words to fit our day. He sang to Mama, "Let me call you Sweaty, I'm in love with you." We laughed our heads off. Then it was "Swing Low, Sweat Chariot," then "Ninety-nine

Bottles of Sweat on the Wall." This actually kept us distracted for twenty or thirty minutes. Then we got tired of singing.

"How much farther?" Joe wailed. "Please tell me! Aren't we almost there?"

Eventually Joe and I invented a new game that actually kept us interested for as long as we were allowed to play it. It was called Fighting in the Back Seat. It was amazing how you could slide around on those sweaty plastic seat covers and how hard it was, when you were wet and slick all over, to catch hold of one another. It was a good game, but Mama made us stop playing it very quickly.

Mama was now at the end of her patience. "Play Cow Poker!" she ordered. "Just settle down back there and play Cow Poker."

Cow Poker was the ultimate game designed to occupy bored children on a long car trip. It was a step above Find the Alphabet on Road Signs. The game started simply enough. The sides of the road were divided. I quickly claimed the right side and Joe got the left. We then each counted the cows on our side of the road ... forever. The first one to get to a certain number—say, one hundred cows—was the winner. We knew that this was going to be a long trip when Mama's instructions included, "The first one to get to a million wins!"

Real Cow Poker was a game of changing, mostly escalating, rules. Every time we got tired of simply counting cows (which first came by the time I had thirty-one and Joe had nineteen), Mama would introduce a new rule to recapture our interest.

"I'm tired of this!" Joe whined.

At that moment Mama, who had just seen some horses up ahead, said, "Two points for each horse," and we were off again. Each time the game almost ran down, Mama invented a new variant. "Five points each for a mule ... Take one off for a dog and two off for a cat ... Buzzards count ten ..."—for a little while we rode with our heads out the window looking at the sky—"If you see a church on your side, it doubles your score ... If you pass a cemetery, your cows are dead!"

It was pure genius. With her variable-rule Cow Poker, she kept us counting for miles, into the hundreds.

Finally Mama dredged up the ultimate addition to the game. In those days, before Disneyworld, before Busch Gardens, before Six Flags Over *Anything,* the most advertised tourist attraction in the entire Southeast was Rock City, Tennessee, located "high atop Lookout Mountain." You could "See Seven States! Go through the Fat Man's Squeeze! Feed the pet deer!" and enjoy a host of other temptations by visiting Rock City, where man had improved on the work of the very creator Himself.

The Rock City marketing and advertising people had devised a very clever and widespread plan of saturated advertising. They painted barns for farmers. All over the Southeast farmers had their barns painted by the Rock City barn painters. The only catch was that once the barn was painted, the words SEE ROCK CITY were then added to one side of the barn roof, depending on where the best view from the highway was obtained. (I never did see a Rock City barn that didn't just happen to be beside a highway.)

When we had finally tired of calculating the results of sighting cows, horses, mules, buzzards, churches, and cemeteries, Mama had a stroke of genius.

"Now boys, if either one of you sees a Rock City barn, *on either side of the road,* just shout out 'See Rock City!,' and you automatically win the game, and we will stop and get everybody a Co-Cola!"

This was just too good. We now looked out the windows and counted with a hopeful vengeance.

Finally, though, even this ran out. It ran out when I quit in a pout because Joe was cheating. I would be at least a hundred cows ahead. We would pass a barn that was as plain as anything, and then, just as we were going around a curve and leaving the barn behind, Joe would look out the back window and yell out "See Rock City," and swear that the just-passed barn had been painted on the back side. I pitched such a fit over this that Daddy, now way down into Georgia, actually pulled the Plymouth off the road, turned around, and went back so we could check the barn out. There was no SEE ROCK CITY painted there, and I refused to play any more with such a cheater.

So now we were back to sweating and fighting again. Our long afternoon driving through Georgia was frequently punctuated by *"Now* how much farther is it?"

Finally, both Mama and Daddy wore out. Daddy had wanted to get to the Florida state line before stopping for the night, but Mama's ultimatum won out. "The next town," she said, "the next town, whatever it is, the next town is it. We are stopping there to spend the night!"

Nahunta, Georgia. That's where we burned out. At five o'clock in the south Georgia afternoon, it was twice as hot as it had ever been in Sulpher Springs in all of our lives. Mama spotted a motel, limply pointed, and said, "That's the place." Daddy pulled the Plymouth off the road and onto the cemented parking lot of the Bel-Air Motel.

The Bel-Air Motel was U-shaped and in the front center of the U was the office/restaurant. "We can even eat supper here," Mama added, "and ... look!" She was pointing to a green neon sign in the restaurant window that proudly proclaimed *Air Conditioned!!!* in flowing cursive script.

"Let's check in and then go straight to supper," Mama suggested as she wiped the sweat off her forehead. "We can get cooled off in that air conditioning and then we'll feel more like unloading the car and taking everything into our room later."

Having never been in an air-conditioned building, we eagerly hurried toward this new experience. Hot, drippy, sweat-headed, and wearing nothing but sandals, shorts, and summer shirts, we plunged in the door of the restaurant and were met with a blast of cold air you could have hung meat in. Joe shuddered, and you could hear Mama suck in her breath. The cold blast of the air conditioning system was too much for our little sweat-covered bodies.

In less than a minute we had all forgotten the long, sweaty, plastic seat-covered Georgia afternoon and were huddled with our teeth chattering in a cold plastic-covered corner booth of the restaurant. Mama and Daddy ordered coffee and Joe and I asked for hot chocolate.

Mama had listened very carefully to Mrs. Cole, our neighbor, back when she had given all the advice about packing: "It's *hot, hot, hot!*" And so there was not in any of our suitcases a jacket, a sweater, or even so much as a pair of long pants or a long-sleeved shirt to be had. Suspended between North Carolina and Florida, we were in air-conditioned purgatory.

"Let's hurry and eat and get on into our nice, warm room." Mama didn't have to force us. Once we had finished our supper of hot soup and hot chocolate, we eagerly returned to the outside heat only to make a new discovery. The approach of darkness had brought another invention that none of us from the North Carolina mountains had ever experienced: three-pound striped south Georgia mosquitos. A small squad of them could have carried off a six-year-old. Slapping right and left, we pulled our suitcases out of the car and headed for the motel room.

The motel room was apparently on the same air conditioning system as the restaurant, and it was certainly just as cold. Air came out of a vent in the wall, deliberately aimed straight at both beds, full blast. It was Joe who made the suggestion, "Turn it down! No, turn it off!" But Mama, with a response I was to hear hundreds of times in countless variations through the years of my life, responded, "Turn it down? We don't know anything about air conditioning. We don't know how to turn it down." And without so much as looking for a switch or a dial, we abandoned ourselves to the cold.

Daddy didn't say anything for a few minutes. Then he had an idea. "I know how to warm up, boys. How about a good, hot shower for both of you?" That sounded great. Joe and I went into the bathroom and started to undress while Daddy turned on the water in the big tubless motel shower to let it run hot and even start to steam the room a little bit. As the water ran hot and began to steam, we discovered another south Georgia treat: sulfur water. Joe and I were instantly holding our noses as the steaming hot running water, heavily laden with rotten-egg-smelling sulfur fumes, filled the small bathroom with its smell.

We were trapped: sulfur steam in the bathroom, meat-hanging cold in the motel room, heat and mosquitos outside. Mama opened the door to air out the sulfur smell and let in some heat. Instead of heat, the light in the room drew in flocks of mosquitos. We turned off the lights, hoping that the mosquitos couldn't see us in the dark. They could.

We spent that night with our heads under the cover to keep the mosquitos out of our ears, and with the door propped open with a chair to let heat into the room and air out the sulfur smell.

The next morning we loaded the car to get on our way, filled with the excitement of knowing that we were almost to Florida. At Mama's suggestion we decided to drive a little bit and then stop for breakfast so as not to freeze to death in that same motel cafe. We all agreed, and in no time we were in Florida.

The entire family cheered when we crossed the Florida state line. We had started so early in the morning on this day that we were hardly sweating yet. None of us realized that we still had a long way to go to get to all of the places Mr. Cole had told us to be sure to visit.

Just over the Florida line we began to see restaurants and fruit stands. All of them advertised orange juice, and several had signs that read *Orange Juice: All You Can Drink for Twenty-Five Cents.* Mama pointed out these promising signs, and we stopped for breakfast at the next fruit stand we saw.

Once inside, Daddy paid a dollar to a man who looked like he hadn't shaved for about three days or changed his shirt in longer than that. The man poured all four of us little paper cups of orange juice and we each drank ours down. Daddy held his cup back out to the man and said, "That was good, how about a refill?"

"You want some more?" the orange juice man asked.

"Yes. I expect all four of us could use another cup. Those cups aren't very big, you know."

"If you want some more orange juice," the man went on, "it'll be another dollar."

Daddy began to turn red around his neck, knowing that he had been had but not sure how. He went on: "The sign says, 'All you can drink for twenty-five cents.' I want a refill."

"Well, buddy"—the orange juice man was getting hostile by now—"that's all you can drink for twenty-five cents ...

you want more? That will be *another* twenty-five cents, or a dollar for your whole family."

At that moment, the entire family vacation changed. Things would never be the same between Florida and our family after that. From then on, Daddy seemed determined to spend as little money in Florida as possible, and not much more time than money.

Daddy grabbed all of us and led us out of the fruit store. We got in the car and tore out of there. With no breakfast and none of us daring to mention it, we headed for St. Augustine and got there by lunchtime. Mr. Cole had told us to be sure to see Ripley's Believe It or Not, so we got directions and went straight to it without even eating lunch to begin with. Daddy seemed to be excited about this because he always liked the cartoon-like Believe It or Not features in the newspaper.

We parked the car and went up to the building. There were large poster-sized pictures and advertisements all over the outside of the building. We could see right there all the things there were to look forward to on the inside: "See the two-headed calf ... See the man with four eyes ... See the White House made out of pennies ... See the woman with a tongue so long she can part her hair with it!"

There were pictures of all kinds of things from all over the world, and they were posted all along the wall of the walkway that led to the ticket booth. There was a picture of a violin made entirely out of toothpicks, a picture of a man who ate light bulbs, and even a picture of a man who could smoke a cigarette and blow the smoke out his ears and eyeballs! We looked without any hurry at all, as long as we wanted to. We studied those pictures all the way to the ticket booth.

Once the pictures ran out and we were right at the ticket booth, the ticket saleslady looked at us and said, "How many? Two adults and two children?"

Without looking at her, Daddy turned to us and asked, "Are you beginning to get hungry now?" We were starving.

In unison Joe and I both said, "Yes! We are about to starve to death!"

"Then why don't we go get something to eat?" he went on.

As we started toward the car, it was Joe who asked. "Are we going to come back after lunch and go inside?"

Daddy quickly answered, "Of course not! Why, you have to *pay* to go inside. And besides, what could they possibly have in there that we haven't already seen in these pictures on the walls? The building isn't big enough to hold much more than that." He must have seen in this act some secret and twisted sort of revenge against the orange juice man.

During the course of the afternoon he drove us past The Fountain of Youth, the Old Jail, and Castle of San Marcos, all the while trying to convince Joe and me that all those cars parked in the various parking lots beside these tempting places just belonged to all the people who worked there. Through it all, Mama never said a thing. It was pointless.

The entire visit to St. Augustine, including lunch, took less than two hours and less than ten dollars. We headed south toward Daytona Beach, in search of Marineland, our real main goal of the trip.

The Plymouth was getting low on gas, so we stopped to fill up the car and check everything out at an Esso station just on the south edge of St. Augustine. While the station attendant was cleaning the windshield, Daddy leaned his head out the window and asked, "About how far is it to Marineland?"

"Marineland?" the attendant stopped wiping and his eyes met Daddy's with a questioning look.

"Yeah," Daddy went on, "Marineland. We want to take these boys down there. I heard they've got a pretty good show."

"Oh," the gas man said, "you don't want to go there. Why, sir, that's just a tourist trap. The whole thing is just set up to look good on the outside and take your money once they get you on the inside. No sir, I wouldn't go there."

My heart was sinking as the gas man talked on.

"However…" He paused, then smiled. "Sir, if you want to see the *real* thing, then me and my brother's got a alligator farm, a real one, about twenty minutes from here. We don't usually let people see what's going on there. But since you're customers of mine, I might could call my brother and tell him it would be fine to let you in. If he sounds like he likes you as much as I do, we'll let all of you see the whole thing for ten dollars, cash!"

Daddy said, "Oh, boys, how about it? Wouldn't you really like to see the *real* thing?"

The gas man disappeared to call his brother, then returned momentarily to inform us that we had been accepted. He drew Daddy a crude map on the back of a greasy-looking used envelope and we set off to find "the real thing."

About twenty minutes of map-following later, we turned down a weedy sand road and spotted the spitting image of the gas pumper, waiting to open the gate for us.

The brother introduced himself to us as Big George, collected the ten-dollar bill from Daddy, and pointed to where we should park. Through all of this Mama had not said a word. She was just giving Daddy her silent deep-freeze look all the time, which he in turn was ignoring.

Even before we got out of the car, the odor was unbeliev-able. The whole place reeked with a nauseating odor that was hanging thickly in the still and humid air. The sicker we looked from the smell, the more Daddy proudly marched around and proclaimed, "It is the *real* thing, boys. Even smells right!" Mama was by now holding a cloth handker-chief over her nose and gagging like she was holding back on a good chance to throw up.

We were shown a big pit of mud, multilayered sleeping alligators, and a lot of stuff that had at some time come out of the alligators. The pit seemed to be where most of the evil smell was coming from. Big George told us he was going to wrestle an alligator and "put it to sleep." He waded into the smelly mess and grabbed a big sleepy-looking creature by the tail. Then he pulled it out of the mire and onto the open ground close to where we were.

Mama screamed through the handkerchief, "Get back, *please!* Get hold of those children!" Daddy just laughed.

Big George fell on the alligator's back. He grabbed it around the neck and rolled around and around on the ground with it. He seemed to be trying to thrash around a whole lot harder than the alligator was. Through the whole wrestling match the alligator looked like he just wanted to be left alone so he could go back to sleep.

Finally Big George flipped the tired-looking alligator over on its back, held it down, and began rubbing it under the neck. In a minute the alligator was completely still. Joe-brother said, "Is it dead? Did he kill it?"

Big George stood up and proudly proclaimed, "That's my specialty, folks, the Japanese sleeper hold! Now, you-all wanna see some snakes?"

"This is enough," Mama pulled at Daddy's elbow. He laughed and headed out behind Big George. We followed.

Big George took us over to what looked like a round well with a wooden lid on it. "Stand back. They might be hungry," he said. He took the lid off, and before we even saw them we heard the rattles of a whole pit full of writhing, squirming, twisting rattlesnakes. "I feed them rats," he said, as if to assure us that, not being rats, we were safe.

"Want to see me milk a snake?" These were all rhetorical questions, as there seemed to be no choice but to keep going until the show was over or at least until Big George got tired of us.

We all watched as he caught a big rattler using a little lasso on the end of a stick, held it by the back of its head, and "milked" venom from its big fangs by hooking them over the edge of what looked like a little juice glass. Joe and I were fascinated, but Mama didn't seem to be any more interested in snake milking than she had been in alligator wrestling. If fact, she was at this moment finished with Big George, the Real Thing Alligator Farm, and maybe even with us, as she gripped the handkerchief tightly over her nose, marched away, and told Daddy she would be waiting in the car whenever we "got tired of this show."

Daddy seemed at last to get her message, and pretty soon he was thanking Big George. We rejoined Mama in the car and headed on toward Daytona Beach to look for a place to spend the night.

Having no experience at all with either planning or carrying out vacations, we of course had no room reservations. And since this was one of the first weeks that school was out for the summer (all up and down the East Coast, it seemed) there was not a room to be had in all of Daytona Beach. Joe and I saw the sunlight rapidly running out on our first trip to the beach as we drove from one motel to another just to read, or be told in the office if there was no outside sign, that all rooms were full. Mama was quiet.

Finally we saw a brand new motel. It didn't look finished enough to be open for business, but Daddy tried.

He came back to the car smiling. "We're in luck!" he said. "Tonight is the first night things have been finished enough to rent out rooms. Why, we're going to be their first customers. They're going to go buy some sheets and make up our beds right now."

While the beds were being made up for the first time in a room in which the paint was not yet dry on the walls, we walked down to the beach and across the wide sand and for the first time in six generations, since our ancestors came over from Scotland, someone in our family saw the ocean. We waded in the edge and tasted the water. The tide was coming in, and we picked up shells and walked up and down in front of our new motel.

Once we were back in the room, Mama made the announcement. "We can't stay here!" was all she said. I looked around the room trying to figure out what was unsafe or unacceptable about the new motel we had ended up in.

"Why can't we stay here?" Daddy asked.

"Don't you remember when we were out there next to that ocean? Didn't you see," she went on, "that every time those waves came in, they came closer to where we are right now than the time before? If that keeps happening all night, why, this whole place will be washed away by tomorrow! No wonder this motel just opened … anything built right here has to wash away."

Three of us spent the night, asleep, in the new motel room, while Mama spent the night, awake, waiting to warn us to leave when the waves got close enough.

Early the next morning, we loaded everything into the Plymouth and headed back toward home and the mountains of North Carolina.

We spent a long day sweating, fighting, and playing Cow Poker as we passed back by Marineland, back by Big George's alligator farm, back by St. Augustine without even looking twice. We quickly drove by all of the state-line fruit stands with their all-you-can-drink signs; we passed Nahunta, Georgia, and finally spent the night on the edge of Atlanta.

The next day brought more sweating, fighting, and Cow Poker. After a four-day vacation, all four days of which we had spent in the car, we were almost home!

Once we entered North Carolina, Joe really started in with "How much farther is it?"

Mama's answer was, "One more game of Cow Poker and we're home!"

So we started our final game. Both of us secretly knew that we would win this game because both of us knew that, just short of the driveway to our new house, there was a big barn that had SEE ROCK CITY painted right on the side. As we separately pretended to be trying very hard and doing our best to stay ahead, we each secretly planned to be the first one to spot the Rock City barn.

Almost home now, both Joe and I were hanging over the back of the front seat to get a better view of the roadside. Finally we came around the last curve, the Plymouth straightened, and there it was, in full view.

At exactly the same time Joe and I called out together, *"SEE ROCK CITY!"*

And without missing a beat, Daddy said, "Why not? We still have three days left in our vacation!"

And so, without even stopping at home, we drove right on past our own driveway and continued for four more hours to Chattanooga, Tennessee, to see Rock City.

We got to Chattanooga too late to get in that day, but, now being experienced motel patrons, we got a room and enjoyed the evening. It was cool enough in Chattanooga that day that we didn't need any air conditioning.

The next morning, early, we had breakfast and waited in line to get our tickets when Rock City opened for the day. As soon as we walked in through the turnstile, Mama got tears in her eyes.

"Oh, look!" she said.

Ahead of us were huge granite boulders that looked for all the world like the mountain at Grandmother's house where we had knocked the bottom out of the old Plymouth to begin with. A narrow walkway led us down between the biggest of these gigantic rocks.

"This," Mama went on, "looks just like where I lived as a little girl. We used to play on rocks just like these! Oh, this is just wonderful! It's so much like home!"

Everything in Rock City reminded Mama of where we had all grown up: the deer in the park, the moss on the rocks, the waterfalls. In a man-made cavern there were even lighted tableau scenes of fairy tales that were her favorite memories from both her own childhood and ours.

Finally we came to a gigantic overlook where the signs said, SEE SEVEN STATES, and arrows pointed in seven directions toward those states. Mama got herself lined up on the arrow that pointed toward North Carolina, strained her eyes, and said, "This is so wonderful! I can almost see all the way home! This is where we should have come to begin with … it is almost as good as being home!"

I wish I knew, in later years, how much money that one trip to Florida actually saved my parents. It turned out in the end to be such a remarkable vacation, that in all their lives, they never had to take another one. After all, when you discover that the place you really want to be is at home, why pay to go somewhere else?

Beverly Davidson ...
Love from Afar

1956–58

*T*he day I fell in love was Tuesday, the day after Labor
Day, 1956. It was about ten minutes after ten in the
morning, and I was worthless for days afterwards.

The day after Labor Day was always the first day of the
school year in Nantahala County. This year I was beginning
the eighth grade. In a system with a seventh- and eighth-
grade junior high school and a ninth- through twelfth-grade
high school, being an eighth-grader was almost as good as
being a high school senior.

This year, for the first time, we changed classes, "getting
ready for high school," our homeroom teacher, Old Miss
Mockley, said. We only made two changes, though. Except
for special classes like phys ed, band, and art, I spent half the
day in language arts (which included North Carolina history) with Old Miss Mockley. The science and math half of

the day, which was much more pleasant, I spent with Mr. Wylie Jonas.

On this first day of the school year we went to our homeroom session where Old Miss Mockley told us that there would be a morning assembly with Mr. Underhill— principal of the combined Sulpher Springs Junior/Senior High, all on the same campus—who would impart all of the rules and "get the year off to a good start." Since Davey Martin and I both had Mr. Jonas for science and math in the mornings, it was from his class that we went to the assembly.

Mr. Jonas told us from the start that he would treat us like adults until we did something to prove that we were not. While most of the other teachers made students march into assembly and sit in alphabetical order, he let us choose our own order and sit next to friends (with the threat that this privilege would be taken away if he saw just one person talking or even wiggling too much).

There was no school auditorium at Sulpher Springs Junior/Senior High School, so assemblies had to be held in the gym.

The gym had folding pull-out bleachers on both sides. One side would not hold us all, so the plan for assemblies was that eighth graders would come in and sit on one side, then the new seventh graders would come in and sit on the other. Under the basketball goal at the far end stood a microphone, where Mr. Underhill would deliver the sermon for the day.

Mr. Jonas and Old Miss Mockley were not the only eighth-grade teachers. There were four teams of two teachers each, eight teachers in all, and there were nearly two hundred and fifty eighth graders in this newly consolidated west-end-of-the-county school.

At five minutes before ten, Mr. Jonas started us toward the gym. Of course, it took not five minutes but at least fifteen until the entire hoard of hormonally advantaged eighth graders was herded, yelled at, and yanked back into line, as we walked on the seats of the bleachers (as we had been told not to do), made as much noise as we could get away with, and finally settled into place to watch the new seventh graders come in.

Since this was the first assembly of the new year, we were all eagerly watching to see what this year's crop of seventh graders would look like ... especially the girls. We all remembered the way last year's eighth graders had stared at us when we had been herded in on our first assembly day the year before.

"Fresh meat!" Davey Martin whispered to me as we looked across the wide gym floor and watched. One by one the new seventh graders came in the end door and paraded down the floor to take their seats in the bleachers opposite us. They were wide-eyed with fear while the corps of seventh-grade teachers accompanied their entry by, very loudly, uttering "Shhhh! ... Shhhhh! ... Shhhhhhh!" over and over again.

Suddenly I saw her! Right there on the very front row in the bleachers opposite us. The loveliest, most delicately gorgeous creature ever to be molded by the gentle hands of the creator! My breath failed me as I saw the seventh-grade clear creaminess of her golden complexion beneath her straight-bobbed, full, almost white blonde hair. I was instantly and totally committed to live my life, from this moment on, in pursuit of such purity, such beauty, such imagined goodness!

Recovering my breath, I turned to Davey Martin, discreetly pointed across the gym floor, and asked, "Who is *that?*"

Davey's reply was the dumbest, stupidest comment anyone on the face of the earth ever uttered since human life had evolved. He simply said, *"Who?"*

"Can't you see?" I was exasperated and disgusted with him. "Right there in the front row, that *beautiful* girl!"

"Oh, her." Now Davey was catching on. "That is Beverly Davidson. Her daddy is a lawyer."

That last information was almost annoying. I didn't care what her daddy was. All I knew was that, from this day forward, I was to be devoted to her. And I was.

But this was eighth grade. And so, while my emotional devotion and joy were complete, the possibility of my actually *speaking* to Beverly Davidson, let alone telling her how I felt, was out of the question.

And so began a year of whispered relationship. I had friends and so did Beverly Davidson, so there was a sort of unacknowledged junior high grapevine through which important communications took place, never directly, but fourth-handedly as messages were conveyed from me to my friends to her friends to her, and eventually back again.

The total content of the eighth- to seventh-grade messages was, "He likes you ... do you like him?"—answered not by a yes or a no, but by another question: "She likes you ... do you like her?" This seemed to indicate the first message had either not gotten through or had been somehow ignored for the sake of maintaining control of the grapevine conversation to begin with.

Of course, there were times that we saw one another from afar, even times when we accidently passed in the hall. But at these times both parties were required to pretend that the other simply did not exist—or if existence was inevitable, that it did not matter in the least.

My daddy loved to listen to Hank Williams on the AM radio. Daddy was always singing Hank Williams songs as he worked around the house, and suddenly one of these songs began to describe my love life.

> *Kaw Liga was a wooden Indian, standing by the door,*
> *He fell in love with an Indian maid*
>   *over in the antique store ...*

The Hank Williams song went on to tell how Kaw Liga sat silently by, never telling the antique Indian maiden how he felt about her, and how one day a wealthy customer bought her and took her away before Kaw Liga could ever muster the nerve to speak to her.

My life was haunted by my certainty that I was the mirror image of the wooden cigar-store Indian, who had just about as much intelligence as I had at this particular time in my life. No image was more properly descriptive of my eighth-grade love life than the picture of that old wooden Indian pining his life away over an object of affection he could never even speak to, let alone actually build a relationship with. It was a miserable year.

For the summer after the eighth grade, I planned an escape from myself. Unable to live with the possibility of sitting around for the entire summer not knowing what Beverly Davidson was doing, I decided to fill the summer with so much activity that I wouldn't have time to think. I picked the most fun—and at the same time scariest—thing I could think of, and I went for it.

I applied for a summer job at Camp Zebulon Vance, the regional Boy Scout camp, and was accepted to be a kitchen steward for the summer season. I later found out that this was a fancy title for "cook's helper," but it was too late by then. At least I was going to a different world, a world in which I would be so preoccupied that there would not even be time to think of Beverly Davidson.

It didn't work!

First of all, the more I did the menial work of cook's helper, the more time my underoccupied mind had to think of the girl I was so in love with.

I got up each morning at five o'clock to go to the kitchen and meet Mrs. Deerbone. She was a large woman who cooked for the entire camp. Her husband, Stony, was the caretaker and overall maintenance man for the camp. Mama was relieved to find out that Mrs. Deerbone was to be my boss. She and Mama had gone to elementary school together, though to save my life I couldn't see my mother as being even in the same generation as Mrs. Deerbone. This woman seemed like she had been around since Daniel Boone was a Boy Scout.

We had a set menu for each day of the week, meaning that for the entire ten weeks of the summer session, every Monday was the same, as was every Tuesday, and so on. Monday morning always got off to a bad start, as Monday morning was scrambled egg day. I still remembered the "soft food" scrambled eggs that had been brought to my hospital room during the great tonsil-yanking episode, and I didn't like eggs any more now than I had then.

So on that first Monday morning, when Mrs. Deerbone instructed me "Go into the walk-in refrigerator and get thirty dozen eggs. Then break them into one of those giant kettles over there and beat them all up"—when she gave me those directions, I knew my summer plan had been a big mistake.

The undersized, government surplus, cold-storage eggs were as cold as ice, and before I had finished breaking the first two dozen my fingers were frozen. By the time I got to the end I knew why Mrs. Deerbone had an assistant to do the dirty work.

Mama had always told me that when I was in a bad fix I should try to think of pleasant things that were a long way away from where I was. The most pleasant thing I could think of was Beverly Davidson, and she was certainly, in every possible way, a long way away from where I was. The worse things got in the kitchen, the more terribly intensely I thought of beautiful Beverly Davidson!

Yes, I thought of her on Mondays when I had to break the thirty dozen eggs every single week. I thought of her after every meal when I had to supervise, cajole, threaten, and almost whip the weekly campers into taking their turns at scraping the dirty plates and washing and sterilizing the dishes in a primitive army-surplus outdoor gas sterilizer. I thought about Beverly on Wednesdays when I emptied the meat-baited fly traps and buried the gallons of dead and rotting flies in the woods. I thought of her when I had to clean out the grease trap that caught and held all of the coagulated cooking fat from the kitchen. No matter what I was doing, I could not keep from thinking of Beverly. Now I really was like poor that poor old wooden Indian because she was indeed as far away as that antique maiden.

That was the first of my summer problems. There were others.

No one had told me about homesickness.

My living quarters for the summer at Camp Zebulon Vance consisted of a tent pitched on a wooden platform that served as a floor. The tent had two cots and a sort of army-surplus cabinet for clothes and other things. The worst thing of all was that I had to share the tent with Bobby Jensen, that horrible boy whom I had first known in Mrs. Rosemary's kindergarten class. Bobby Jensen turned out to be Mrs. Deerbone's second assistant.

If I had had any idea in this entire world that Bobby Jensen had been anywhere around camp, I never would have applied for the job. Now he had turned out to be not only there but my tent mate to boot.

Bobby Jensen hated work so much that I ended up doing half of his jobs before it was all over. I hated Bobby Jensen almost every minute of that summer. He took over the whole tent like it was his own.

There was no electricity in the tent, and when it got dark, it was purely black in there. All there was to come home to at night was either a tent mate whom I hated or a totally dark and empty tent if Bobby happened to be somewhere else. I was happier if the tent happened to be empty.

There was no light to read or do anything else by, unless you had a flashlight, which never lasted very long at all in the days before alkaline batteries. All there was to do was to go to bed and, since it was not really very late at night yet, think about things. That's when the homesickness was pleased to take over!

I died a thousand deaths. I died over times I had been ugly to my mama, times I had ignored my daddy, times I had hated my brother, things done and things not done. It was miserable.

And then, just as I thought I was going to die, the image of Beverly Davidson would enter the picture. In some imaginary world she would be entering the tent to join and take care of me. For a few moments the mental picture was warm and pleasant, but then it wouldn't hold together and the sharp knives of reality that cut this fantasy to shreds ruined the entire picture. Beverly Davidson became the most intense part of the entire homesickness package.

I made numerous deathbed homesickness promises that summer: I would go to church every Sunday (and Sunday school too), I would never abuse my brother again, I would always appreciate my parents, and, if I lived until school started back in the fall, I would truly talk face to face with Beverly Davidson.

On one very desperate day, I actually wrote Beverly Davidson a Camp Zebulon Vance postcard. It said:

> Having a wonderful summer. Wish you were here (ha! ha!). I miss all of my school friends. *[This was to take the personal-sounding edge off of it.]* See you when school starts.

I signed it, "Your friend, Hawk."

I mailed the postcard to: "Beverly Davidson, c/o Mr. Davidson, Attorney-at-Law, Sulpher Springs, North Carolina (please forward)." I went through the entire summer not knowing whether it got there or not. Postcards don't have return addresses, so even my failure was undocumented. After this, however, the homesick-fantasy-nightmare nights were exacerbated by the feeling that I had through the postcard crossed an improper line of intimacy and had done something morally horrible. That summer lasted forever.

Finally the term of homesickness and nightmares came to its end. Summer camp was over. I went home and, one week later, entered Sulpher Springs High School, a new ninth grader.

I had not realized in all my summer dreaming that, being now in high school, I was in a different set of buildings from the junior high. I hardly even saw Beverly Davidson. Oh, I might see her once in a while when the eighth graders were late leaving the lunchroom and she was still in there when I went to lunch, but it was a year of love from afar.

One day I heard my daddy going around the house singing about poor old Kaw Liga again. I decided then and there that it was time for me to do something about all of this frustrated and unexpressed affection.

After staying awake most of the night, after thinking about it almost all of the next day at school, I made my move. That afternoon, I called Beverly Davidson on the telephone.

"Hello," I started, "Beverly? ... this is Hawk..."

Silence.

Then she said, "Oh, I wondered if you would ever call me. Thank you for the postcard you sent me from camp this summer. I'll bet you had a great time working there!"

I didn't hear a word that she was saying. All I knew was that she was still on the phone and I had to go on with my plan or I would die.

"Beverly," I pushed on, scared to keep going but knowing that now that I was in, I did not dare stop. "There's something I have to tell you."

"What?" she played right into it.

Then I did it. I said those words: "I love you!"

Without even a moment of hesitation, just like she knew exactly what I was going to say, just like she had rehearsed or been coached on this moment since the day she was born, she said right back to me: "That's a compliment!"

Now what was I supposed to do? Later on I wondered just exactly what I thought or even hoped she would say. If she had returned my words, I would have died on the spot. If she had responded with hostility or disgust, maybe I would have been able to begin to get her out of my system once and for all. But with "That's a compliment!" I was hanging forever, in that horrible land between acceptance and rejection, not having any idea in the world what she was thinking or what those words really meant.

Without saying another word, I dropped the phone, ran in the bathroom, and spent the entire afternoon hanging between throwing up and not throwing up. I couldn't even get sick without doing it halfway!

For a few weeks after that, I wasn't sure that I wanted to see Beverly at school. I actually lingered around on the outside of the lunchroom until I was sure that all the eighth graders had left, because I knew that if I accidently ran into her I would be instantly sick.

On one of those days, while I was waiting for the eighth graders to clear out, I was standing just around the corner from the lunchroom door. I heard a voice behind me say, "Hello, Hawk!" When I turned around there was a little black-haired girl I did not ever remember seeing in my life. I said hello in return and then turned my back on her to keep my self-protective vigil. For a moment I wondered how that little girl knew my name, but when I saw her rejoin the eighth-grade class leaving the lunchroom, I knew for certain that the entire grade had heard about my telephone call to Beverly. Surely they were all talking about me!

For the rest of the ninth grade I parked my love for Beverly Davidson. I had ruined it, I knew, with the telephone call. There began to actually be days when I hardly thought of her at all.

Our ninth-grade American history teacher was Miss Roberta Turbyfill. She had been teaching since the Civil War was a current event and was a devoted member of both the Daughters of the American Revolution and the United Daughters of the Confederacy. In the spring of each year, the Daughters of the American Revolution sponsored a "declamation contest." If you wanted to get a good grade in Miss

Turbyfill's class, you signed up to be in the declamation contest, on the spot! I signed up the first day she told us about it.

The way the declamation contest worked was that Miss Turbyfill had a desk drawer full of old speeches made by selected famous Americans. They were selected by the perpetual officers of the D.A.R., with occasional editorial corrections, slipped in by those whose memberships also overlapped with the United Daughters of the Confederacy.

Those who agreed to be a part of the D.A.R. Declamation Contest were assigned a speech by Miss Turbyfill. We were to memorize the speech and, on the day of the contest, deliver it to the history classes in a special assembly program.

There were several prizes to be awarded. The main prize was that if you did this at all your history grade with Miss Turbyfill went up by at least a full grade point. If you happened to come in second, you would also get some little book of poems, picked out by the D.A.R. committee. The first-prize winner would get a $17.75 United States Savings Bond, which, if kept to infinity, would be worth a full $25!

I didn't care about the two main prizes. I just wanted a better grade in history.

There were no girls in the declamation contest. Whether this was because, in the eyes of the D.A.R., only men had been famous Americans, or because all the girls in Miss Turbyfill's class got good grades anyway, I couldn't figure out.

Miss Turbyfill handed me my selected speech: "Slavery is Dead" by South Carolina's John C. Calhoun. As I read the speech I realized that *slavery is dead* was not a proclamation—no, it was a downright lament! But if I wanted a good grade in American history, I had to memorize it perfectly, and then deliver it like I actually believed it!

Anything for a good grade: I started memorizing that awful speech a word, then a sentence at a time. By the day of the contest, I knew the first half of it quite well, the next fourth fairly well, and had made it to the very end twice! If I could just manage to get through it one more time, I would not care at all who won the old savings bond.

The great day came. I put on my light blue Sunday suit, a white shirt and a red spotted bow tie. The assembly for the contest was to be second period, and there wouldn't really be time to get fixed up for it at school. All through homeroom and first period everyone in the contest worried, continuing to learn his speech a little better during the final hour.

Those of us in the contest were instructed to gather in the gym the last ten minutes of first period to be in our seats and ready when the audience came in. There were five of us in all, the total number having thinned out from the fourteen who started by nine dropouts who either got scared or made no progress at all at rote memorization of outdated politicking.

There in the gym we met the judging committee from the Daughters of the American Revolution, three old powdered blue-haired ladies whom I already knew from the Methodist Church. They wore hats and gloves, and I was glad I had my Sunday suit on. These three sat in the front row with Miss Turbyfill and stared at us while we got ready to make the speeches to the history class assembly. By the time we all got properly scared, the bell rang and the audience started filing in.

I had assumed that when we were told the audience would be made up of "the history classes" that Miss Turbyfill meant the high school history classes. But to my horror, the first group I saw was made of eighth graders, and there, on the very front row of the left-hand bleachers, was Beverly

Davidson, my broken heart's love. All the words and thoughts that John C. Calhoun ever had about slavery or anything else went straight out of my head. In that moment I could not have stood up and said my own name, let alone make a speech.

After trying for the past months to put space between Beverly Davidson and myself, this unexpected proximity was raising my temperature. I was sweating all over. Luckily, I had the last turn. I sat as still as I could and hoped that, by the time it was my turn, I would be in some way competent again.

Mousie Gray was first. Mousie, a slight, brown-haired boy whose real name was Hiram, Junior, was supposed to give Washington's second inaugural address. Even as short as that was, he got about two sentences into it and totally froze. Mousie just stood there, trying to remember ... as, one piece at a time, his world fell apart. Kids in the audience started wiggling, then giggling. Miss Turbyfill started turning red—from embarrassment for Mousie or for herself, I never knew which. The three D.A.R. judges started whispering. Finally Mousie eeked out, "I'm sorry ..." and sat down.

Next came Nicky Lewis. He was supposed to be Andrew Jackson running for president. He actually made it about halfway through his speech before his memory ran out. Having watched Mousie suffer, Nicky decided to make a clean break and get it over with. After a pause of no more than two seconds, which came right in the middle of one of Andrew Jackson's most complex thoughts, Nicky threw up his hands and said, *"That's all, folks!"* and it was over like a Bugs Bunny cartoon.

Davey Martin was next, and he didn't do any better than the rest. He tried to present Henry Clay's defense of the Missouri Compromise, but it was Davey's own memory that was compromised, and he too sat down short of his planned finish.

So far, not one single speech had been completed to the end. The students in the audience loved it. Assemblies were supposed to be boring, but not this one. They got great joy out of watching such wholesale slaughter for their own entertainment. When I had first seen Beverly Davidson come in, I had been very glad to be last on the slate to give me a chance to regroup, but now, as the audience was getting whipped up to rowdiness, I was beginning to regret that I had not already had my chance to fail and get it over with.

While Daniel Putnam was trying to get through Zebulon Pike's expeditions to the sources of the Mississippi, I noticed that the little black-haired girl who had spoken to me by name outside the lunchroom that day was sitting right beside Beverly Davidson. I leaned over to Davey, who by now had started to breathe again, and asked, "Who is that sitting beside Beverly Davidson?"

"That's Brenda Davenport." Davey knew everybody. "I think she's one of Beverly's best friends. But it may be that they always sit together because they come next to one another in the alphabet."

So that was it! This little black-haired girl was a spy for Beverly! During all this time that I thought I had blown it with Beverly, she had had her best friend checking on me to be sure I was still there! My heart came to life again.

Suddenly I heard a door slam. Daniel Putnam had actually run out of the gym in the middle of Zebulon Pike's expedition rather than listen to the laughter that erupted from the audience when he, like all the others before him, stopped short of the end. With Daniel's exit, it was my turn.

I stood up, proud in my blue suit and red bow tie, and walked toward the standing microphone in the middle of the floor. I was back in love now, ready to make a run for it with John C. Calhoun's speech. It was time to start.

"My speech is 'Slavery is Dead,' by that great American *and Southern gentleman*"—this was for Miss Turbyfill and the judges—"Mister John C. Calhoun." And I was on my way!

In my excitement, powered by a high-test rush of adrenalin, I raced through the first three or four minutes of the speech. Then I could feel myself starting to run down. First I was thinking very deliberately about each sentence, then about each word. I was reaching hard into memory for the words that needed to come next. Then my battery just went flat dead. At the end of one sentence I felt like a car out of gas at the bottom of a long hill. I had gone as far as I could go, and had not one idea in this world what John C. Calhoun meant me to say next.

In that moment several things happened: I thought of the embarrassment I had just witnessed in my peers who had failed to complete their speeches, a kind of embarrassment I would do anything to avoid. I thought of the three D.A.R. judges, and I knew from the way they had listened so far that they actually had no idea what John C. Calhoun might have said, as long as it sounded flowery and Southern. I looked at Miss Turbyfill and felt sorry for her that all her prize students had let her down. Finally, I looked at Beverly Davidson and knew that I could never allow myself to appear as anything other than brilliant and competent in her presence.

And so, without a moment's hesitation, I took a big breath, and John C. Calhoun just kept talking, as I simply made up the rest of the speech on the spot. John C. Calhoun said not only things he had never said, he said things he had not even thought of. He waxed and waned and came to an eloquent and masterful end. I bowed deeply, giving Mr. Calhoun all the credit.

Miss Turbyfill either never knew the difference or was so relieved that one of her students had finally made it to the end that she led the applause, *standing!* The three judges stood and applauded. The students applauded and that little black-haired friend of Beverly's, that Brenda Davenport, jumped up and down and clapped louder than all the rest.

When it was all over, I won the $25 savings bond, and I made an *A* in American history for the spring semester.

This great victory gave me such a high that I was back on the track of love again. I had done what poor old Kaw Liga had not done: I had made my speech and I had made it to the end (one way or another). Now I was ready to take on anything. I was going to ask Beverly Davidson for a date!

This summer I did not go back to work at Camp Zebulon Vance. Instead, Davey Martin and I worked together running the miniature golf course behind the Big Horse Drive In Restaurant. And I made plans for love.

I told Davey all about my plan to somehow have a date with Beverly Davidson. The one problem with the entire plan was that I was only fifteen years old and, though I had been driving Jeeps, tractors, pickup trucks—anything with wheels—off the road for years (every kid who grew up in farming country did the same), I was not allowed to drive legally on the public roads for another year. Luckily, though, since we now lived in town, I could try to arrange a "walking date."

It was Davey who made the suggestion. "Why don't you call her and ask her if she wants to go to a movie with you? You could walk up to her house and then walk her into town to the movie, then back again!"

"That's a great idea," I thanked him. "But where does she live?" I realized that in all of my years of fantasy daydreaming I had no idea where Beverly Davidson lived, or whether it was close enough into town to be able to walk to a movie or not.

When I shared my ignorance with Davey, he simply said, "Well, call her up and *ask her,* silly! You won't know anything unless you ask!"

So, fearful but determined, I made the resolution: before the first real Saturday of summer, I was going to ask Beverly Davidson to go to a movie, *if* she lived close enough to walk.

Davey told me I needed to call her at least three days ahead of time because it took girls a long time to get ready. He knew about these things; he had two sisters. At his urging, I decided Wednesday was the day to call Beverly and try to make the date.

Wednesday was a day of misery. I got up thinking, *What time should I call? What if I call too early and they are still asleep? What if I call and her daddy answers the telephone? What if I call too late and she has already gone somewhere for the day?* Every moment was filled with misery.

Finally I decided that the right moment to call was eleven in the morning. Davey and I did not go to work at the miniature golf course until two o'clock in the afternoon, so this would give me a chance to recover from whatever happened before it was time to go to work.

I went to the telephone. I had the number memorized well, having called it—not in reality but in my imagination— a million times. Finally, with sweaty hands, I picked up the black telephone and dialed the number.

It rang once … twice … then three times … then …

"Hello?" It was Beverly's voice!

"Beverly? … This is Hawk!"

"Oh, Hawk! I thought you would never call back!"

I couldn't believe it. Could I have been so wrong after the last call? Had she been waiting by the phone for the last year?

"Well ..." I had practiced this speech in my head a million times. "Well ... I was just wondering if you would like to go to a movie with me on Saturday afternoon. I don't have to work that day and *Song of the South* is playing at the Plaza Theater."

"Oh ... oh ... oh ..." she almost squealed, "oh, Hawk ... I would just *love* to! But I didn't know you had your driver's license."

"I don't, Beverly." I thought this would be the end of it all. "We would have to walk. I don't even know where you live or if it would be close enough, but we would have to walk. I won't get my driver's license until next summer."

"That's OK," she went on, as I breathed a sigh of relief. "It would be just fine to walk. We live at one-thirteen Cherry Street, and it's not far at all to the Plaza Theater, just about fifteen minutes right up into town. We walk up there all the time!"

"Well, the movie starts at two o'clock. How about if I come to your house about twenty minutes after one. That way we can get some popcorn and have time to get a good seat, too."

And so the great plan was made. I reported gleefully to Davey that afternoon all that had gone on, about how she *wanted* to go with me and sounded like she had wanted to for a long time. My world was going to turn out all right.

Davey seemed almost as thrilled as I was. "That's great! I think I'll even show up at that movie and watch to see how you get along! You wouldn't mind that, would you?"

What could I say? He was my best friend. Besides, since I couldn't possibly tell my parents the real truth about my

Saturday plans, it would be good to have the "Davey and I are going to a movie" alibi ready in case it was needed.

I didn't sleep at all Friday night. On Saturday morning I tried to stay in bed as late as possible so as not to give Mama a hint that anything funny was going on. After breakfast, I voluntarily washed the car for her. In part this was to distract her with my goodness, but it was also due in part to some sort of male genetic imprint that said, "You wash the car to get ready for a date," even if I didn't even have a driver's license.

Besides, getting wet and dirty washing the car then gave me an acceptable excuse to take a second bath, something I would never have done under normal circumstances. After the bath the big problem was: what to wear? No high school prom queen ever worried more about her dress than I did about what to wear that day. Should I dress up, like for church on Sunday? But if I did that, Mama would never believe the "Davey and I are going to a movie" story. Should I be casual? How would Beverly Davidson know that I was serious? It was an awful dilemma.

Finally I decided to wear good pants and a dress shirt. If Mama said anything about it, I would just say, "Well, I just took a bath. I might as well be cleaned up all over!" I knew she would like that. I also slipped my red bow tie into my pants pocket. It was the kind that clips on the collar of your shirt, so I knew that I could put it on once I was out of sight of the house. I knew that Beverly's daddy was a lawyer and that my great-uncle Zeb who was a lawyer wore bow ties, so maybe this would be a smart thing to do.

I estimated that it would take about twenty minutes to get to Beverly's house from our house. I ate lunch in a hurry and told Mama that I would be back after the movie was over, and, with bow tie in pocket, I was off.

As soon as Beverly had told me that 113 Cherry Street was "a brick house with a steep roof and a red front door," I knew the exact house it was without even thinking about the numbers. Every time Daddy circled the block to come home after church on Sundays, we passed that house. And to think that my true love had been in there all that time without my even knowing it. *Well*, I thought, *now I do.*

It only took me about fifteen minutes to get to the right block on Cherry Street, so to keep from being early—Davey had told me never to be early!—I lingered around the post office corner for five minutes. Then I marched straight for the house.

"Kaw Liga" was long abandoned as my theme song by now. Now I was humming with Patsy Cline as, in my head, I could hear her singing "I Was So Wrong for So Long."

With a last-minute touch to be sure that the red bow tie was in place, I marched up the walk of 113 Cherry Street and pushed the doorbell button. My heart thumped against the wall of my chest as I heard footsteps inside the house.

The door swung open, and Beverly Davidson said, "Hello! You are right on time!"

Only it was not Beverly Davidson. Instead of the fair, blonde object of affection I had been in love with for nearly two years, there in the door stood that little black-haired girl I thought was Brenda Davenport!

Suddenly, Pasty Cline laughed in my head: "I was *so* wrong, for so long!" And I began to realize all that had happened. I realized that on that first day of the eighth grade, when I had punched Davey Martin and said, "Who is that?," he had thought I was looking at a different girl and had honestly said, "That's Beverly Davidson." She was, after all, sitting, alphabetically correct, right beside the real Brenda Davenport, who had the soft, blonde hair!

In that door-opening moment, two years of life passed before the eyes of embarrassed memory. I had passed "I like you ... do you like me?" messages back and forth to the wrong girl! I had dreamed and fantasized about the wrong girl! I had sent a summer camp postcard to the wrong girl! I had made the "I love you!" telephone call to the *wrong girl!*

No wonder *this* Beverly Davidson had called me by name at school and had led the applause when I made up the end of John C. Calhoun's speech! Every time she had a chance she was responding to messages she kept getting from me, and I never noticed.

Suddenly, I was back to being that poor old wooden Indian again. At all costs now, I had to hide my feelings—though the heartsickness had been momentarily replaced by confusion and bewilderment. But all I said was, "Well, Beverly, are you ready to go?"

And with the *new* Beverly Davidson, who would be my own chosen girlfriend for most of the next two years, I set out for the Plaza Theater.

Davey was there, of course, and he never knew that anything was wrong. He had had the right girl in his mind for me all the time and simply did not know how totally stupid I had been for nearly two years. And, true to poor old Kaw Liga to the very end, I never told Davey the truth either.

Everybody Goes to the Beach

1958–60

*A*fter the ill-fated Florida vacation that terminated at Rock City, I lived with the acceptance that I would probably never see the ocean again. Things changed in high school.

By the time my class was in the tenth grade, reports and rumors began to drift down the ranks from juniors and seniors about "going to the beach for Easter." At first I thought these to be stories of what some individual family planned to do (everybody didn't dream of Rock City the way Mama did, I realized). But as the talk continued, I came to realize that, no, there were actual groups of eleventh- and twelfth-grade students who, *on their own*, were going to Myrtle Beach, South Carolina, for the Easter holiday break.

Davey Martin and I decided that we wanted to do this—some day, in some imaginable world, where dreams come true. We both knew that my mama and daddy would never let it happen in this world.

The reason Mama and Daddy were the key to the imagined trip was that Davey lived with his grandmother—Mazza, we called her—and she didn't drive. So unless he could somehow talk one of his aunts or uncles into giving us a car for the proposed beach trip, my parents' new Plymouth was the only choice.

We knew from the start that the plan was a long shot, so we started working on it early in the tenth grade, aiming not for that year—no, we didn't even have our driver's licenses yet—but for the spring of our junior year, a full year and a half away. Both of us had learned that my mother was subject to battle attrition; if we could just wear her out over eighteen months (as I had done long ago with the birthday party business) we might have a chance.

We started right in with a full frontal attack. One night Davey and Billy Stockwell were both over at our house when out of the blue Davey said straight to my mama, "Why don't you go to the beach with us for Easter this year? We're going to have a lot of fun!"

"Why, thank you for asking, Davey. Who's going? Your grandmother and your aunt Millie?" Mama sounded genuinely flattered.

"Why, no ma'am ... they're not going ... it's just the three of *us*—me and Hawk and Billy!" Davey grinned at Mama.

Mama sucked air like her lungs were going to explode! "You boys can just get that out of your minds *right now!* You have no business in this world thinking you can go off to the beach! It must be three hundred miles down there ... and besides that, where would you stay?"

That was the end of the discussion for then.

It was in this moment that I knew we would eventually win. If Mama had simply walked out of the room laughing and shaking her head, we would have been in trouble. But she did not. She had argued back! This meant that we had her attention, and when we had her attention, I knew, we were still in the fight! We pushed on with hope and courage.

Davey, Billy and I did not spend the entire year talking about going to Myrtle Beach. No, we just did it in front of Mama enough that she *thought* that was all we talked about. In fact, she once said to us, "Is that all you boys ever think about?"

"Well," I replied smugly, "what else is there to think about?" and I gave her a tenth-grade look.

Davey Martin turned to Mama and said, "I hate to have to tell you this, but *everybody* goes to the beach!"

"Well, *you're* not!"

We truly had her attention now! It was becoming quite clear to us that sooner or later Mama would realize she could either be locked in an eternal argument or she could let us go and have it all over with. We were going to win!

The battle itself was great fun. Gradually, as we argued on through the weeks and months, we learned two things. First, we learned that we would probably have better luck with Daddy. He even admitted, with hindsight, that he had enjoyed the brief trip to Florida. (Now we really had shifted the balance of power!) The second thing we learned was that pure and simple storytelling worked a whole lot better than begging, even on Mama.

After our tenth grade Easter break came and went (by this time Davey and Billy both had their driver's licenses and I looked forward to getting mine in June), instead of begging, we began to tell Mama stories of carefully selected episodes from other people's beach trips. It was actually Davey Martin, not me, who discovered this power.

Siding up to Mama, who had just given him a piece of chocolate cake, Davey started into conversation. "Did I tell you about that Easter sunrise service?"

"No, Davey," Mama fell right into the trap. "Did you go?"

"I didn't get to go this year, but it sounded so inspiring and beautiful that I sure would like to go next year. Sandra Trout's family went and her mama told me all about it."

"Well," Mama was asking for it now, "tell me about it."

"The Trouts got there real early in the morning and just as the sun came up a choir began to sing. They even had a band and trumpets to play for the rising of the sun. There was a lot of special music, and just a little bit of preaching. By the time it was over, the sun was all the way up and then, they said, the whole day was just beautiful!" He began to lay it on thick: "Mrs. Trout said that after that sunrise service, why, Easter would have been a beautiful day even if it had rained! Yes, I sure would like to go next year!"

Davey's part was finished. Mama picked it right up.

"That sounds so nice, Davey, I think you ought to go next year, and … why don't you take Hawk with you? I think it would be good for him.

"Oh, by the way, where did you say that the sunrise service was held? Was it the one over at Cherokee or the one out by Tuscola Lake?"

Davey grinned, "Oh, no, ma'am, the *real good one* wasn't either one of those … no, the real good one is down at Myrtle Beach! They have it right out on the beach every Easter! Oh, do you really think we ought to go next year?"

Mama knew she had been had. She looked at Davey and frowned. Then she slowly said, "I will not even dignify that question with an answer!"

Now we knew we were winning. This time she didn't even say no.

On the first day of June, 1959, I got my driver's license. Now Davey, Billy, and I could all three legally drive on the public roads of North Carolina. If we truly hoped to have any chance at all of going to the beach next Easter, our present job was to convince my mother that we were the safest, most careful, most mature, most responsible drivers who had ever been licensed in the state.

There were two cars in our family now. Sometime after Mama got her driver's license Daddy had come home one day with an old fluid drive 1948 DeSoto he had bought off the back row of Uncle Ferrell's used cars for one hundred dollars. The DeSoto ran a year or so, then was sold as junk for fifteen dollars. "Eighty-five dollars a year is not a bad price for transportation," Daddy had allowed, and since that time we had had a progression of hundred-dollar second cars from Uncle Ferrell's back lot.

Mama drove the "new car," which, this year, really was new, a 1958 Plymouth, the last car left in Uncle Ferrell's year-end inventory. Mama had given in at last to automatic transmission. The new Plymouth had push buttons to select the gears, even a radio. It was the first model year to have dual headlights! The year-end Plymouth was such a bargain that Mama didn't even fuss about the color: purple and white! The top of the Plymouth was white, the middle (including the giant rear-fender tail fins) was purple, and the bottom halves of the doors were white again.

Part of my proof of automotive responsibility was the constant washing and polishing of both the new Plymouth and Daddy's current old clunker. Davey, Billy and I hoped that Mama would reason that no one who took such good care of cars would possibly drive unsafely!

We also spent an inordinate amount of time reporting to Mama everything bad that ever happened to any of our newly licensed driving schoolmates. We never missed a chance to make ourselves look better by comparison.

"Mary Barkley got a speeding ticket!" I proudly told Mama, with a look that stated my own disapproval of such reckless irresponsibility. "And James Callaway wasn't paying attention to what he was doing and ran his mama's Buick right into a telephone pole *in the middle of the school parking lot!*"

"He must have been showing off!" Mama added, and I solemnly shook my head in an assent of both agreement and condemnation.

Looking back now, it is hard to believe that three sixteen-year-old boys spent over a year planning what would be, even if it happened, no more than a long weekend, but we did. Perhaps it was a combination of hormonal hope and ignorant fantasy that kept us going. This was, after all, more than NASA had to go on to sustain them through years of planning the first moon shot.

After school started back, and the fall of the year plodded on, we kept up our dreams—and our assault on Mama's veto. Then, around Christmastime, two things happened that helped us blast the door of hope open once and for all.

Davey Martin came rushing over to our house in the afternoon to report that his uncle Tom and aunt Alicia were visiting for Christmas. Uncle Tom was a career Air Force pilot, and Davey's grandmother's house was always their home for the holidays.

"Guess what?" Davey said to our whole family. "Uncle Tom is retiring in January. He's put in twenty years, and he can retire now and still start his own business."

"That's great!" Mama said. "I guess they'll be moving back here for good now." (Mama always thought that Davey needed more parental guidance. Now maybe he would get it from his uncle and aunt, and Mama wouldn't feel like she had to raise him along with raising Joe and me.)

"*Oh no!*" Davey went on. "They're not moving here ... they're going to live at Myrtle Beach! That's where Uncle Tom was stationed when they first got married, and they've always wanted to go back. Why, they've bought a house there already. They'll be moving in by the first of February, and *they have already invited all of us to stay with them when we go to the beach for Easter!* Isn't that wonderful? That solves what you were worrying about, doesn't it? Now we will have a good, safe place to stay!"

Mama looked so beaten that she couldn't even open her mouth. Then Daddy, who had been silent on the matter all these months, weighed in.

"What if," he started slowly, looking at Mama more than at us when he did, "what if Davey's grandmother wanted to go down to Myrtle Beach to visit with Tom and Alicia, and these boys just took her down there and then stayed to bring her back? That way Mazza would get to visit their new house, the boys would get to go to the beach like they want to go, and they would have a chaperone at the same time!"

"I'll think about it," was Mama's reply, but, we knew in the depths of our hearts that we had finally won.

The last barrier to our plan was removed New Year's Eve by none other than Sandra Trout's mother, the same one who had been quoted in the report of the Easter sunrise service that had served as a weapon in one of the first battles. The church was crowded more for the New Year's Eve service than on a normal Sunday morning. Since our usual fourth-row-on-the-right seats were taken, we slipped into a row nearer the back and Mama ended up right beside Mrs. Trout.

Then, just to have something to talk about, Mama reported the fact that we wanted very badly to go to the beach. Mrs. Trout said, "Oh, that would be wonderful. We always take a group of Sandra's friends, and it would be *so nice* to have some fine hometown boys down there for them to have a good time with. I'd be glad to help watch over them if that would keep you from worrying."

"Well ..." Mama expressed her doubt, "I'm still not sure it's the right thing for them to do ..."

Mrs. Trout answered, almost aggressively, "Oh, let them go! *Everybody goes to the beach!* You can't hold on to them forever!"

Davey, Billy, and I sat right there listening. After this, we were as good as on our way!

And so, with Easter vacation still over three months away, the die was cast. School would let out for the spring break at the end of the day on Thursday, the day before Good Friday. Both Good Friday and Easter Monday would be school holidays, so, with the weekend thrown in free, the entire holiday would be four days long. After a lot of begging on our part, Mama agreed that we could leave directly after school on Thursday so that we would reach Myrtle Beach by bedtime on Thursday night. We would then have three full days before we had to start for home on Monday morning in order to be home to, in Mama's words, "get a good night's rest before going back to school where you belong on Tuesday."

In reality, bringing Mazza along was just like adding another kid, not at all like securing us with the chaperone

Mama expected. Mazza had raised her own entire family of four boys and three girls before she ever took on the task of raising Davey Martin when his mother, her oldest daughter, was killed in a car wreck. Davey was three at the time, and she had already had enough experience to learn that, like weeds, children grow up a lot stronger if they are not cultivated too much. Mazza was more an enabler than a governor.

Everything we ever did she thought was funny instead of just stupid. She was always game to try new things herself. Mama never wanted us to do anything we had not done before. If she had her way, we never would have done much of anything, since for kids almost every experience is a first-time thing. So all in all, we were delighted to have Mazza along. We could count on her to really help us make decisions, not to just say no no matter what the question was.

From the start it was assumed that we would go to the beach in the purple and white Plymouth.

Mama actually corresponded with Davey's aunt Alicia to be sure that we really were invited, that we really were not going to be any trouble, that there really was room for everybody to sleep without causing an inconvenience, and that she really would be sure that we behaved. She could have called on the telephone, but that was long distance, and "we don't know how to do that" was her answer to that suggestion.

We started packing on the weekend before Easter. The entire Palm Sunday weekend, the day that Jesus came to town riding on an ass with nearly nothing to his name, we made our plans to leave town in a Plymouth with a gigantic trunk that was still not big enough to hold all the things we thought we needed to take for a three-day weekend.

The trunk space problem actually started with Mama. She decided that it would be too much for Davey Martin's

Aunt Alicia to have to feed all of us for the whole weekend, so she bought an entire ham to bake and send along. Even before the ham was baked, she had to solve the problem of transporting the ham safely—Mama was scared to death of food poisoning. We ended up borrowing a gigantic fishing cooler from Uncle Ferrell.

That cooler must have held fifteen gallons and filled the main central part of the Plymouth trunk all on its own. It did smell somewhat like fish, but, packed with ice, it would hold the baked ham and an assortment of vegetables and jellies Mama was just sure were not available at Myrtle Beach. Now, where were three boys and a chaperone grandmother going to put all the things we were sure *we* needed?

We decided to build our own car-top baggage carrier. Starting with two bars intended for hauling a canoe, we built a plywood box and bolted it to the canoe bars. We spent all day Saturday doing this, including painting the roof-top box with red enamel (never thinking at all about how the red color would look on top of the purple and white Plymouth) and scrounging up a little tarp to cover everything and plenty of rope to tie it all down with.

As each day of the following week went on, Davey Martin, Billy, and I gradually assembled enough clothing, luggage, and other miscellaneous gear for a six-month safari spanning three seasons of the year. Finally, on Wednesday night, it was all assembled, loaded up, and—except for the ham, which was still baking—we were ready.

I hardly slept at all that night. The next day, I discovered that Davey Martin and Billy had also had sleepless nights. Mazza had slept like a baby. The next day seemed like the longest school day in history. Finally, though, the three o'clock bell rang and Daddy was waiting for us in his most recent second car, a 1950 Pontiac. We picked up Mazza, who brought only one tiny suitcase, checked the oil in the Plymouth, and—with Mama crying, "Hawk... *please* be careful ... I am not sure you should be doing this!"—we got in the car to leave.

"Oh, Mama!" I answered almost in disgust. *"Everybody goes to the beach* ... Don't worry! Mazza will take care of us!" Mazza just laughed, and we were off!

Never in my entire life, before or since, have I ever felt the sense of absolute freedom and release that I felt as we drove on our way for that long-hoped-for weekend. Here were my two best friends, and here was Mazza, the one adult in the world who was more likely to try new things than we were. Ahead of us was nothing but pure freedom and adventure.

On the weekend before, Daddy had bought us road maps of North and South Carolina at the Esso station. We had spent a good bit of time each night during the week studying the map. The chosen route was 344 miles, down through Hendersonville into South Carolina, then along State Highway 9 all the way across the state, just south of the border, until we dropped on down to the beach. Daddy had suggested this route since there were few big towns and no real cities along the way to slow us down.

We left with a full tank of gas—eighteen gallons was the tank's capacity. I had calculated that the Plymouth got nearly twenty miles per gallon, so Davey and I were optimistic that we could make it all the way to the beach on one tank of gas. Since we were on our way by three-thirty in the afternoon, it seemed reasonable that, even with a stop for supper, we could get to Davey's Uncle Tom's house by eleven o'clock. Everything was going exactly according to plan.

Mazza loved to sing hymns. For miles and miles we sang as we left the mountains of North Carolina and began to skim the South Carolina foothills, the day melting away into the pre-daylight-saving-time darkness by about seven o'clock. We were amazed at how warm the air felt, even after dark, as we reached the lowlands of South Carolina toward suppertime.

By the time we had driven for four hours we began to see the signs: SOUTH OF THE BORDER... *Pedro, he sez, stop and eat with me!!!* The signs were painted in garish fluorescent paint on four by eight sheets of plywood, posted, it seemed, every mile or two. *Twenty-six miles to Pedro ... Just twenty-five more miles ... You'll be there in twenty-four minutes ... Pedro Sez "Twenty-three and eat with me!"* We were all four determined to eat supper at this "South Of the Border" place, whatever it was, even if it took a slight detour to get there.

South of the Border turned out to be at Dillon, South Carolina, just south of the North Carolina–South Carolina line. We could see the lights in the sky even before we saw the gigantic plethora of neon signs that announced, labeled, and advertised every magnetic dimension of this roadside attraction. South of the Border consisted of a motel (complete with plaster of Paris animals on the lawn), a Mexican-themed restaurant (with more plaster of Paris animals), a carousel, an indoor miniature golf course, and an assortment of gigantic gift shops. We pulled right in, in front of the restaurant.

As we got out of the car and headed for the restaurant, we couldn't help but notice people staring at the purple and white Plymouth with the red homemade luggage carrier strapped to the top.

After a supper of chicken fried steak and Boston cream pie, we wasted a good bit of time walking all around South of the Border visiting all of the attractions and gift shops. Nobody bought anything, though. We were saving all of our money for Myrtle Beach.

Back in the car at nine o'clock, we figured that we had another two hours of driving ahead of us. By now we were tired of riding, tired of each other, tired of singing hymns, so we started tuning in the radio. Suddenly, in the South Carolina night, out of the silent dark, we hit an extremely powerful AM station: WAPE, Jacksonville, Florida.

When WAPE went on directional power at sundown, the big Florida station reached all up and down the eastern seaboard. The station identification theme for WAPE was: "You're listening to WAPE, Jacksonville, Florida, *WAPE, the big APE ... aaahhhhh, uhuuhhh-uhuuhhh-uhuuuu, aaahhhh ...*" with an ape imitation that Victor Mature on his best day would have been envious of.

The first time we heard "the big APE" Mazza went crazy! She loved it. "*Aaahhhhh, uhuuhhh-uhuuhhh-uhuuuu, aaahhhh ...*" The radio announcer would play the ape sound, then, "*aaahhhhh, uhuuhhh-uhuuhhh-uhuuuu, aaahhhh ...*" Mazza would repeat in complete and wonderful imitation. Then she and all the rest of us would collapse in uncontrollable laughter. Were we ever glad that she was sent along as our chaperone! We were having an absolutely great time.

We had only taken a tiny detour to eat supper at South of the Border, and even with our messing around there, we were looking forward to reaching Myrtle Beach by eleven. Listening to WAPE, laughing and rolling around, we headed down toward and through the town of Conway and then the last little stretch on to the beach.

Davey and I had been watching the gas gauge carefully for the whole trip. Back at South of the Border, we had been tempted to fill up at the gas station decorated with plaster of Paris burros, but our game was to see if we could get to Myrtle Beach on one tank of gas. When we had checked the gas, we had more than a quarter tank—plenty for the rest of our trip. After all, there seemed to be gas stations every-where! If it really got close to empty, we would fill up.

By the time we were leaving Conway, the last outpost, the gas needle was halfway between one-quarter and empty. But Myrtle Beach was only about thirty more miles, so we went on. By now we could smell the salt air very well and we were pretty sure we could hear the ocean. On we went, the gas gauge sinking lower and lower.

Suddenly the road widened to four lanes, and we came to the city limits of Myrtle Beach. Davey Martin, Billy, and I cheered. Mazza made the big ape sound and laughed. We all slapped one another on the shoulders. "We did it! We did it!" we said, over and over again.

Since Billy had never seen the ocean before, we drove straight toward it and stopped the Plymouth in a little cul-de-sac at the edge of the sand where, though we could not see much in the dark, we could at least feel the sea breeze and smell the air. As we came back toward the main highway, we saw the edges of the Myrtle Beach pavilion area with its carnival rides and lights. Wow! Were we ever going to have fun!

Davey Martin's Uncle Tom and Aunt Alicia actually lived at Ocean Drive, a separate little town about a dozen undeveloped miles north of Myrtle Beach proper. Mazza pulled out the written directions, and at a quarter to eleven we headed north on Highway 17 to find our beach home at Ocean Drive. We all knew that we would come back to the pavilion area the next night.

Highway 17 bypassed most of the beachfront develop-ment at Myrtle Beach, and by the time we were on the north side of town, we were on an empty, unpopulated, and almost deserted road. The map indicated we had ten more miles to go.

In our excitement at getting to the beach, in our excitement at feeling the sea breeze, in our excitement at looking at neon lights and listening to the carousel organ from afar, in our making plans about the next three days, we forgot all about looking at the gasoline gauge. We never noticed that it had now fallen below the empty line.

Suddenly the purple and white Plymouth coughed, jerked to life briefly again, coughed four times in a row, and finally shut down, totally and completely dead! All I had time to do was pull off on the shoulder of the road to get clear of the pavement. All four of us knew exactly what had happened.

Davey, Billy, and I were dead silent and embarrassed. But Mazza was laughing! " *Aaahhhhh, uhuuhhh-uhuuhhh-uhuuuu, aaahhhh …*" she screeched. "You big apes! *You ran out of gas!*" then she made the ape sound and laughed out loud again. Her laughter settled us down and we began to try to figure out what to do.

"Just look right up there," Mazza was pointing. "Right there's a little store with a gas pump outside … I'll bet they've even got a can to carry gas in." We looked and saw the little store, no more than a quarter mile up the road ahead of us. Billy stayed with Mazza in the car while Davey and I hiked out toward the store.

Suddenly the lights at the little store went out, and before we could do anything, someone came out the door, locked it, and drove away for the night in an old pickup truck. It was exactly eleven p.m. Now there was nothing in sight with lights on, and we were completely in the dark.

Davey and I walked back to the car, where the four of us made a plan. Mazza told us that she was not scared to stay by herself; besides, she said, "Nobody can steal the car … it's out of gas!" She told us that we would feel better and be smarter if we all walked together to try to find gas. She reminded us that we had passed some open businesses a mile or two back, and if nothing was open that we should find a telephone and call Uncle Tom. He could come and pick us up and we could come back with gas in the morning. It was a reasonable plan.

We left the keys in the car so that Mazza could listen to WAPE on the radio, but, we told her, if we were not back in half an hour she should turn it off so she wouldn't run the battery down. After telling Mazza to keep all the doors locked, we took off, walking back in the direction from which we had come.

When the night's adventures were all over, there were two different stories of what had happened. One story was told by Mazza. The other was told by the Windy Hill, South Carolina, police chief.

According to Mazza, we had not been gone very long when it all happened. She had all of the car doors locked and was happily listening to WAPE. "Maybe," she said later, "maybe I *was* making the ape sounds ... but I *wasn't* doing all those things they said I was doing.

"I was just listening to the radio and a car pulled off the road and stopped behind our car. When some people got out of it, I thought that maybe you-all were back, and so I just kept listening. Then whoever it was that got out of that car started pecking on the windows and shining flashlights in my eyes.

"That scared me, and I switched off the radio and got down in the floor where they couldn't shine that light in my eyes. The next thing I knew, the car was moving, and I was the only one in it!"

The police chief's report was quite different. According to him, he and his deputy had seen this weird purple and white Plymouth with all kinds of things tied on the top of it. The car seemed to be abandoned beside the road, and so they stopped to investigate. When they got close to the car, they heard something coming from the inside that sounded like a big gorilla or maybe like Tarzan himself.

The police chief swore that when they slipped up and shined their lights in the car, they saw an old woman braying like an ape and beating herself on the chest with her fists. Then, they said, she got down in the floor just like she was a chimpanzee!

They figured that she had either escaped from some-where or had been hauled off and abandoned by somebody, but that whatever the story was, she might be dangerous. So, instead of trying to get into the Plymouth or even trying to talk to Mazza, the police chief had called the city tow truck dispatcher and had the Plymouth towed in to the police station where he could assemble a group of "reinforcements" and investigate this thing in the light!

In the meantime we finally did get to a store. It was closed, but there was a pay phone on the outside. So we called Uncle Tom and waited while he came to pick us up. After he got us in the car he said, "Now where did you-all run out of gas? I came right down the main highway and I didn't see anything."

"Oh, you must have," Davey replied. "The car is right on the side of the road and with that red plywood box on top of it you couldn't miss it." Pretty soon, though, we discovered why Uncle Tom had not seen the car. The Plymouth was gone! We were in a total panic, imagining that every kind of thing had happened to Mazza.

"Oh, what will we tell Mama?" I said to the others. "Mazza came to take care of us, and now we have lost her!"

"Now settle down, boys," Uncle Tom said. "There's got to be some reason for this. Let's just go to the Windy Hill police station. It's the closest to where you left the car."

When we got there, there was a standoff. Four men were gathered around the car, trying to get Mazza to roll down a window or unlock a door. She was inside, refusing by now to cooperate with any strangers at all.

When Mazza saw us, she let out a yell, *"Aaahhhhh, uhuuhhh-uhuuhhh-uhuuuu, aaahhhh ... Where have you been, you big apes?"*

We fell apart with laughter.

Uncle Tom told the police chief that Mazza was out on an Easter leave from Dix Mental Hospital in Raleigh, but that he was her son and would be responsible for her. The police chief didn't even ask any questions. He was so glad to get this crazy woman off his hands that he just said, "Take her!" and disappeared into the station.

Finally, after putting the two gallons of gas Uncle Tom had brought into the Plymouth, we went on to Uncle Tom's house. We must have laughed for two hours telling Aunt Alicia all about what had happened.

We slept late the next morning to make up for our late night adventures. While Mazza started her visit with Uncle Tom and Aunt Alicia, Davey, Billy, and I were up and off to play on the beach.

Except for my one night in Daytona Beach, none of us had ever been to the beach before, but Mama had sent us well prepared. That she did not know any more about the beach than the rest of us didn't stop her.

"Now," she had warned us the week before, "I don't want the three of you getting blistered in that sun." So she had gone straight to Conard's Drugstore. In the North Carolina mountains, there was very little need for suntan protection and all Dr. Conard sold was two versions of Coppertone, lotion and oil. Mama bought both.

Each day for the rest of the week until we left, we had to hear her read us the directions from the Coppertone bottles. "Apply liberally and often ... stay in the sun only fifteen minutes on the first day ... then increase fifteen minutes each day for an even tan ..." There on the Coppertone bottle was a picture of a little girl with her bathing suit pulled down just enough to reveal her white bottom in contrast to her tan. The little girl, like a newspaper cartoon, had a bubble of words coming from her mouth: *"Tan, don't burn, get a Coppertone tan!"* Mama's one worry was that maybe she had not bought enough lotion and oil for us.

We were very serious sunbathers that first day on the beach. We simply greased ourselves with the lotion and oil. We timed ourselves for fifteen minutes, and went back inside the house and cooled off for an hour. Then we regreased ourselves and went back out for another fifteen minutes.

By the time the day was over we had used the entire two bottles of Coppertone and had spent no more that two hours, total, on the beach, and that in well-greased fifteen-minute intervals. By that night none of us showed the least trace of ever having been in the sun in our lives. We were disgusted. What was the point of even going to the beach if we didn't go home at least pink enough to make all our pale friends jealous?

That night, the three of us boys were invited to have supper in Myrtle Beach proper with Sandra Trout's parents. Sandra's mother picked us up at five-thirty in her gigantic chrome-laden 1958 Buick station wagon. She had also agreed to bring us back to Uncle Tom's by eleven o'clock so that Mazza, Uncle Tom, and Aunt Alicia could have an evening out on their own in the meantime.

The Trouts had let Sandra bring Beverly Davidson and
Brenda Davenport with her to the beach where they rented
the same big house they always rented. It was there that Mrs.
Trout took us to meet the girls. Even though Beverly and I
had cooled down a lot, we were still good friends. It looked
like we would be paired with the girls for the evening:
Beverly with me, Sandra with Davey, and, by default, Billy
with Brenda.

From the rented house, we crossed the street and walked
down to a big, old Chinese restaurant. I had never been to
such a place before in my life. Inside was a goldfish pond
bigger than the one in the Rosemarys' yard. A little bridge
curved over it. The restaurant was filled with indoor plants
and trees that made it look like a jungle, and torches burned
everywhere on the tops of bamboo poles. I had no idea what
we were eating—Mrs. Trout ordered for all of us, and we
shared our food—but it was one of the best times I had ever
had.

By the time we spent over an hour eating, then went back
to the Trouts' rental house and visited, I was ready to go back
to Uncle Tom's. I had purely exhausted myself, pretending
that this was just the kind of thing I was familiar with doing
almost every day.

The next morning we were up and ready to head for the
beach again. But when we looked out the window, it was
raining! We wasted the day by getting in the Plymouth and,
following Aunt Alicia's suggestion, driving down to Brook-
green Gardens (hoping the rain would stop, but it did not),
then coming back up to Myrtle Beach and prowling for hours
through a gigantic gift shop called the Gay Dolphin. We
drove back to Uncle Tom's, arriving just as it finally stopped
raining about five in the afternoon.

"Boys," Uncle Tom started in, "do you have big plans for tonight?" We just shook our heads. We had had a worthless day. "Then you ought to go to the pavilion and have a big time!"

"Are you sure about that?" Aunt Alicia put in. "It might be dangerous down there on a Saturday night!"

"Oh, Alicia, they'll be OK. They need to have a good fun night on their own while they are here! We won't even wait up for you, boys. You just come on in when you get home and we'll probably all be in bed." And with that, we were set free for the night!

After putting on our nicest casual clothes, we headed into the center of Myrtle Beach and parked the car. First on our agenda was finding a place to eat supper.

Billy spotted a place called Down the Hatch. It had some wild-sounding and very loud music coming up out the door and we headed there. It smelled like cigarette smoke and beer even outside the door. We decided it was the place for us. But when we tried to go inside, it was so dark we couldn't see. When a big beefy guy with an anchor tattooed on his bicep said, "Get out of here, you little turd-knockers! You don't belong in here!" we hurried down the street and ate outside at the Dairy Queen.

The pavilion area in the center of Myrtle Beach was lively and bustling. The three of us started to consume the center of Myrtle Beach gradually and gently. After the Dairy Queen supper, we headed for the open-all-night, dinosaur-inhabited miniature golf course, with its live parrots and windmills and waterfalls with colored water. We must have played both of the eighteen-hole courses twice before we moved on.

Next we stood in awed wonder while a huge antique German player organ, complete with automated drums, bells, and exposed gold-painted organ pipes, played a selection of songs ranging from the "Blue Danube Waltz" to "The Stars and Stripes Forever." Near the organ was a gorgeous turn-of-the-century carousel, its Wurlitzer merry-go-round music competing with the organ. With no shame at all at being the only teenagers among hoards of children, Davey, Billy, and I rode the carousel three times before we were sated.

After the carousel came bumper cars, the Ferris wheel (which absolutely took my breath away every time it went over the top on its rounds), and a very jerky little roller coaster called The Wild Mouse. By now the three of us were so brave we thought we were ready for anything.

But we also were hungry again. There were all kinds of food concessions. I didn't like the looks of candied apples and, though curious, I knew that the cotton candy couldn't be at all filling if you were actually hungry. Even when we had only gone as far away from home as an occasional trip to Asheville, Mama had forever warned me against eating what she called "strange hot dogs," so the greasy chili-topped hot dogs were out. We checked out all the food stands.

Then we saw the Dip Topper. The Dip Topper, we discovered, sold soft ice cream "with a little extra." Inside the stand was a long row of pots, each filled with a different color of some kind of molten stuff. Each was labeled with a different flavor, and, as we watched other customers order, the now-filled swirly cones of soft ice cream were dipped in the molten stuff. As the server thrust them out into the air, the outer crust of topping, artificially colored to match the supposed flavor, was already hardened. All three of us agreed that this was the thing we needed.

I was first to order. I chose a "large cone of chocolate with lime dip-top." What I got was absolutely six inches tall above the cone and covered with a twisted green covering that made it look like the steeple of a weathered copper Russian church. It was beautiful.

I had to start eating fast, even while Davey and Billy ordered, because the soft chocolate ice cream was already beginning to run out of the sides of the coating and down the outside of the cone. I ate as fast as I could, not missing a single drip. As I slurped, Davey and Billy began doing the same thing. We all thought this to be the finest treat we had ever had and wondered why someone didn't open a Dip Topper in Sulpher Springs.

Right beside the Dip Topper was the Tilt-a-World, a ride we had, so far, been a little bit shy about riding.

We watched as all the victims surrendered their tickets and entered an opening onto a circular plate about thirty feet in diameter. The plate was actually made of expanded metal mesh so that when you stood on it you could also see through to the ground. It functioned kind of like a cake pan. It had an eight-foot high curving wall made of the same metal mesh all around its perimeter.

The victims stood with their backs to the mesh wall and faced the center. There were actually little niches in the perimeter wall to keep the victims spaced out evenly and separated from one another. When the ride started up, the big mesh cake pan full of people began to turn. It turned faster and faster and faster until it was all just a blur. Then when all of the victims were pressed tight against the sides by centrifugal force, the floor of the whirling machine slowly began to drop away, and there you were, stuck to the outside wall by sheer force, with nothing but open air under your feet.

Then the best part of all started. With all of the riders stuck fast by force, the entire spinning contraption began to tilt up on its edge until people were now spinning not around and around but up and down, until the whole process reversed itself and it all came back to earth again.

Emboldened by the Wild Mouse and the Ferris wheel, rejuvenated by the dip-top ice cream, the three of us decided it was time to take on the Tilt-a-World. We bought three tickets and stood in line, getting dizzy just watching a couple of loads in front of us spin around and around in sparkling lights. Then, at last, it was our time to load up. The three of us spread out instead of getting side by side, so that we could all see one another through the whole course of the ride.

Finally, the entrance door clanked shut, and the Tilt-a-World started turning. Soon we were spinning so fast that the entire world blurred into a stew of colored lights. Since the people on the opposite side of the ride always stayed in their same place and didn't seem to move at all, it began to feel like *we* were the ones who were still and the entire world was spinning out of control. By now the force on my body was so harsh that it felt like I couldn't get a deep breath and my brain was mashed into the back of my head. Still, I was sure that I would fall down into the machinery when the floor started dropping away ... but I didn't.

Just when it seemed that nothing could be more disorienting than what was already happening, the world started to turn over at the same time! I suddenly realized that the Tilt-a-World was tipping us up on our sides. Now it seemed like the circular pattern we had been taking turned into an ellipse. Each time we went up it felt like we slowed down and almost stopped—I was sure we were going to fall out—then when we went back down the speed and pressure were unbearable. Suddenly my stomach began to notice the abuse we had entered into together, and began to register its inability to continue the abuse and retain the just-eaten green dip-top ice cream cone I had just given it.

Just as I thought, *I'm going to get sick*, I saw Davey Martin throw up.

It looked like, by some mysterious force of gravity, the throw-up just hung there in the air and spun around in weightlessness. We were going around so fast that my side of the ride moved out of harm's way just as Davey's side got to the bottom of the cycle in time to receive the load he had let go of at the top!

As soon as the ride stopped, Billy and I ran into each other as we stumbled for the exit. We made it just into the shadows behind the Dip Topper before we returned to the earth all that we had just paid for. Davey Martin joined us, a real mess.

One of the great mysteries of biology to me has always been how throwing up actually makes you feel better. Once it was all over, we were howling hysterically, euphoric at the experience we had just had! Davey cleaned up in the bathroom, and soon we were off again, weakened and shaky to be sure, but not about to give up on the evening's adventures.

By now we had taken all the rides we had any interest in taking, so we settled into spending the rest of our time on games of chance. We wasted money throwing off-center-weighted balls at lead milk bottles that you couldn't have knocked over with a bowling ball. We threw darts at balloons that were being blown around by an under-the-counter fan so that none of them stayed in place long enough to be hit.

As we played along, each of us seemed to pick certain games we liked more than others, and so gradually we separated, with a plan to meet back at midnight in time to head for Uncle Tom's house.

Davey headed for Skee-Ball bowling, where you automatically got tickets from your score to later exchange for prizes. Billy went for tossing hoops on Coke bottles. I stopped at a place where you paid your money and then got to pick three ducks out of the flock circulating in a flowing stream of water. Some of the ducks had numbers on the bottoms of them, each corresponding to a prize.

Any time you picked up all three of your ducks and didn't get a single one with a prize number on the bottom, you were given a plastic Hawaiian lei as a sort of consolation prize. So far I had spent three dollars and had three of these loser's leis hanging around my neck. It was time to give up on the ducks. As I turned to walk away from the duck booth, I bumped chest to chest into a strange, smiling girl who had to be a year or two older than I was and ten or twenty years more experienced and aggressive. Since she was blocking my path, I just stood there.

"Hi!" she said. "My name's Melody ... I've just been needing one of these!" As she made this proclamation, she picked up the leis, and, without lifting them from my head, she put them also over hers! Now we were locked together with our faces no more than four inches apart.

"Want to go for a walk on the beach?" Melody said.

What choice did I have? She had my leis! If I had any hope of getting them back, I had to go with her.

We walked on the beach, neck to neck, soon holding hands, then arms around waists. Melody steered me to a dark corner past the end of the lighted boardwalk, and there she began to answer questions I had not even thought about asking. Later I rationalized that I must have been weak from losing my Dip Topper, so all the things that happened on the beach that night were not really my fault.

After exchanging addresses with Melody, who turned out to be a freshman at Coker College, I broke loose and went back to the pavilion to wait for Davey and Billy. Twelve o'clock came and went, and neither of them returned.

Finally at about twelve-forty-five, Billy came back. He was all smeared with lipstick. "Where have you been?" I asked, more out of jealousy than anger. "And where is Davey?"

"Well," he started, "he and I happened to run into Sandra Trout and Beverly Davidson. He took off with Sandra and I don't know where they ended up." He was blushing by now, and, I recognized the color of Beverly's favorite lipstick. By the time he finally confessed that they had made what he called "a new connection," Beverly was no longer even my casual girlfriend.

Finally, at about one-thirty in the morning, just about when the clean-up crew was leaving the amusement park, Davey Martin, disheveled and worn out, came dragging up the steps from the beach.

"Where in the world have you been?" Billy and I asked in unison.

"Oh ... The time just got away from me ... Sandra and I were just talking down on the porch of the house where her family is staying ... you know, she's a very intelligent *woman!*"

Billy and I both stomped away in disgust, and the three of us went home for the night.

We missed the Easter sunrise service. There was no way any of us could get up the next morning after the night we had had. It was nearly ten o'clock on a bright sunny day when we finally saw the light of Easter morning.

Uncle Tom came up to the breakfast table and made us an offer. "What are you boys going to do today?"

"We would like to try again to get a suntan," I said.

"Well," he offered, "I've got an idea. I've got a little fishing boat with a ten-horsepower engine tied up back on the inland waterway. If you boys want to, you can take it and ride up and down the waterway and see what you see.

"Actually, you could take it and go down into Myrtle Beach for lunch and then come back again. That wouldn't take more than a couple of hours, and, back there on the Waterway it's a lot more protected from the wind than on the beach. How about it?"

We all thought this to be a good idea. Mazza and Aunt Alicia and Uncle Tom were taking a little trip to introduce Mazza to some of their friends around the area, so we would be out of the way for a while if we did this.

This time we didn't even take the suntan lotion. Our Friday on the beach had produced no visible suntans, so we were determined to get all the sun we could on this, our last day. Besides, riding in a little boat on the water couldn't possibly be as dangerous as being out on the white sand on the beach. After all, today was a cool day.

Uncle Tom took us over to the Ocean Drive Inland Waterway Marina. The Intracoastal Waterway ran all the way down through the Carolinas, and along here it was just a couple of miles back from the beach itself. We dipped out the small bit of water that had settled in the bottom of the little boat during the Saturday rain and wiped the bottom nearly dry with an old towel. We watched as he taught us to start the outboard engine, then he watched as we started it to be sure that we knew how. He checked to see that the gas tank was almost full, and, telling us to have a good time, Uncle Tom sent us off on our own for the day.

The little boat was like an open metal rowboat, not more than twenty feet long, undecorated in any way. But it was just right for three mountain boys who had never even dreamed of being in a boat before. Davey took the stern position first, the position for steering the outboard motor. We planned to go south, thinking that there might be more to see down toward Myrtle Beach. We could find a place to stop and have lunch, mess around for a while, then come back in the afternoon.

The Waterway had some Easter traffic on it, but not very much. As we headed south, we occasionally met a big yacht heading north from Florida's winter toward the coming spring of New England. We waved to the rich retirees as though we were their equals—after all, we too had a boat!

The Waterway had fairly high banks along the sides. As we went along, we realized that those high banks sheltered us from the wind. With its heavy air and the humidity, our environment had a nearly tropical feeling. Gradually we shed our outer clothes, down to nothing but our bathing suits and winter-white skin.

When there were no other boats in sight, we acted stupid with the little boat. Taking turns driving, we revved the engine and ran the boat in circles and smacked through our own wake. Only our own inexperience could have actually made such innocuous attempts at danger seem exciting.

Gradually Davey and Billy began to grumble about getting hungry. So was I. We boated flat-out toward the south and soon came into sight of a big marina on the left side of the Waterway, where we stopped and tied up for lunch.

The three of us got big, greasy hamburgers and french fries. It was good to put some normal food in our stomachs after the dip-top cones of the night before. After eating, we walked all around and looked at the big yachts tied up there. It was great fun to imagine what was inside them, what it would be like to actually have one of these gigantic things and be able to go from Maine to Florida every year.

Finally we got back into the boat, motored over to the gas tanks, and paid to refill the red outboard-motor gas can. Then we headed back north.

We had no awareness that when we turned back to head in the other direction, we were, in fact, doing something like turning meat on a charcoal grill. Unknown to us on this partly cloudy Easter Sunday, we were already badly sunburned on one side and were now poised to take care of our other sides as well.

By the time we were halfway back to where we had started, Billy began touching his stomach with his finger and telling us he thought he had gotten a pretty good tan. "Look at this!" he said excitedly, as he pulled down the waistband of his bathing trunks. We saw the radical difference in color in his obviously red stomach and his protected white skin. When the other two of us tried the same experiment, we got the same results. In part it seemed funny. We didn't hurt, after all, and I wondered what Mama's big-deal fear about sunburn was. But we knew we were getting burned, so we had no choice but to try to get back as soon as we could.

The adventure ended miserably. It was so hot and steamy in the boat that it was almost dizzying when we put on our clothes. Yet without some protection, we could actually feel the sun burning us more and more. Finally we got back to the Ocean Drive Marina, tied the boat up, and called Uncle Tom to come get us.

"You boys are *red,*" he said, as he drove us home. "We better get something to put on that."

"You boys are *red,*" Aunt Alicia said, when we walked in the kitchen door. "We better get something to put on that!"

Mazza heard us come in, and she came out from the guest room where she was staying. "You boys are *red ... we really better get something to put on that!"* By now, we knew that we were badly burned.

It was an absolutely miserable night. As the evening went on, we got redder and redder and could feel the heat more and more. Having no experience with sunburn, I did not know that the real pain would accelerate after the sun went down.

At Aunt Alicia's urging, Uncle Tom went to the drugstore and came back with an assortment of remedies. We spent the evening being alternately lotioned with Solarcaine and greased with cocoa butter. I ended up sleeping only in my undershorts, on top of the sheet. None of us got much sleep.

Easter Monday was the day of our return. We all hurt so much that we didn't stay in bed at all late. After breakfast, we began to pack the Plymouth. For some reason we couldn't seem to get all the things we had brought with us back into the space they had come in to begin with. Finally we were loaded, with long strands of Spanish moss streaming from the homemade roof-top carrier as extra proof that we had been to the beach.

Aunt Alicia gave us some old towels to put on the car seats. This was partly because the towels felt a lot better than the plastic seat covers on our sunburns, and partly so that we could grease ourselves with the sunburn remedies without sliding around on the seats. Mazza was giggling and laughing nonstop at all of our arrangements for getting home. Davey finally got short with her. "If you felt the way we did, you wouldn't laugh!" She must not have felt the way we did, because that made her laugh harder than ever.

Finally, about ten o'clock in the morning, we headed back toward the mountains of North Carolina.

The trip home seemed to take twice as long as the trip down had. Even with the sunburns, we had all had the time of our lives. It was really hard to be heading back for home. I knew Mama would pepper me with a million questions, and I was already trying out how to field them. Maybe she would be so mad that we had gotten sunburned that she wouldn't even ask about anything else.

Mazza reached over and tuned in the radio. She searched the AM dial until she found The Big Ape. Then she showed us how she had beat her chest and made the ape sounds when the policeman had shined the flashlight in her eyes.

"You really did that?" Davey asked her.

"Of course I did! I had to do something! With that light in my eyes I couldn't see that he was a policeman. He might have been a rapist or something, and so I tried to look like something he wouldn't want to mess with!"

We were riding on the towels with our shirts off. Billy was so sunburned that he had unfastened the top of his shorts and unzipped them so they wouldn't rub his stomach. He was wearing green shorts that had mountains and trees in the pattern and, with the sunburn and those shorts, he looked like a July sunset.

Eventually, the Big Ape ran out on us, and the boredom set in again. We started trying to invent games to pass the time. Billy had won a big stuffed dog at the pavilion. He put it on his lap and started to play ventriloquist with it.

He was doing the ventriloquist act when we passed a car with two little girls riding in the back seat. The girls stared at the big dog and, on the spur of the moment, Billy stuck the dog's head out the window and barked at the car as we passed it. The driver, who had to be the mother of the little girls, swerved like she was going to run off of the road. It was great! Mazza laughed her head off.

Mazza was wearing an Air Force cap that Uncle Tom had given her. It had gold braid on the bill and a gold band around it. She pulled the Air Force cap off and put it on the dog. "That'll make him look a lot better," she said. "Now he can bark like a general!"

The next few cars we passed were barked at by Billy as he held the Air Force-hatted dog out the window while we passed. At least this incentive to pass all the cars we could would get us home faster.

We were almost to Hendersonville now. We had eaten lunch way up through South Carolina (deciding not to stop at South of the Border this time), and now, at nearly five in the afternoon, we were not much more than another hour from home. I was driving, and we passed a car loaded with girls who looked like they were headed home from the beach just like we were. What a good car to bark at!

Billy slapped the Air Force cap on the dog, stuck almost the entire stuffed animal out the window, and let out, "BOW—OW—OWOWOW—BOW—OW—OWWW!" as we passed the load of girls.

Just as I cut the Plymouth back into the right-hand lane, the wind caught the cap on the dog's head and blew it off. I saw the Air Force cap fly back through the air, and I quickly pulled off the road into a wide spot just ahead. Billy jumped out the back door of the car to retrieve the cap, but forgot that after lunch he had again unfastened the waistband of his shorts and unzipped them for the sake of his sunburned stomach. Just as the whole carload of girls passed by, his shorts dropped totally to the ground around his ankles and he fell flat on his face in the gravel!

If that was not bad enough, the carload of girls had also run over the Air Force cap and flattened it with black tire marks! Billy got up, chagrined, just as the girls in the other car stuck their heads out the window and barked, "BOW—

OW—OW!" He pulled up his shorts and came back to the Plymouth, now skinned up as well as sunburned.

It was six-thirty when we got home, and, just as I expected, Mama was sitting at the living room window watching the driveway. I got ready for the barrage of questions, determined to be truthful, but selectively enough not to give away anything of importance. I hoped that Mazza would have the discretion not to say too much.

"Oh, boys," Mama cried out. *"You made it!"*

How embarrassing! Of course we made it.

"How did my boys do?" The question was directed to Mazza.

"They were just wonderful," Mazza laughed. "They sure took good care of me! I wouldn't have made it if it hadn't been for these boys. They are good ones ... They were never out of my *vision* for one moment on the whole trip!"

Wow, I thought. *She is smart! You can keep someone in your vision when they are out of your sight!* I took Mazza's cleverness as the pattern for my answers.

"Now, Hawk," Mama went on, "did you meet any new girls down there?"

"Well, ma'am," Davey Martin answered this one, "he didn't even try! There were girls from Sulpher Springs down there, you know!" That was the truth, too!

Mama kept asking, "You didn't get sick eating any strange food, did you?"

"Oh, no ma'am," Billy took this one. "We didn't get sick on any *food* at all. We all ate the same things and we always talked about it before we tried it out!" It was, after all, the Tilt-a-World that was to blame, not the Dip-Toppers!

I thought we were about to satisfy her. Then she threw one straight at me. "And Hawk ... *How was the sunrise service?"*

I really had to think fast on that one. "Everybody who was there thought it was the best one they had ever had! See, it rained on Saturday, but Sunday was a beautiful day!"

Every single word of every answer was absolutely true, right down to declaration that we had made it all the way to Myrtle Beach on one tank of gas. We were so good at telling the truth that we even volunteered a lot of information that she never even asked about. Mama was so pleased that she didn't even get after us for the sunburns.

Finally, she sent me to take Billy, Davey, and Mazza home. The last thing she said to all of us that day was, "Well, boys, it looks like you were right! Now that I let you-all go, I guess everybody does go to the beach!"

Stanley, the Easter Bunny

1959–61

*U*ntil the early 1980s, North Carolina—and many other largely rural states—employed high school students as school bus drivers. Thousands of boys and girls all over the state were safely transported to school each day by drivers who were sixteen, seventeen, at most, eighteen years old. Then, out of fears spawned by a new era of litigation as an American pastime, the student driver era ended and only adults were employed to pilot the big buses—now yellow, a dilution of their former orange—to and from school.

Actually, the new plan brought a great loss. When students drove, the safety record was very good. Driving a bus was a great honor in the 1950s and 1960s, and it paid well for a part-time job. It was hard to find a responsible adult who would take such a part-time job and even begin to do it as well as a student.

I spent my last two years at Sulpher Springs High School as a Nantahala County, North Carolina, school bus driver. It is impossible for me to remember a time when I didn't know how to drive. When you grow up in a rural area with tractors and trucks and Jeeps on farms everywhere, you just end up crawling up on them, sitting in laps of uncles, grandfathers, and fathers, and eventually driving before you even realize that you have learned anything. I remember turning the car around in the driveway at Plott Creek before we moved from there, before I was twelve years old. I remember that Joe and I both begged to drive down the farm roads whenever we went to visit our grandparents or aunts and uncles. Knowing how to drive was a very natural thing.

On the day of my sixteenth birthday, June 1, 1959, I drove Mama to town—she had to ride with me to make it legal for me to drive there with a learner's permit—and took the test for my driver's license. It was no trouble at all. I knew the answers to all the questions on the written test and I had been for years doing all of the things the examiner had me do for the road test. I was now a licensed driver, which meant that I could do on the paved public roads what I had been practicing on the farm and country lanes.

One month later, on the day after the Fourth of July, I went to the high school and started taking the two-week course to get my school bus driver's license. It had not been a long-term plan of mine to do this. It was Davey Martin who suggested it. He had called to tell me he was going to get his bus license and suggest that maybe we could both do it. So it was on the spur of the moment that the two of us met Mr. Joe Bennett and signed up to be bus drivers.

We were trained in groups of four. Besides Davey and me, the terror of kindergarten and Boy Scout camp, Bobby Jensen, was in our group. The fourth member of the team turned out to be the first black person my age I had ever met or even seen up close in my life: Stanley Easter.

The entire black population of Nantahala County was about five percent of a total of less than twenty thousand. That meant that the number of black school-age children in the entire county added up to less than two hundred, a number spread through twelve grades that totaled less than the consolidated white high school graduating class. Somehow the few black people I had had exposure to were either small children or old people. It was almost a shock to see someone exactly my own age who was black!

Stanley Easter was to be one fourth of our bus driving team, this integrated training being the briefest first step toward eventual desegregation of all levels of public education, which was not to be achieved for another half dozen years to come.

All through the years, Nantahala County had practiced busing—not to overcome, but to preserve segregation. Black children were bused from wherever they lived, all over the county, to a single black school which was located about ten miles outside Sulpher Springs, in the rural community of Pigeon River. There were black children who lived right across the street from Sulpher Springs Elementary School who were picked up there and bused the ten miles to their "own" school.

I realized that while Stanley Easter was going to be trained to drive school buses with the other three of us, he would never, in my public school lifetime, be driving either the same buses or hauling the same children I was to haul.

Right from the start, it was Bobby Jensen who was the outsider in our group of four. Davey and Stanley and I started to become great friends. It seemed a shame that it was to be a two-week friendship only.

Actually, his color was not Stanley Easter's only notice-able difference from me. He had the biggest biceps I had ever seen. Stanley had learned to drive the same way that Davey and I had—early in life and on the farm. We found out that his daddy had spent his life as a dairyman on a farm belong-ing to the Smathers family below Pigeon River. Stanley had driven tractors and trucks of every shape and size, not for fun, but because he had been working long and hard for as long as he could remember. He told us that he got his big muscles from throwing hay bales from the truck to the hay-loft, and if that wasn't enough he bench-pressed calves just for the fun of it!

On the other hand, Bobby Jensen could hardly drive a car, let alone a school bus. He was a pure town boy, who had had to take driver's training just to get his driver's license to begin with.

During the classroom part of the course, before we hit the road, Mr. Joe Bennett had told us again and again that more school bus accidents were caused by dogs than by anything else in the world. He said that most dogs just couldn't resist chasing the big orange buses and that out of nowhere a dog of any size or shape was liable to come into the road behind and often in front of a moving bus.

The problem was that, just like car drivers, the bus driver's first tendency was to swerve so as to not run over the dog. The difference was that, with a big, heavy bus, all loaded with loose children, if you swerved, the children would shift like a load of cattle, and the bus, now unbalanced and out of control, often turned over or at least went off the road.

"Go for the dog!" Mr. Bennett advised. "If a dog runs out in the road in front of you, just go for it! It won't hurt the school bus. It's a whole lot more important to keep your children safe than to save a dog's life, so, if one runs out in front of you, just grip the wheel, grit your teeth, and go for it!"

Two days into road training, Bobby Jensen drove the bus for the first time. We were driving over all of the school bus routes in Nantahala County so that we would be tried out on every actual place where a bus might have to go. On the second day we were in the north end of the county and Bobby was driving about twenty-five miles an hour on a flat, gravel road that ran alongside a long, equally flat corn field. The July corn was mostly full by now and higher than our heads.

Up ahead, there was a break in the cornfield where a small frame house sat, close by the side of the road. Just as we got to the edge of the yard, a mongrel hound dog came to life from under the front porch and headed toward the school bus. Bobby, remembering Mr. Bennett's talk on dogs, took his advice and decided to "go for it."

Before any of us, including Mr. Bennett, had time to react, Bobby had turned the wheel and headed for the dog. In the seconds it took for Mr. Bennett to realize what was happening, dive for the dashboard, and cut off the ignition switch, Bobby had followed the dog out of the road, across the corner of the small yard, and had plowed the big, orange vehicle two bus lengths into the soft, green cornfield.

During those same seconds, Stanley Easter had turned white, I had almost wet my pants, Davey Martin was on his back on the floor laughing his head off, and the hound had safely escaped back under the porch of the house. Mr. Bennett couldn't talk. He just gazed up from the floor of the bus and *looked* at Bobby!

"What'sa matter, Coach?" Bobby said, almost offhand-edly. "The bus didn't turn over. Hey, I would've saved the children *and* the dog!"

It seemed to me that the worst part of the whole disaster for Mr. Bennett was that he had to go up to the very house the dog came from, admit that he was the bus-driving teacher, and ask to use the telephone to call the bus garage so that the tow truck could come and pull the bus backwards out of the soft dirt of the July cornfield we had mired up in.

We all heard Mr. Bennett talking to the tow truck driver: "If I were closer to retirement, I'd just leave the damn thing in there and go home. I never have had a day to end like this in my life!"

Needless to say, Bobby Jensen was out of the bus-driving program.

So now our class was down to three, which meant that each of us got to drive more than before Bobby dogged out on us. Since the three of us already had a lot of experience driving big farm trucks which, if not as long, were certainly wider than the school bus, we spent most of our time just learning all of the routes in Nantahala County, while Mr. Bennett read and worked the crossword puzzle in the daily Asheville newspaper.

The driving part of the course lasted two full weeks, which gave us a lot of time to learn about each other. We found out from Stanley that he was just as scared of girls as we were, that he was as scared of his mama as I was of mine, and, that, even though he played football for the Pigeon Eagles, he liked the rest of school a whole lot better than he liked football.

I told Daddy about him, including Stanley's hopes of going to college. Daddy told me that if Stanley was really a good football player, he might get to go to one of the "little colored schools," but that a real college wouldn't take a chance on him.

The final level of trust came when Stanley Easter told us that his family's nickname for him was the Easter Bunny.

"With a last name like Easter," he said, "it was bound to happen. And besides, I was born on April the fourth, which wasn't Easter that year, but close to it."

Stanley also told us that he was very proud of his last name. It had come, he said, because his great-great-grandfather, who was a slave, actually had been born on an Easter Sunday. For people from two different worlds, we did not seem to be that far apart.

At the end of the two-week driving time, all three of us got our certificates, put our names on the list to get a route of our own when school started, and Davey and I said goodbye to the Easter Bunny.

The week before school started I got my assignment, including instructions about when to come to the bus garage to check over and pick up my own bus. I was to drive Bus No. 40, a 1950 International chassis finished as a school bus by Thomas Bus Company in High Point, North Carolina. Already nine years old, this giant old bus was the largest size in use in the county and I was to fill it up, not just once, but four times each morning and afternoon for the coming two school years.

On the scheduled day I eagerly asked Mama to drive me to the school bus garage where I reported in to the chief bus mechanic, Mr. Dale Richardson, who showed me No. 40. The old International had just been repainted bright orange, and on the outside at least, it looked great. Inside it wasn't bad either. The summer before, the bench-seat bottoms and backs had been recovered in brown plastic and everything else on the inside of the bus was either painted green or plated with chrome.

When I took it over, No. 40 had 81,000 miles on the odometer, which was, in fact, no mileage at all, considering that the engine speed on all North Carolina school buses was governed to keep the bus from ever going faster than thirty-five miles per hour, and, in its entire history, the big engine in this bus had never been revved even halfway to its red-line speed. At this rate, these buses could run forever.

Mr. Richardson showed me all around the bus. He showed me the spare tire and the tire chains, which were both fastened up under the tail end of the big bus. He assured me that I would never need to use either one. If the bus ever did have a flat tire, the garage truck would come and change it, and, he said, school would always let out in bad weather long before the tire chains were ever needed. "It's just that a few years ago one of the school board members had a tire business and he talked them into buying all of that stuff for the buses. I'll bet he made enough to retire off of that!"

We got in the bus and I was shown all the controls. I already knew all of this stuff, of course, from the classes, but I listened anyway because Mr. Richardson seemed to be so interested in telling me everything in his own way. He even gave me a new broom, which had had about one-third of the handle sawed off of it to make it easier to sweep the bus with. He told me that he expected me to sweep the bus out every day, and that the garage men would wash the bus once a week and that they would keep the gas filled up and the oil checked.

As I looked around the bus that was to be mine, I noticed the announcement stenciled over the rearview mirror: *Maximum Capacity 92: 78 seated, 14 standing. No Standing Forward of the White Line.* Mr. Richardson saw me looking at the announcement, and he answered the question that must have been on my face.

"Yeah, it'll hold that many. Seventy-eight in the seats—that's thirteen seats on each side with *three* to a seat—then fourteen more standing up in the aisle. If you ask me, you could stand more up than that, but it's hard to fit three in a seat after they get to about the sixth grade. I reckon it all comes out in the wash!" I didn't see what in the world the wash had to do with anything right now.

Mr. Richardson handed me a map of my route and the worn keys—only one set, no allowance for losing them—and then he turned No. 40 over to me. "Take it home today, and in the next day or two take it out and drive over the route. This route's been taking other drivers about an hour and thirty-five minutes to make, so, on the first day you ought to be at the first stop by about ten minutes 'til seven."

I started to climb onto the bus and Mr. Richardson called to me once again. "Oh, Hawk," he wiped his forehead with the back of his hand as he talked, "you'll want to play around a little with the brakes." I looked puzzled. "There's a vacuum booster on the brakes and the vacuum pressure don't hold real good … there's a gauge on the dashboard you can look at. After you've pulled a long hill, you may not have much for brakes … hit the gas and let off a few times to build it up … you'll catch on to it!"

Even with the warning, the first time I touched the brakes after coasting down the long hill from the bus garage, I almost stood the big bus on its nose. The bus had no seat belts, and I slid out of the seat and right onto the floor under the steering wheel. When I finally looked at the dashboard and found the vacuum gauge, the needle was flat against the MAX post. I would learn to keep my eye on it from now on.

Just after leaving the bus garage on the way from school toward home I had to pull a long mile-and-a-half hill into the middle of town before coming on through town to our house. Unloaded and with no stops, the big bus pulled the hill at twenty-five miles an hour in third gear. But all the way up the hill, I could see the needle on the vacuum gauge slowly dropping. By the time I got to the Haywood Street stop sign at the top of the long pull, the brake pedal went flat to the floor.

This was no real problem since I was headed uphill. When I pushed the clutch in, the heavy bus stopped on its own, and all I had to do was slip it into first gear the moment it came to its full stop, catch it with the clutch to keep it from rolling backwards, and ride the clutch until traffic was clear and I could pull out and on my way. But I did realize that this might be a problem if you had to go back down a long hill immediately after going up one.

I was fully aware that this was my first time ever to drive a school bus "solo." Mr. Bennett had always been there before. And the 1950 International was somewhat different from the new '59 Chevy we had learned to drive in bus drivers' school. Going over the route could wait until tomorrow: just getting No. 40 home would be enough for me for today.

That night I proudly and conscientiously mopped the inside of the bus, then with a stepladder and a bottle of Glass Wax I cleaned every one of the windows inside and out. At the Esso station I had even bought an air freshener shaped like a pine tree, and I carefully suspended it from the rear-view mirror.

I gave Mama, Daddy, and Joe a tour of the bus, and when Joe asked if he could ride with me the next day when I went over the route, I was mature: instead of saying, "Of course not, are you an idiot," I politely said, "I'm so sorry, but that would be against the rules."

I studied the route map that night. After breakfast the next day, I took the big bus over the course I would follow well over three hundred times in the next two years.

No. 40 was one of two buses that had routes running from the top of Clyde Valley all the way into town to Sulpher Springs High School. No.39, the other Clyde Valley bus, started at the top of the valley and came straight down the paved highway, picking up children who gathered themselves into clots about every half-mile along the road.

My bus had what was by far the more interesting Clyde Valley route. No. 40 picked up all of the kids who lived on the half dozen or so dirt roads that ran up and dead-ended in various creekside coves along the sides of the bigger main valley. On these roads the houses were far apart and the kids were picked up only one or two at a time.

The beginning of the run was at the top of Wedder's Creek, where the bus had to pull a long two-mile unpaved hill. There was no trouble pulling the hill in second gear with no load on board. I wondered what would happen if we were loaded.

All the way up the long hill I watched the vacuum pressure drop on the dashboard gauge. It was below five pounds when I got to the top. Having driven all these roads in bus driving school, I knew there was a level turnaround place on the right side at the top to back the bus into before going back down the hill.

This was a cinch. All you had to do was wait until the exact moment when the bus stopped, double-clutch it into first gear, and ride the clutch to slow it as you turned the wheel and let it drift gently back into the turnaround place. Once there, the bus was perpendicular to the hillside and it sat still all on its own while I alternately revved the engine and let off on the gas until the vacuum gauge came up to ten pounds.

Going down the hill in second gear, the pressure actually kept increasing. Everything was fine as long as I, instead of riding the brake, kept pumping it gently to take advantage of the growing vacuum pressure. I had, I was sure, mastered the system.

It took me just over forty-five minutes to drive the route with no one on board, so, I was quite sure I could do it in an hour and a half with all the stopping and starting added in.

Our house had a long concrete driveway that went uphill from the road to the garage. I carefully backed the bus up the driveway and parked it on the grass beside the garage. In cold weather this parking position turned out to be most helpful. Once the temperature dropped below thirty degrees, the old six-volt battery could not muster enough kick to turn the engine over. It was a big help to be able to roll down the driveway with the switch on and then let the clutch out in second gear until at least most of the cylinders were firing by the time you reached the road at the bottom.

I hardly slept on the night before school started. Davey Martin came over to my house, and we talked half the night. He had been given bus No. 22 which went from Gomorrah through Riverside and back.

For the first time since summer we talked about Stanley Easter and wondered if he had gotten a bus route for the year. We decided to try calling Stanley on the telephone to find out, but there were no Easters listed in the Nantahala County telephone book. When we told Daddy what we were doing he said, "Aw, boys, I don't reckon colored people would have a telephone ... especially *country* colored people." I had never even thought about that before.

The next morning I was up at five-thirty, on the way by six-fifteen, and so far ahead of time that I had to pull off by the side of the road up in Clyde Valley and wait for fifteen minutes so the children at my first stop wouldn't find out that I didn't even know when to leave home. I was ready.

There was one little boy waiting to be picked up at the top of the hill. I would learn later that his name was Hallie Cosby, but on this first day I never found out. I backed the bus into the turnaround place and opened the door, and Hallie Cosby climbed on.

"Good morning!" I said. "I'm your bus driver," Hallie Cosby just stared at me like one of us was from another planet, said nothing at all, and sat down in the seat immediately behind my driver's seat, a position which he was to occupy every time he rode the bus for the next two years.

Later on I was told by the other kids, "Hallie don't talk."

"What do you mean?" I asked them. "Is he deaf or something?"

"He just don't talk," a little girl named Sandra Campbell replied. Arthur Setzer—about a fifth grader, I guessed—offered, "I bet he ain't got no vocal cores!" None of these kids seemed to know *why*. Actually, nobody seemed to know Hallie well enough to even guess why he didn't talk. The only consensus of agreement was, simply, "Hallie don't talk."

Being an eighth grader, Hallie turned out to be not only the first passenger I picked up each day, he was also one of the few students whom I had on the bus for the entire trip to the combined Sulpher Springs Junior/Senior High School. I did not realize on that first day that I was not simply to haul one load of students to one school; rather, by the time I arrived at the Junior/Senior High School at 8:25, I had moved four loads totaling more than 200 students to four different schools.

During the first seven miles of the route, I picked up a full load of students on three dirt roads, then stopped at Clyde Valley Elementary School. At this point all of the elementary students got off while the junior and senior high students stayed on. Now the bus was three-fourths empty again.

As the route went on for the next eight miles, I again filled up the bus and, when I now stopped at Mauney Lake Elementary School, about forty elementary students got off and about twenty older students stayed on. From there, the next nine miles, the process was repeated one more time, until, when I stopped at Sulpher Springs Elementary in town, only thirty younger students got off and now about sixty junior and senior high students were still on the bus. At this same stop, nearly thirty junior and senior high students, who lived near enough to the elementary school to walk there, boarded No. 40, and the big bus, full for the fourth time, traveled the last three miles to Sulpher Springs Junior/Senior High School, arriving just five minutes before the first bell rang.

I carried out this process as a matter of assumed course and did not realize until years later either the massive responsibility I was, as a sixteen-year-old, carrying out, or the sheer genius of the route-maker who, since I was paid forty-three dollars every twenty days, had me moving pupils to and from school for little more than a penny per student per day!

On the very first day of school, as I made the leg of the run from Mauney Lake school toward Sulpher Springs Elementary, I met another school bus headed in the opposite direction. The bus was as big as No. 40, but older and in need of repainting.

For just a moment I wondered why this strange bus was going in the wrong direction, but as soon as I saw that it was loaded with black children, I knew. This bus was headed for the back side of Nantahala County, headed for tiny Pigeon River School, picking up black children who lived in sight of the same schools I hauled white children to.

As this other bus approached, the driver flashed the headlights, *Flash … flash … flash-flash-flash*—and I could quickly see that the bus driver was none other than Stanley Easter. He and I both smiled and waved, and, from that day on we met, morning and afternoon, on almost the same stretch of road, and flashed our headlights as a silent salute of comradeship with one another.

During the fall football season, there would occasionally be a tiny back-page mention of the Pigeon Eagles football team when they won a game in Black 1-A conference play. Whenever this team was mentioned, Stanley Easter's name was featured as the one who had either led in yards rushing or who had scored the winning touchdown or both. I showed these articles to Mama and Daddy, and Daddy always said, "One of those little colored schools will snap that boy up, sure enough … he's a big'un!"

What I wondered was how Stanley Easter could drive a school bus morning and afternoon and still get in enough time at football practice to not only play but to be the leading scorer, while he was still only in the eleventh grade.

There were great adventures along the way in bus driving. One of the things that I soon discovered was that the route was run much more quickly if you could make the stops as the bus traveled downhill rather than uphill. I discovered this the first afternoon when it took two full hours to undo the same trip I had made in an hour and a half in the morning.

This was the difference: in the mornings, when I stopped to pick up children as the bus traveled down Wedder's Creek road toward school, the heavy bus, after the downhill stop, was almost immediately back up to its thirty-five mile-an-hour maximun speed. But, on that first afternoon, as I let the children off one at a time on the way back up the long hill, I could never even get the bus out of first gear after starting back up, and it crept, roaring and groaning, at about five miles per hour slowly up the hill to the next stop. Two and a half miles of this crawling took over thirty minutes!

I quickly convinced the kids that if they would all sit still as we went all the way to the top of Wedder's Creek without stopping on the way, we could zoom up that hill at fifteen miles an hour in second gear compared to the bare crawl in first if we stopped on the way up. Then I could let them off on the way back down the hill and we would, in this clever way, cut a full twenty minutes off the afternoon trip home.

Because of this new plan, Hallie Cosby, who was the first one onto the bus in the morning, was not the last off in the afternoon. No, all of the kids on the whole long Wedder's Creek hill road rode right past their own houses to the very top with non-talking Hallie. He got off at the turnaround, then the others got off as we went back down the hill.

In about the middle of October, about six weeks into the school year, I arrived at the top of the route one morning and Hallie was not there. I waited for a full five minutes, revving the engine in part to build the brakes up and in part to be sure that Hallie could hear that the bus was there. Finally I was sure he wasn't coming and I started on down the hill, picking up the others, whom I was getting to know pretty well by now.

When I picked up Arthur Setzer, I asked, "Do you know if Hallie's sick or something? He didn't come out this morning."

Arthur just shyly looked at the floor, seemed to giggle, and didn't give me an answer.

I kept asking other children and kept getting giggles until, finally, Sandra Campbell was brave enough to fill me in.

"He's in the hospital," she said. "Broke his leg!"

"Wow," I said. "What happened to him? Did he fall off of something?" The others were all giggling a lot by now.

"Yeah," she said. "He fell through a fence."

What had happened, I finally found out, was that on the Saturday before, Hallie had been helping his daddy and his uncle work a moonshine still not very far from their house. It seems that Sheriff Tate was out snooping around and found the whiskey still, all fired up, while nobody was there. The sheriff hid out and waited, knowing that the owners would be back soon.

When Hallie and the two men got to the still, Sheriff Tate stepped out, and Hallie's daddy and uncle ran off and left him. "They knew," Sandra explained, "that Hallie couldn't talk and witness against them even if he did get caught." Well, Hallie had tried to run and fell through an old dilapidated fence and broke his leg.

He was out of school another day or so with his leg—and another week, it turned out, because of embarrassment. Then he was back again.

None of us ever had any real discipline problems as student bus drivers. Our instructions were very clear: if we had any trouble on the way home in the afternoon, we were simply to turn the bus around and take everyone all the way back to school. Once back at school, the students would have to call their parents to come to school to get them. Anyone who ever had to go through this once never misbehaved again; the other kids on the bus wouldn't allow it, they all wanted to go home! Of course, there was never any trouble in the mornings because we were, after all, on our way *toward* school, and, the first person to meet the bus at school when we got there was always the principal.

Davey and I now had a wonderful new dimension to our friendship. Almost every day we would call each other when we got home and exchange our adventures of the day. I was a little jealous because he always seemed to have more exciting and daring adventures than I ever had with No. 40.

On Davey's route up through Gomorrah, his run went past a little tourist attraction called Gomorrah Gardens Reptile Center. Locally we all called Gomorrah Gardens "the snake farm." It was a second-class tourist trap that featured big fluorescent-painted plywood road signs, which, for miles in either direction, told you how many miles it was to Gomorrah Gardens. We all knew that the snake farm would pay fifty cents a foot for nonpoisonous snakes and a dollar a foot for deadly ones. We often joked about going out in the mountains to "hunt rattlesnakes and make some money," but we all knew that this was just empty talk.

In addition to many snakes, one caged bear, turkey buzzards in a terrible-smelling cage, and a pair of penned-up wildcats, the snake farm had a half-dozen peacocks and peahens who walked about freely inside the fence.

One afternoon I got home to find the telephone already ringing. It was Davey calling, eager to tell me of his afternoon bus adventure.

"I got a peacock!" he proclaimed. "I got a peacock. Come on over here and I'll give you some feathers!"

I hurried over to his house to hear the great story face to face.

"If I hadn't remembered Mr. Bennett's advice, I might've wrecked the bus!" he said proudly. "I was coming down the dirt road that comes right around the back of the snake farm. I had already let everybody off who lived on that road and was headed back for the paved highway with the last few kids when it happened.

"There must have been a hole in the back fence of the snake farm, and one of those big peacocks just got out. Just as we hit that straight stretch of road, that peacock came right out in the road in front of me, just like it was trying to see if it could get across the road before the bus got there.

"I remembered what happened with Bobby Jensen and that dog, so I didn't jerk the wheel or anything. I just held on and went straight ahead and thought, *If it doesn't move, it's dead!* It didn't move."

Davey went on to tell how the few children left on the bus begged to stop and get the feathers they saw flying up in the air as the peacock was hit. They did stop (it was past the summer season and nobody was anywhere around the snake farm right now), and Davey himself came home with fourteen perfect peacock tail feathers—and a promise from the other children not to show theirs to anybody.

"You dummy!" I said. "How is anybody going to hide a peacock feather?" We never did know whether they somehow *did* manage to hide the feathers, or that their parents felt the same way we did about the snake farm and just didn't care. Nothing bad ever came from the peacock business, and I went home with two peacock feathers.

It was a great year, that junior year in high school. Davey and I drove our buses and were closer to being adults than we would ever be again for years to come. We looked forward to our senior year at Sulpher Springs High School, where, once again, the two of us expected to be driving Nos. 40 and 22.

Something happened that summer, however, that changed all that. Davey Martin, my best friend, the friend whom I trusted more than anyone else in the world, went to the bad! Davey Martin fell in love!

The culprit was Sandra Trout, the girl who had kept Davey out late on the great beach trip at Easter. Sandra Trout, whose father was the one surgeon at the Nantahala County Memorial Hospital. Sandra Trout, who lived in a beautiful house and was herself, in a word, beautiful!

Once Davey fell in love, he became totally worthless as a friend. He would rather be "doing something" with Sandra than doing *anything* with the rest of the world. And when he did happen to end up with me, all he did was talk about Sandra, Sandra, Sandra. It was disgusting.

The lowest blow came near the end of the summer. The time came for us to go pick up our school buses for the new year. Mama was planning to give me a ride up to the school bus garage to meet with Mr. Richardson and get No. 40 back for the year. I called Davey on the telephone to see if he wanted to go at the same time.

"Well," he seemed to sound like he was smiling while he told me, "you go on up there and get that old bus. I'm not going to be driving this year. I've got other things to concentrate on ... important things!"

I couldn't believe what I heard! It was the last straw.

As it turned out, giving up the bus route was not entirely Davey's own idea. It seems that his life had been taken over not only by Sandra Trout but also by her parents, especially her surgeon father, Dr. Trout.

Sandra's father had gone to Harvard, and everyone in town knew it. It was almost impossible for anyone to ever have a conversation with Dr. Trout without at some point having to hear the words, "When I was at Harvard ..." followed by a school story. His Harvard diploma hung right on the wall, not in his private office but right out in the reception room where it was hard not to see it (though most residents of Nantahala County, not being able to read Latin, had no idea what the big, framed certificate was all about).

When I talked to Davey about a week after school started, the real plan for his life came out. We were just beginning to talk about applying for colleges for the next year when everything suddenly became clear to me.

"Dr. Trout says," Davey began, "that nobody born in Nantahala County has ever been admitted to Harvard. He says that he doesn't even think that anybody from Nantahala County has ever even applied."

I was carefully listening now, for what I knew was coming next.

"Dr. Trout says that with his coaching and a lot of hard work, he thinks that maybe I could get accepted and that if somebody from a place as remote as this ever got accepted, they would have to give him a scholarship. That's the real reason I'm not going to drive a bus this year. I'm going to work for Dr. Trout in the lab at the hospital after school and on some Saturdays, and he's going to help me with my schoolwork and coach me through applying to Harvard."

"Harvard?" I couldn't believe it. "What in the world is wrong with you? You don't have any business even thinking about something like that. It's that girl, isn't it? That doctor's got you married already and he's going to be ashamed of you if he can't take over your life and make you into something he wants you to be."

Davey looked so much like he had been slapped that I knew I had, even if by pure accident, stumbled close to the truth. "Why doesn't he send his own daughter to Harvard? Don't they take women?"

"I honestly don't know … if they take women, that is. Sandra wants to go to some girls' school up there close, and Dr. Trout really thinks that this is a good idea."

And so the tone of the year was set. Davey, Sandra, and Dr. Trout spent every available moment together, with Dr. Trout single-handedly planning the future for all of them. I, with no best friend, having spent all of last year with either Davey or No. 40, began the process of applying to Davidson College, an old North Carolina school which was surely as far from home as I had any business trying to go.

No. 40 occupied almost all of my free time and energy. I did play in the Sulpher Springs High School band, but that was mostly a weekend commitment. From before daylight until the edge of dark, I contented myself with the company of silent Hallie Cosby, and Sandra Campbell and Arthur Setzer, now a year older and wiser, as well as over two hundred more just like them. And, yes, I kept waving to Stanley Easter morning and afternoon, though my recollection of the friendship we had started in bus driving school was only the very palest of memories.

In February I was accepted to Davidson College and began to watch Mama make her own plans for my departure. And lo and behold, in March, it was Dr. Trout who announced that "Davey Martin has just become the first person ever born in this county to be accepted at Harvard University for the class of 1965." He didn't even mention that his own daughter had, all on her own, applied to and been accepted at Wellesley—a place none of us had ever heard of at the time anyway. I guessed that this was the end of the road for Davey and me.

It was in April that the most wonderful and memorable event of my entire bus driving career happened. In fact, it was perhaps the most memorable event of my entire high school career. It all started when, in the middle of a school day, I got sick at school.

It was in the middle of Mrs. Turner's senior English class last period of the afternoon. I had been feeling flush all day, and was beginning to get a little bit woozy, when, all of a sudden, without notice, I felt a wave of nausea that was so quick and so powerful that there was not even time to ask for permission to leave the room. I simply ran for the door, knowing that my illness would cover every excuse I needed later. I barely made it to the bathroom and was losing several meals at once when Davey, whom Mrs. Turner sent to "find out whatever is going on with that young man," came in and saw the problem. He left me and went back to report to Mrs. Turner.

When Davey returned to the bathroom to see what he could do for me, I realized that there was no way I could drive No. 40. "Go to the bus garage," I begged, "And tell Mr. Richardson what happened … I *can't* drive that bus!"

As things finally turned out, Mama came to school to pick me up, and Davey, not driving a bus of his own this year, agreed with Mr. Richardson to be my temporary substitute driver for No. 40.

Thinking about all of this later, I am still certain that I had, at one time or another, told Davey about how long hills depleted the vacuum pressure for the brake booster. With hindsight, I also wondered how he had not figured the brakes out for himself on the first part of the route. But either information was lacking, or Davey's brain was elsewhere (probably with Sandra Trout), or, as he insisted, something mechanical really did go wrong.

Davey got to the top of Wedder's Creek hill, pushed in the clutch, and gravity stopped the big bus. He slipped the bus out of gear, turned the wheel to the right, and No. 40 obediently rolled back to the right into the turnaround place. As it came to a stop, on its own, Davey took advantage of the last movement to turn the big non-powered steering wheel to the left. In that moment everything started to go wrong.

As Hallie Cosby got up from his seat to come to the door to get off, the big orange bus started rolling forward, with—unknown to my friend, substitute driver, and future Harvard student—the vacuum gauge flat on zero.

Davey put his foot on the brake, and the pedal went flat to the floor as No. 40, now with a mind of her own, rolled faster and faster with every passing moment.

If Davey Martin had ever pumped the brake pedal just once, or if he had even let up on it enough to take advantage of the now-increasing downhill vacuum pressure, everything would have been fine. But, in sheer panic, his foot was now frozen to the floor, and instead of pumping, he just tried to push even harder against the floorboard. It didn't work. The big bus didn't even pretend to slow down. Davey held it in the road but had no hopes of making it safely to the bottom of the mountain.

All of a sudden someone was yelling. "Hit dem pines, wild man! Hit dem pines! Hit dem pines, wild man! Hit dem pines!"

Everyone in the bus stared in silent disbelief as Hallie Cosby, making the first audible sounds anyone had ever heard come from him, jumped up and down in the aisle of the bus beside the driver's seat and pointed to a soft-looking grove of hemlock bushes located along the right side of the road not fifty yards ahead.

Davey later admitted that there was not enough time to actually think through a decision. Maybe his brain did remember the driver's class bus sinking slowly into the soft cornfield when Bobby Jensen went for the dog, and maybe not. Whatever thought process went on, the "pines" did seem to be the softest and safest thing to run into before the bus gained enough speed to be totally out of control, and so, Davey did indeed "hit dem pines"!

No. 40 slowed as it plowed through the young hemlocks, came out on the other side, and landed softly in the shallow mire where Hallie's daddy and uncle dumped the spent mash from the moonshine still they had hidden there. Running the big bus into a pillow couldn't have provided a softer landing. Most of the dozen riders still left on the bus didn't even fall out of their seats throughout the whole crash landing.

I later realized that the worst thing about being sick on that day was that I was not able to go up to Wedder's Creek to see my drunken bus before it was pulled out of the mash-mire.

Hallie didn't say a word after the bus came to its safe stop. He just got off the bus, waded out of the mash, and walked home, as did the other kids still left on the bus.

The next day Mr. Poindexter, the principal, called Hallie into the office for a conference about the entire bus business.

"Hallie," Mr. Poindexter started off, "we didn't even know you could talk. Why hadn't you ever said anything before yesterday afternoon?"

Hallie's reply was simple. "They wadn't never nothing needed saying." And that was that.

No. 40 was not hurt at all by the drunken trip through the hemlocks, and in just a few days both of us were back on the road again. The orange bus did, though, have an interesting odor for the rest of the year. And Davey Martin, my former best friend, the boyfriend of Dr. Trout's daughter, now accepted to enter Harvard as a freshman in September, never drove another school bus again.

We graduated on the fourth day of June, 1961. I told the old bus goodbye. Never in my life would I again have another job that involved such actual responsibility as this job had. Davey and I spent our summers getting ready in our own separate ways to say goodbye to Sulpher Springs and, finally, to one another.

In September Davey Martin, loaded up in Dr. Trout's latest Buick station wagon, left for Massachusetts. He was headed for his date with destiny, all planned by his girl-friend's father. I packed up, with Mama's help, and went on my more proper way to Davidson College, in the flatlands of the same state in which I had been born and always lived.

Before my first day at freshman orientation was over, I knew that I was in a different world. It was 1961 and this was a Southern, male-only, liberal arts school for the white and well-cultivated sons of the South. As I abandoned my blue jeans and flannel shirt and quickly bought a yellow Gant shirt and Bass Weejuns so I would at least appear to fit in, I knew that there were many things about my mountain childhood that I would not only leave behind but about which I would positively lie to cover up my uncultured upbringing.

One of the things I would never admit to my sophisti-cated freshman classmates was my history as a North Caro-lina school bus driver. As I realized this, I chuckled to myself, knowing how many more things Davey Martin would try to cover up in order to be accepted up at Harvard. I began to live out a fresh, clean—if somewhat revised from reality—personal history.

We were fresh in the first year of what was to be the brief presidency of John F. Kennedy. The hottest elective course open to freshmen on campus was a political science course called "Current Politics: The Pulse of Washington." I signed up for the course, partly because it sounded interesting and partly because it offered a Thanksgiving trip to Washington. I was in such a ripe mood to get away from home that this prospect sounded great to me.

Mama cried on the telephone when I told her that I wouldn't be home for Thanksgiving. In the middle of my attempt to explain my desire to "broaden my horizons," she kept talking about "forgetting where you came from." It was with a mixture of feelings that my first trip to our nation's capital drew near.

The political science class went up on a chartered bus on Wednesday afternoon. I felt like the king of the world as we came over the last ridge in Virginia and looked down on the Pentagon and on across to the city of monuments, now lighted in the darkness of our night arrival.

We were staying in dormitory rooms at American University, rooms emptied by students who had gone home for this holiday. There were students from other visiting colleges staying in the same dorm. They were, we discovered, there for the same reason we had come.

We were left to wander on our own on Thanksgiving day, and it was then that my Davidson roommate and I met up with the boys from Harvard. They were staying in the dormitory room next to where we were staying, and after forming a quick friendship, the four of us decided to go to the Washington Monument and then get a pizza together.

All four of us talked about college and about Washington and about politics and about John Kennedy, just like we knew what we were talking about. We waited in line in a stiff wind that blew all around the Washington Monument until, after an hour, we rode to the top and then walked back down. Then it was off to get a bite to eat.

At the pizza parlor, one of the Harvard boys said, "Where are you guys from?"

"Davidson College," I answered quickly. "You-all know that."

"That's not what I mean," the new Harvard friend went on. "Where are you *really* from? Like, where did you grow up?" It was the awful question that I did not at all want to deal with in front of these new, sophisticated friends.

I tried to get off with a generically vague answer. "North Carolina."

The Harvard questioner persisted. "What part?"

I was not about to say "Sulpher Springs." At the time that was the stupidest place in the world I thought anybody could be from—so stupid the name was even spelled wrong. After a long pause, I finally said, "Close to Asheville." It was as close to the truth as I was going to get.

"Close to Asheville?" one of them asked. "Is it anywhere close to a place called *Sulpher Springs?*"

My heart almost stopped! Where in the world did they hear about Sulpher Springs?

The other one chimed in. "Yeah! We've got a classmate from Sulpher Springs, North Carolina. He's the coolest guy you ever met. You know what? He says he drove a school bus in high school! Isn't that about the coolest thing you've ever heard of?"

All my fears melted. So Davey had not lied about where he came from, and these guys really didn't think that Sulpher Springs, North Carolina, was stupid after all. All of a sudden I felt terribly homesick, and Nantahala County was the only place in the world that seemed worth talking about. I swelled with pride.

"Well," I started in, "you won't believe this, but I am from Sulpher Springs too, and I also drove a school bus, and that classmate of yours is my very best friend in all the world. We grew up together and we even got our bus drivers' licenses at the same time!"

"Oh, yeah!" They were really talking now. "He told us all about bus driver's school. Did that guy really chase after that dog with a school bus and end up in a cornfield? That's the funniest thing I ever heard!"

"It sure did happen." I was loving this. "It happened just the way he told you. It was the funniest thing you've ever seen in your life. You should have seen the farmer when he came running out of his house and saw the bus."

We were all laughing. "So you were best friends, huh?"

"I guess we still are," I went on. "Say, did he ever tell you about running my school bus into a hole full of moonshine mash? Now that was really the funniest."

The two of them looked at each other. "No," one of the Harvard boys shook his head. "We never heard of that."

"You mean"—I was laughing on my own now, just remembering the whole story—"he didn't tell you about having no brakes, and about dumb Hallie Cosby, who had never spoken a word in his life yelling, 'Hit dem pines, wild man' and saving the bus?"

They were still looking blank and shaking their heads. So, I thought, old Davey didn't tell everything! I'm going to let the cat out of the bag!

"You mean," I laughed, "that Davey Martin didn't tell you that he wrecked my school bus?" I waited for their response.

"Davey Martin?" one of the Harvard boys asked. "Who's Davey Martin? The guy we're talking about is Stanley Easter. Calls himself the Easter Bunny. He's the smartest guy in the freshman class ... made over fifteen hundred on his SATs ... he's on a full academic scholarship!"

After a moment of dead silence, which was accompanied by a whole lifetime of thoughts and attitudes rearranging themselves in my head, the other Harvard freshman added, almost as an afterthought, "There is a Davey Martin in our class ... but he says he's from 'up above Atlanta.'"

Walking Through Sulpher Springs

THANKSGIVING DAY, 1962

*M*y sophomore year I *did* go home from college for Thanksgiving. In fact, I had now become so proud of where I was from that I could hardly wait to get home. I no longer had to lie about where I was from. Now I was "that kid from the mountains ... the one who used to drive a school bus," and the world of childhood was quickly becoming a dear place to visit.

Joe was a freshman at North Carolina State. He and I had gotten home within an hour of each other on Wednesday night and now, after eating ourselves silly on Thanksgiving day, we were deciding what to do for the afternoon.

Ever since childhood at the old house our family had habitually taken long walks around town. This was an unseasonably beautiful November day, and it was Mama who made the suggestion: "It's such a warm and pretty day. Why don't we just go on one of our walks around town?" We all agreed, and so off we went on a ramble through the place where we had lived forever.

This was not like the old walk from Plott Creek, where most of the way walking time was spent just getting from our house to the edge of town. No, the new house was already in town, so we were looking, remembering, and visiting as soon as we left our own driveway.

We started down the street and almost immediately looked across to the Coles' house to see if anyone might be home. The Coles' house was all dark, and Mama told us that they had decided to go to Florida for the whole winter. Out of the blue, Joe and I both said, "It's hot, hot, hot down there," and we all burst into laughter.

"Remember those awful plastic seat covers?" I asked Mama and Daddy.

"It wasn't my idea to get them!" Daddy said, taking up for himself. "Your mama thought we were going to ruin those new seats on the first day. But you know, everybody had those things back then ... it was just the thing to do."

Mama took over. "I guess that growing up in the Depression, we just took so much extra care of what we had that sometimes it got right silly. But I never will forget that Florida vacation!" Her eyes sparkled and she laughed out loud. "I'd still rather see Rock City!"

It really was a beautiful Thanksgiving afternoon as we walked the few blocks up Maple to Cherry Street. After turning there and walking another couple of blocks we were on Main Street of Sulpher Springs, forever our home town.

Right there on the Main Street corner was the bank, where Daddy would continue to go to work until he retired six years later. "Hey," he said to me, "did I tell you that Roy Batchelor died? It was just about two or three weeks ago."

"Oh boy," I remembered. "I'm sorry to hear that. I would like to have seen him again. Do you know what I did one time when I was supposed to be cleaning the board room?"

Daddy laughed. "You mean the time you stopped up the toilet with paper, and old Dr. Baker saved your life?"

"How did you know about that?" I was amazed.

"Didn't you know? Blind men tell no lies! I'll bet Roy told a hundred people about that day. He always said you were the funniest sight he had ever seen!"

"Guess what?" Daddy went on. "Ardis Carpenter's daughter, Suzie, has just gone to work as a new teller. She's the first black person we've ever hired." Even as I listened to this reported sign of progress, I realized that her father had worked at cleaning the bank for forty years, yet he was not referred to at all in this employment report.

"Do you still buy those calves and put them in the lobby?" Joe asked.

"No," Daddy answered, almost wistfully. "After Mr. McCrae died and Paul Robinson got to be the president he cut that out. I reckon the health department wouldn't allow it anymore anyway. We don't even have spittoons anymore. Times have changed, boys, whether you know it or not."

The barber shop was long gone as we passed the street in front of the bank, but as we walked around the corner, the dental office was in the same place. Dr. Franklin's name was gone now. So was Dr. Caldwell's name. He had been dead for years, and the two new dentists who had bought the office probably didn't even know the story of Dr. Franklin. That's too bad, I thought, still wondering all these years later what had gone wrong and, for a moment, what had ever become of that pretty Donna Sue.

It was not a long walk to the end of Main Street. From there we looped back past the church. There in the yard, already strung with lights, was the biggest Christmas tree in town. Each year the town utility workers strung it with colored lights as big as the light bulbs we used at home.

The lights were turned on this Thanksgiving afternoon, and we all stopped to admire the tree. "I can't remember how long they have strung up this old tree," Daddy said. "It seems like it's been lit up every year as long as I can remember."

"You know what I remember?" I volunteered. "I remember the first time I ever saw the lights being put up on it. I was in Mrs. Rosemary's kindergarten class and we spent the whole morning watching from the second-story window above our classroom. The town workers used the fire truck to get all the way to the top of the big tree. We were really quiet because we all thought Mrs. Rosemary had slipped us up into a part of the church where we weren't supposed to be.

"That tree seemed every bit as big back then as it does now."

The afternoon was cooling now, and Mama suggested that we stop in Conard's Drugstore and get hot chocolate. It was the only place of business in town that had opened on Thanksgiving afternoon.

We sat at the soda fountain, and when Dr. Conard's helper (now he actually had hired help!) came to us and said, "What do you'uns wont?" I recognized the voice before I did the face. She did not recognize us though, and, as she went back into the little kitchen to fix the hot chocolate we all ordered, I whispered to Mama, "Is that—?"

"Yes," Mama said, "that is Barbara Blackwelder. She started to work here when she got out of high school, finally, this year!" When Barbara came back, we tried to visit, but only a very little bit of what we had to talk about still touched the both of us.

Soon the hot chocolate was gone and we headed for home.

We were almost back when an old, rusty-red Chevrolet pickup truck pulled out from a stop sign up ahead of us. The old truck spewed blue oil-burning smoke as the driver accelerated, then shifted into second gear.

Then, as I watched it come toward us, I saw the headlights flash an old familiar pattern: *flash … flash … flash-flash-flash*, and just at the same time I saw Stanley Easter throw up his hand and wave! Riding in the front seat with him, squeezed in to fit the narrow seat, I could see his mother and his two little sisters. As the truck passed I saw, riding in the bed of the truck, because there was no more room to fit inside, Stanley's father and his one little brother.

We waved to them and they waved to us, and, centered in the back window of the old truck, framed by their callous-handed waves, we saw the red decal that proudly proclaimed: HARVARD.

Other Books from August House Publishers

White Wolf Woman
and Other Native American Transformation Myths
Teresa Pijoan explores the common spirit which binds together
all forms of life through more than 40 transformation myths.

Hardback ISBN 0-87483-201-2
Paperback ISBN 0-87483-200-4

American Indians'
Kitchen-Table Stories
Contemporary Conversations with Cherokee, Sioux,
Hopi, Osage, Navajo, Zuni, and Members of Other Nations
Keith Cunningham collects more than 200 narratives
from conversations with contemporary Native American storytellers.

Hardback ISBN 0-87483-203-9
Paperback ISBN 0-87483-202-0

Rachel the Clever
and Other Jewish Folktales
Forty-six tales brought to America by immigrants from
countries and regions as diverse as the stories.
Collected and retold by Josepha Sherman.

Hardback ISBN 0-87483-306-X
Paperback ISBN 0-87483-307-8

African-American Folktales
Stories from the black oral tradition that transcend color and culture
collected and edited by Richard and Judy Dockrey Young.

Hardback ISBN 0-87483-308-6
Paperback ISBN 0-87483-309-4

August House Publishers
P.O. Box 3223, Little Rock, Arkansas 72203
1-800-284-8784

HIGH ATOP
LOOKOUT MTN.

A SPECIAL
GIFT TICKET

FOR YOU AND YOUR FAMILY TO
SEE ROCK CITY

— ADMIT —
2 ADULTS & 2 CHILDREN

NOT VALID WITH OTHER DISCOUNTS • VALID MAY-SEPTEMBER ONLY

FOR MORE INFO, CALL OR WRITE:

SEE ROCK CITY, INC.
LOOKOUT MTN., GA 30750

1400 PATTEN RD.
706-820-7531